Corrupted by a Gangsta 4

**Lock Down Publications and
Ca$h Presents**
Corrupted by a Gangsta 4
A Novel by Destiny Skai

Lock Down Publications
P.O. Box 870494
Mesquite, Tx 75187

Visit our website
www.lockdownpublications.com

Copyright 2019 by Destiny Skai

First Edition August 2019
Printed in the United States of America

This is a work of fiction. Names, characters, places, and incidents either are products of the author's imagination or are used fictitiously. Any similarity to actual events or locales or persons, living or dead, is entirely coincidental.

Lock Down Publications
Like our page on Facebook: Lock Down Publications @
www.facebook.com/lockdownpublications.ldp
Cover design and layout by: **Dynasty Cover Me**
Book interior design by: **Shawn Walker**
Edited by**: Kiera Northington**

Stay Connected with Us!

Text **LOCKDOWN** to 22828 to stay up-to-date with
new releases, sneak peaks, contests and more…

Submission Guideline.

Submit the first three chapters of your completed manuscript to ldpsubmissions@gmail.com, subject line: Your book's title. The manuscript must be in a .doc file and sent as an attachment. Document should be in Times New Roman, double spaced and in size 12 font. Also, provide your synopsis and full contact information. If sending multiple submissions, they must each be in a separate email.

Have a story but no way to send it electronically? You can still submit to LDP/Ca$h Presents. Send in the first three chapters, written or typed, of your completed manuscript to:

LDP: Submissions Dept
Po Box 870494
Mesquite, Tx 75187

DO NOT send original manuscript. Must be a duplicate.

Provide your synopsis and a cover letter containing your full contact information.

Thanks for considering LDP and Ca$h Presents.

Previously

Silence took over the room for a few seconds, but Janae walked in, talking to Demarcus. "Janae," Shan's voice was hoarse.

"Yes, Mommy?" Her eyes were bloodshot red when she walked up to the bed and held her mother's hand.

"I love you so much."

"I love you too."

"And I'm so sorry I'm not going to be here to see you go off to college." As Shan continued to talk, we were all in heavy tears, including Nae's boyfriend. I continued to hold her hand.

"When I gave birth to you, I promised myself I was going to be the best mother I could be. I always had plans for you to go to college and become a better woman than I am."

"You're a great mother and this is not your fault." Janae sniffled. "I promise to make you proud of me."

"I'm already proud of you, so don't ever doubt that. You've been the perfect daughter."

Shan closed her eyes and looked away. "I just wish I made better choices when it came down to your father. I'm the reason he was missing from your life like that. You could've had so much more if it wasn't for me being so young, dumb and selfish. I hope you can forgive me."

"I'm not upset and it's not your fault he's in prison. Brick has been a good daddy to me, so I'm not missing anything." Janae stepped up and hugged her mother tight. "I never missed a beat in life and that was because of you. I don't know what I'm going to do without you. Why do you have to leave me so soon? I'm not ready, Mommy. My heart can't take this pain."

Janae screamed and made everyone jump. That was my cue to get up and comfort her. Demarcus stood up, but I signaled him to stay seated. The grip she had on Shan was tight as hell, but I managed to pull her away and embrace her.

"Nae, I promise I'll be here for you. I will never leave your side. I will be there to see you graduate from college. I'm going to walk you down the aisle and be in the delivery room when you have kids. This is going to be hard for both of us, but we will get through this together."

"This is not fair. Life is not fair. Why do I have to lose my mother?" she screamed repeatedly.

"Janae? Baby, calm down, please," Shan pleaded.

For the next few minutes, I spent my time consoling her and getting my baby to relax. I knew she was going to need me more than ever.

The monitor Shan was hooked to started to make a loud beeping noise, sending our nerves in a frenzy. Janae and I attended to her mother. Seconds later, the nurse came rushing through the door and to the bed. We stood back and watched her check Shan's vital signs. Silently, I was praying she was going to be okay. This couldn't be her last day on earth.

After the nurse was done, the monitor was back to making its regular noise and we were relieved. The nurse looked at us with a great deal of concern. "Her blood pressure has gone up drastically and her heart is beating irregularly, but she's okay right now."

"Thanks," I replied.

Once the nurse left, we went back to the bed with Shan. It seemed like she was tired and ready to give up on life. That didn't sit well with me, and I was going to talk to her about going to another hospital. Now wasn't the time, so I put it in the back of my mind for the next day.

"I need you two to listen to what I'm about to say." Shan looked me and Janae in the eyes. "Brick, I appreciate everything you've done for us over the years, and I know you will keep your word. Please take care of my baby girl."

"I got her, Shan. I promise."

"There is something I need to say before this monitor goes off and I die for real this time."

Whenever I left the hospital, I knew I was going to need a stiff drink and a shoulder to cry on. Never in life did I think I would be saying goodbye to my first love.

"My intentions were always good with you, Brick, and you know I loved you to death. You were my first and I wished you were my only, but life had other plans for us. Janae, you are the air that I breathe and always remember, I never meant to hurt you."

"Hurt me how?" Janae asked.

Shan wiped her falling tears and looked me in the eyes. "Janae is your daughter."

"Huh?" My ears couldn't believe what they were hearing and apparently, Janae couldn't either because her mouth was wide open. "My daughter?" I repeated. "Are you sure?"

"Yes. Do you remember the very last time I saw you and we had sex?"

I nodded my head.

"A few weeks later, I found out I was pregnant. I didn't have the guts to tell you the truth, so I slept with him to cover it up. I did that so you wouldn't ask questions. I'm sorry y'all. Don't hate me."

Janae walked away and sat next to Demarcus.

"Shan, I don't hate you, but why didn't you tell me this years ago? You know I would've taken care of my responsibilities."

"You wasn't ready to be a father, because you wasn't ready to be in a relationship. I knew how that was going to turn out, so I kept it a secret." Shan shook her head from side to side. "I'm sorry for disrupting your life with this, and I hope this doesn't ruin your relationship. For Janae's sake, I couldn't go to the grave with this secret. All I ask is that you don't hate me."

The secret she laid out on the table like a Sunday dinner was enough to feed a thousand men. It was certainly a lot to take in and I needed to sit down. So, I lay down in the bed with Shan and held her in my arms.

"I'm not mad at you and I don't hate you. Back then, I was wild and I could see how my reckless behavior drove you to think I wasn't ready. My only problem is, why didn't you tell me sooner? I've been here all her life and I feel like that was something I needed to know."

"I been wanted to tell you, but every time I got close to saying those words, I lost my nerve. If you want to take a DNA test to confirm, you can do so. But, I know without a doubt, that you're her father and I'm sorry for not telling you sooner."

Shan's words were sincere and I knew it came from the heart. We stared in each other's eyes and I kissed her gently. "Shan, I love you and I always will. You have my word that I will take care of our daughter. People make mistakes and we were kids. Don't worry about my relationship, I'll handle that. Even if she doesn't accept it, which I highly doubt, because she's not like that at all, I will never abandon her. You have no worries. I'm going to take care of her the same way I take care of Breanna."

"Thank you," she whispered.

"You don't have to thank me. She's my responsibility now."

As I held Shan in my arms, I didn't want to imagine life without her. My words were sincere also, because I still loved her. I just knew we could never be together. The friend zone seemed like it was better for us, so we didn't cross that line. The sound of the monitor beeped long and hard once again, interrupting my stroll down memory lane. When I looked at Shan, her eyes were closed. Placing my hand over her heart, I realized it was no longer beating and in that moment, mine stopped too, temporarily. Tears streamed down my face and my heart broke in a million pieces, as I kissed her forehead.

"I love you, Shan. Sleep in peace, my angel."

"Nooo!" Janae screamed and rushed over to me. I jumped from the bed and took her into my arms. "I want my mommy back."

"Nae, baby, it's going to be okay. Daddy will be here for you as long as I have breath in my body."

I was fine with Janae being my daughter. However, Zuri was another story. I wasn't sure how she was going to take the news, but it wouldn't be long before she found out.

Chapter 1
Zuri

The sound of the gun erupted in the dark, quiet streets so I knew it wouldn't be long before the nosey ass neighbors started peeking from their windows. Quickly, I slammed the trunk and got inside my car and started the engine. To keep from drawing attention to myself, I cruised out the neighborhood at precautionary speed.

As I made my way out to blend in with traffic, a sigh of relief comforted me. However, that was short lived, as I could feel a sharp pain creep through my stomach. On instinct, I placed my hand on my stomach and rubbed it in an effort to soothe my irritated baby.

"Shit," I breathed in and out   I mouth slowly. "This bitch really kicked me in my stomach. I should go back there and fuck her ass up some more."

My plan was not carefully thought out because I was reacting out of anger. Not once had I considered what I would do once I was done with her. If Brick would've done his fuckin' job, this wouldn't be happening.

"Let me call him," I mumbled.

The light turned red, so I was able to look for my phone. Once I had it in my hand, I clicked on his name and pressed send. Brick's phone rang twice before going to the voicemail. I know damn well he didn't send me to the voicemail."

Boom!

I could hear Deja hitting on the trunk and shouting. "Bitch, stop making all that fucking noise because nobody can save you. This hoe irritating as fuck."

Aggravated, I turned on the radio and turned the volume up to the max. What she wasn't about to do was give me a damn headache or get me pulled over.

After driving around for fifteen minutes, Brick still hadn't returned my calls and the pain in my stomach was starting to increase.

"God, no. Please don't let me go in labor." My actions caused me to be in a fucked-up situation. Therefore, my nerves were shot and so was my train of thought.

Something had to give and quickly at that. The gas station was coming up and I needed a Tylenol badly. As bad as I wanted to keep going I couldn't, because as far as I knew, my baby's life could be in danger.

When I pulled in next to the pump, I was relieved that no one else was getting gas just in case Deja started that damn banging again. I turned down the radio and waited a few seconds to make sure she was quiet. Once everything was good, I got out the car and went inside.

"Welcome to Shell." The cashier smiled.

"Hello." I smiled back and made my way to the cooler to get a bottled water. When I made it back to the front, he was still smiling.

"Did you find everything you need?"

"Almost. Can I get a Tylenol pack please?"

"Sure. Will that be all?"

"Yes."

Passing him a bill, I couldn't help but to look outside. That was the moment I almost pissed in my clothes. Coming towards the door was an on-duty cop. Perspiration immediately formed underneath my arms and on my forehead. *Stay calm*, I told myself.

The cop walked in with a stern look on his face, like we missed curfew. "Good evening."

"G-good evening, Officer."

"Is that your car out there?"

That was all I needed to increase the mini heart attack that was surfacing. There was no way a lie would check out, since I was the only one in the store.

"Yes. Is there something wrong?" I did my best to remain calm, but that was hard to do.

"As a matter of fact there is." He pointed towards the door. "I noticed that one of your back tires needs some air. If you give me a moment, I can help you with that."

"Oh, that's okay. I'm headed home to meet my husband, so he can help me with that."

"It's not a problem and besides, it's too dark for a pregnant woman to be driving under those conditions."

"I'm fine, really. I don't live too far from here." The cashier passed me my Tylenol and I exited the store quick, fast and in a damn hurry.

Going to jail wasn't an option. There was no way in hell I could explain this fuck-up to Brick. As soon as I got in the car and pulled off, I could see him standing at the register.

"Damn, that was a close call." My heart was throbbing, right along with the pain in my stomach.

The hotel was too far for me to drive with the pain I was feeling. Nor had Brick attempted to call me back. Maybe he was mad because I was ignoring his calls. So, with that being said, I had no choice but to drive to my house. The chances of anyone coming there were slim to none, but I was willing to take that gamble.

Ten minutes later, I was pulling up in my driveway. I hit the button to unlock the garage, pulled in and let it down behind me. A flashback of the unpleasant night I met Brick played in my mind, just like it happened yesterday. That had to be the absolute craziest night of my entire life. For sure, I thought he was going to kill me and now look at me in love, pregnant and engaged to the fool. True enough, my baby was bat shit crazy, but I loved him to death and there was nothing anyone could do to change my mind. We were going to be together forever.

My phone vibrated hard in the console, scaring the shit out of me. I picked it up with an attitude. "About time you picked up."

"Don't start, bruh. Where the fuck you at?"

"My house."

"What the fuck yo' stupid ass doing there with them kids? See, that's why you was in that shit earlier. Get yo' ass back to that hotel and I'm not playing with you."

"I can't, something happened and you need to get here now."

"What the fuck happened now? Never mind, don't even answer that, 'cause I can only imagine what type of fuck shit you did."

"This is your fault, not mine."

"You a muthafuckin' lie, 'cause I ain't did shit."

"What the fuck ever. Just get here now," I screamed, feeling pain shoot up my back and stomach.

"Zuri, hear me and hear me good. I have never hit you before, but when I get there I'm fucking you up. I think you forgot who I am and what I'm capable of, because you steady pushing. But, it's time for a reminder 'cause you steady trying me."

"That's what you not gone do."

"Okay slick mouth. Keep that same energy. I'll be there in five minutes."

Brick hung up in my ear, but I wasn't stressing over his empty threats. When it came to that he was all talk, so I knew he wasn't going to hit me. Not to mention, I was carrying his child, so he would never bring harm to his own flesh and blood. He wasn't that type of father. I knew that firsthand from observing him with Breanna.

Finally, I tore the pills from the small wrapper and popped them in my mouth. Then, I washed them down with some water before getting out the car. The bathroom was calling my name and I needed to make sure there were no blood spots in my panties.

Rushing to the guest bathroom downstairs, I turned on the lights and pulled down my pants. When I saw nothing was there, I was relieved. However, I still needed to go to the hospital, because I didn't feel right.

The sound of the door slamming made me jump, but I already knew it was Brick. After I washed my hands, I walked out the bathroom and ran directly into his chest.

"Now what was all that fly shit you was talking earlier? Say that shit while I'm standing here," he barked in my face, trying to intimidate me.

I placed my hand on his chest and pushed him away from me. "Back up, because you know I hate when you talk to me all aggressive and shit. We have bigger problems to worry about, aside from me getting snappy with you for a reason."

Brick grabbed me by the throat and pushed me against the wall. "Stop fuckin' playing with me. I'm not one of these fuck niggas you used to dealing with. I'm not ya' faggot-ass daddy. Put some respect on my muthafuckin' name, before I bust yo' ass in the mouth."

The grip he had on me grew tighter and I could feel heat and tears in my eyes. Brick's words were hurtful and I couldn't believe he would say that to me. At that moment, I wished I could disappear into thin air. Placing my hands on his wrist, I tried to move his hand, but he wasn't letting up and I could barely breathe. My lips moved, but there was no sound.

"I can't hear you. What 'chu trying to say?" he mocked. "I'll break yo' fuckin' neck."

Another sharp pain kicked in, causing my knees to buckle. I grabbed my stomach and tried to scream. Still nothing. Brick looked at me sideways right before he let me go.

"What's wrong?"

Although I was winded, I still answered his question. "I'm in pain and I need to go to the hospital."

"That's because you running around town like a silly ass girl who forgot she is pregnant." Brick scanned the room. "Where are the kids?"

He was really pissing me off with all that fly talk and it was time to let him know why I called him over in the first place. Once I caught my breath, I was gone get him together real quick.

14

"No. If you would've taken care of shit from the jump, we wouldn't be in new shit right now. I told you to take care of that bitch after that shit went down at your apartment, but did you do it? No."

"Listen, you can't tell me what to do or how to do it. That shit don't work like that. You dropped two funky ass bodies and now you a killer."

"Well, I started it for you and now you can finish the bitch." Holding my stomach, we stood there and faced off like two enemies.

"What the fuck you talkin' about?"

"I'll show you." My fat ass turned on my heels and waddled to the garage with him in tow. I popped the trunk and he stopped abruptly.

"What the fuck did you do? I know damn well you didn't kidnap this girl."

"Go look."

Brick walked to the back of the car and raised the trunk. When he saw the blood, he immediately pulled her body closer and placed his hand on the side of her neck. The cold stare from his dark eyes made me nervous.

"What the fuck did you do?"

"I shot her, duh. What the fuck does it look like?"

"You killed her."

"So what? She tried to have me, her own fuckin' daughter and our baby killed. You didn't think I would let that slide, do you?"

"No! No! You just fucked everything up. Damn, Zuri. Why the fuck you couldn't just stay in your place? This street shit ain't for you."

"Are you serious right now? You mad with me because I killed the bitch that was coming for me from every angle? You can't be serious."

"Fuck!" He was shouting like a mad man. "That wasn't your place to handle her. It was mine."

"You act like you still loved that bitch or some shit."

"Just shut the fuck up and go in the house while I clean up another mess you made."

"I don't understand you. What type of fuckin' man would let his baby mama slide on doing the shit she did? I'll tell you, a weak ass bitch. That ho' kicked me in the stomach, so I shot her."

Brick cut his eyes at me and I swore I saw the devil himself appear out of nowhere. Swiftly, he raised his hand and struck me in the face with an open palm. He then grabbed my neck with both hands. This time there was no wall and I could feel my body elevate from the floor. In mid-air, he shook me like a rag doll. I was in disbelief.

"You hit me," I screamed in his face.

"Don't you ever in your natural life call me another bitch. Next time it'll be a closed fist. You will need stitches and your stomach pumped for swallowing your goddamn teeth. I don't disrespect you and you won't disrespect me either."

Brick let me go and I doubled over in pain. That shit hurt so bad that I couldn't focus on the fact that he slapped me. "Ah! Ooh."

"Take my car and go to the hospital." He handed me his keys. Once I grabbed them he squeezed my hand lightly.

"Zuri, if something happens to my baby, I will be digging two ditches and not just one. And that's on Gawd! So, you better pray that he's okay and where the fuck are the kids?"

"They with my sister."

My ass stood there crying like I was waiting on a pity party. Brick slammed my trunk and walked past me without a single word or apology. When he got in the car, he rolled the window down.

"What the fuck you waiting on? Go check on my child."

The garage door opened and that was my que to leave. Brick hit the horn, so I froze in place. The reverse lights on my car went out and the driver door opened. Something told me that our argument wasn't over.

"Pop the trunk."

To my surprise, that was all he said to me before emerging from the back of the car and heading back to mine. Under any other circumstances I would've questioned where he was going and what he was about to do, but I decided against it. My imagination told me all I needed to know once I saw him with a bucket, tackle box and a fishing pole.

On my way to the hospital, I prayed my baby was okay and that his father remained safe, while cleaning up the mess I made. In no way, shape or form did I feel bad about my actions. I did what I had to do as a mother. Brick would have to understand my reasons sooner or later. As of now, oh well, the bitch dead now.

Chapter 2
Brick

Zuri had me fucked up, but she was lucky her ass carrying my child, because I would've did some major damage to her for talking to me sideways. Tonight proved she had some issues and wanted that type of reaction out of me. It was like she deliberately pushed my buttons, forcing me out of character. Every muthafucka that knows my name is aware I don't tolerate disrespect from nobody. I wouldn't give a fuck if it was the president of the United States. Don't fuckin' play with me.

This crazy ass girl didn't realize the type of situation she put me in. My ass was guaranteed to be the first suspect, so I had to make sure Deja could never be found. On everything I loved, she better not fuck up my chances of getting full custody. Now I was responsible for getting rid of the dizzy ho's body. My intentions were to get rid of her eventually and I already had a plan in place, but now I had to execute it immediately.

Once Zuri pulled off, I followed her until we hit the main road. In deep thought, I jumped onto I-95 and headed south to I-595, until it was time for me to get off on my exit. Once I handled the business at hand, me and her were going to have a long as talk.

Forty-five minutes later, I was driving through the darkness on I-75, better known as Alligator Alley. The area was very popular for fishing and in some cases, dumping bodies. Tonight, that was my case. Thoroughly, I searched for the darkest spot with a dock. There was no telling what types of predators were roaming the land that time of night.

Getting out the car, I walked up the dock with the flashlight in my hand. At the end, I looked below me and shined the light across the water. Satisfied, I walked back towards the road and opened the passenger door. The bucket was behind the driver's seat, so I had to climb in and get it.

Red and blue lights flickered in the darkness and inside the car. "God, I don't want to kill this innocent man, so please let him go on about his business."

Slowly, I raised up with my hands in front of me. If anything went left I had no choice, but to murk his ass. The state trooper walked towards me with his right hand on his holster and the left one holding a flashlight.

"Hey. What are you doing out here?" he asked with a heavy country accent.

"I like to fish late-night. How about you?"

"Oh, I'm just patrolling the area." He looked puzzled, as he looked around me. "Where's your fishing pole?"

"I have it right here in my back seat."

"And how about a fishing license?"

"I have that too."

"Slowly reach for it and let me see."

With one hand in the air, I used the other to pull my wallet from my back pocket. Good thing I bought one. The trooper slowly approached me and held out his hand. The same one he had on his holster.

"You can put your hands down. I'm not going to shoot you. I just had to make sure you were actually about to fish."

After he checked my license, he passed them back to me. "Be careful out here. These gators been acting up all day."

"Will do, sir. Thank you."

"Have a good night."

"You too."

As he walked to his car, I grabbed the pole and bucket, then headed back up the dock. "At least one of these muthafuckas better be biting tonight."

Inside the bucket was bait, ropes and gloves. From the time I plotted on killing Deja, I made sure my materials stayed handy. That ratchet ass ho' was the reason I got a fishing license in the first place. It was time to get rid of her before anything else occurred. Jogging back to the car, I checked my surroundings and removed my shirt before popping the trunk.

Deja looked at me and attempted to scream. It wasn't too loud, but she started to kick her legs to keep me away from her. That took me by surprise, because I just knew the bitch was dead. I grabbed her by the throat and squeezed hard.

"Bitch, didn't I tell you I was gone kill you? Yo' ass had one muthafuckin' job to do and that was be a mother to my child. Not fuck my cousin. You could've fucked any nigga in Lauderdale and I wouldn't have given a fuck. Now Gucci on his death bed because of you. Then you had the nerve to send yo' fuck ass cousin to hurt my daughter, lady and baby. Bitch, you knew this was coming."

Deja dug her nails into my hand, trying to keep me from strangling her ass. Beside her body lay a tire iron, so I picked it up and bashed her across the head with it. The blow made her release the grip she had on me. Flashbacks of her keeping my daughter away from me during my bid

18

corroded my mind and I went numb. Brutally, I continued to beat her. Blood splatter and brain matter painted the trunk and my tank top.

After an estimated time frame of two minutes, I snapped out of it and dropped the iron back inside the trunk. Deja's face was completely dismembered. No one would recognize who she was without dental records. Scooping her up, I tossed her over my shoulder and slammed the trunk. Mild splashes in the water caused me to pick up the pace and rush to the edge of the dock. If I was lucky, the gators could start on their feast before I left.

With no effort, I tossed Deja's corpse into the body of water and watched it sink slowly. Prepared to walk away, I took a step back and turned on my heels. The violent sound of the water splashing sent me forward, peeking over the edge. I watched closely as the fattest alligator I'd seen in my whole life, chomped down on Deja's body and go under water.

"Guess that muthafucka was hungry." Once I made it back to the car, I tossed the items in the back seat, started up the engine and got the fuck out of Dodge.

Thirty minutes later, I was back in Lauderdale, so I called Zuri to make sure she followed my directions.

"Hello."

"Wae you at?"

"The hospital."

"I know that. Which one?"

"Broward General in labor and delivery."

"Delivery?" I slammed on brakes before I could run a solid red light. "What the fuck you mean, labor and delivery?"

"They might have to do an emergency C-section, because the baby is stressed."

"What the fuck does that mean?" Zuri sucked her teeth, but she didn't answer me. "See, I told yo' ass to stay in the fuckin' house, but no, you wanna run the streets like you sixteen and shit. I should molly whop yo' ass when I get there."

"Excuse me, sir."

"Who is this?"

"This is Nurse Lindsey."

"Yeah?" I huffed heavily in the phone.

"Your fiancée is having contractions and it appears the baby is stressed. Therefore, we will need to do an emergency C-section in order to save him. How quickly can you get here?"

"I'm ten minutes away."

"Okay."

"Brick, please hurry," Zuri whined, "I need you."

"I'm coming, baby, but if my son don't make it, you won't either love."

I hung up on her because she risked my son's life on some revenge type shit, like I wasn't gone handle my business like a G. Women had a tendency to act on emotion and not logic. The stunt she pulled could've made things worse than what they are. Now I would have to deal with the police fucking around with her. All I knew was that my junior better make it. Eight minutes stood between Zuri, Junior and me, so I flushed it all the way there.

***

Zuri

That man of mine was gone drive me to shoot his ass next. I understood that he was mad at me, but I had a perfectly logical explanation for my actions and I expressed that to him. The fight with him would have to happen later, because at the moment, this baby was whooping my ass.

"I need drugs and I need them now." My grip was tight as hell on the metal rail. "This shit hurts."

"Hang tight. We'll start in a few minutes."

"Brick, get your ass here now," I shouted.

For the next five minutes, I was prepped for surgery. My body was in pure agony and I couldn't wait for it to be over. I did my best to keep myself relaxed with breathing exercises, but that shit wasn't working at all. My vagina felt like it wanted to detach from my body on its own.

Suddenly, I saw a tall figure walk through the doors. It was Brick and he didn't look happy at all. The nurse looked at him and smiled.

"Right on time, daddy. We need to get you suited up right now." The nurse picked up a white suit and passed it to him. "Here, put this on."

Brick took the suit from her hand and walked over to the side of my bed. Surprisingly, he leaned down and kissed me on the forehead. "How are you feeling?"

20

"I'm in a lot of pain."

"Remember what I told you." Never taking his eyes off of me, Brick got dressed and grabbed my hand, then kissed it. "I still love you."

The nurse and her assistant pushed me down the hall until we reached our destination. It was cold as hell inside the delivery room. Nobody could tell me that temperature wasn't below zero. After pushing my stretcher in the middle of the room, they put up the light blue tarp. That sight made me nervous as hell, as I had a flashback from watching The Baby Channel. My breathing increased and so did my heart rate. Even my hands were trembling. Brick took my hand into his and kissed my knuckles.

"You're going to be fine, so try and relax. Daddy right here, baby."

"Okay Mommy and Daddy, this procedure will take about ten to fifteen minutes. We'll stitch her up quickly and get her to recovery."

"Okay," Brick replied, while paying close attention to what the doctor was doing.

**

Brick

Being in the delivery room brought back memories of when Breanna was born. The only difference was she was a full-term baby, resulting from a natural birth. Despite all things, I was anxious to meet the prince. The doctor picked up the scalpel, so I took a few steps forward to see what he was doing. And, oh my God, why did I do that?

"Yo, what the fuck?" I blurted out unintentionally.

The doctor looked up and chuckled. "She can't feel it. We numbed her from the waist down."

Apparently, he was right because when I looked at Zuri, she was staring out into space. I mean, she didn't move a muscle, or squeeze my hand. Out of all the heinous shit I'd done in my life, including chopping up Rock, this had to be the absolute worse. Watching the doc cut my girl open didn't sit too well with me. However, it did give me a newfound respect for Zuri because of what she had to endure to give me my son. There wasn't a bitch walking that could make me cheat on my goddess.

After watching the doctor cut through layers of her stomach, I damn near passed out. But, I had to remain tough in front of my lady. As I massaged her hand softly, Doc reached both hands into the opening in her stomach. That was where I drew the line, because I ain't never did no shit like that in all my days of killing. It had me intrigued a little, so I kept watching. Seconds later, he was pulling my baby out by his head. Doc had me fucked up because I didn't hear shit and his face was bluish. I wasn't a medical professional, but I knew what that meant and I was hoping for the best. God knows I didn't want to kill Zuri for causing death upon my child.

"Hey, why he not crying?" My heart was quaking hard in my chest like some African drums.

"What's wrong with the baby?" Zuri panicked.

"He still has fluid in his lungs," the doc replied. "Do you want to cut the umbilical cord?"

"Yeah." I rushed over and took the scissors from his hand. That was the best feeling in the world, but I was still afraid for his safety.

Afterwards, they quickly rushed him over to the warmer. Whatever they were doing was hard for me to see, but I remained calm for Zuri's sake. Seconds turned into a minute, then out the blue, the room was filled with a loud cry. When I looked down at Zuri, she had tears rolling down the side of her face.

"Don't cry, baby. He's okay."

The doctor stepped to the side and I could see the nurse cleaning and swaddling him before she walked my baby over to me. Extending my arms, I took my baby boy into my arms and smiled. Zuri was waiting patiently, so I held him close to her face. On November eleventh at one thirty two in the morning, I became a father for the third time. The only thing left for me to do was tell Zuri about the first child, but that would wait until I was able to take her home. In the meantime, it was all about celebrating the new life we brought into the world. My prince, Brandon Alejandro Riccardo Jr.

Chapter 3
Skeet

It was well after midnight when Kamari hit me up, talking about pick him up from his cousin's spot. I pulled up in front of the complex and hit the horn twice. A minute later, I saw the front door open and Kamari step out, but he wasn't alone. Some female was walking behind him, talking loud and waving her arms in the air. As they got closer I realized it was the same chick from his house.

Kamari ignored everything she was saying and opened the door to the taxi cab. "Man, gone Kyra, you trippin'."

He tried to close the door, but she snatched it back open. "You need to tell me where you going, 'cause I know this nigga ain't no damn cab driver."

"How you know what this man is?" he argued.

"Don't make me call Auntie Anne," Kyra huffed.

"Call, you can call whoever you want to, 'cause I'm out." He looked over at me. "Pull off, bruh."

"Say no mo." I put the car in reverse and took my foot off the brake.

As the car rolled backwards, Kyra finally moved her round ass out the way. She walked away once I put the car in drive and pulled off.

"Fuck wrong witcho peeps, man?" I asked, while slowing down at the stop sign.

"She trippin', that's what. Tryin' to make me stay in the house and shit. I told her I was about to go slidin' wit' a friend."

"She a whole bug, my boy."

"Fuck all that, where we slidin' to?" Kamari sat back in the seat and pulled out a zip of crip.

"Nah, dawg." I snatched it from his hand. "Not in Brick shit. You crazy as fuck and we got work to do. We gotta drop this work off to Big Mike at his shop first. He waiting, so smoke this shit when we get done."

"A'ight bruh, damn."

"You act like you don't know how Brick is." Kamari was gone learn quickly about fuck-ups.

"You right." He snatched the zip back from me. "I'll hold my own shit, thank ya."

Kamari turned up Yo Gotti and bopped to the music.

Twenty minutes later, we were pulling up at Big Mike's shop. The parking lot was well lit and I didn't see anything or anybody out of the ordinary, so I got out the car and grabbed the duffle bag from the trunk. Kamari was right behind me.

"Where yo strap at?" I turned around and questioned him.

He held up his shirt. "On my body, nigga. Fuck you thought?"

"Just checking. Come on." Big Mike was standing behind the counter when I hit the doorbell. He looked through the window before buzzing us in.

"What up, Big Mike?"

"Sup youngin'. Who dis?" Mike scratched his head.

"This my dawg, Mari."

"He workin' for Brick too?"

"Nah, he my shadow." I laughed, tossing the duffle bag on the counter.

"Oh you being funny. What up homie?"

"Sup." Kamari nodded his head.

"Brick got the babies workin' the night shift I see, and what's up with that uniform shirt?" Big Mike laughed, while unzipping the bag and taking the product out.

"Nigga, I ain't been a baby since I jumped off the porch and this my work attire." Kamari was posted against the wall watching the glass door. My eyes were on Mike. Swiftly, he pulled out a knife and poked a hole in one of the keys. Using his finger, he touched the product and rubbed it on his gums.

"Damn! That shit biting."

"Now run me my money, so we can get the fuck up outta here."

Big Mike reached down and came back up with stacks of cash wrapped in rubber bands. He pushed it towards me. "Forty-five bands. Count it."

My math was on point, so it didn't take no time for me to count it up and toss it into the bag. "Next time my boy."

"A'ight shit talker." We slapped hands and I walked off.

"Let's ride my nigga." Kamari opened the door and exited the building.

On our way to the spot, several pedestrians tried flagging down the vehicle, but I kept it moving. There was far too much money in this bitch and I couldn't afford to replace shit.

Kamari was texting on his phone. "Aye, slide by the block party in Parkway before we head back."

"Nah. We got too much money in this car to be reckless like that. I'm not trying to get caught up in no necessary bullshit about this man money."

"Stop being so negative and paranoid all the time. Ain't shit 'bouta jump off. You must've forgot we in a damn taxi cab. We both strapped and we ain't gotta get out the car. I just wanna slide up on my lil baby for five minutes."

The wheels in my head went to spinning and I sucked my teeth the more I thought about it. "Five minutes, nigga, and what street?"

"Sixth Court."

The main reason I stopped was because we were directly around the corner from the spot. Smoothly, I made a sharp right from Sunrise right onto 34th Avenue. In my rearview, I could see a car directly behind me, so I kept my eyes on it. I noticed it minutes prior, but I didn't think much of it since we were on the main road.

"Aye, keep your eyes on that car behind us. They been sliding with us for a minute now."

Kamari looked in the rearview and sat his pistol in his lap. "I'm on they ass if they try to buck."

"That's what I'm talm 'bout."

From the main road, we could hear the music loud and clear and when I hit the corner, that bitch was swangin' hard. The car behind us hit the corner too.

"Shiddd, they comin' to the party too." Kamari continued to look in the rearview.

"That's what they better be doing," I replied, pulling up behind a car that sat in the middle of the street. No matter what was going on, I was still checking out my surroundings. The game was full of snakes, so I kept my grass cut at all times and didn't trust no niggas.

"Aye!" Kamari yelled into the phone. "I'm in the middle of the road in a taxi cab, so come on and bring one of yo homegirls for my brother." He hung up his cell and sat it in his lap.

"They got a nigga boxed in like a vegetable in this muthafucka. This bitch on smash right now."

"Who you telling?" he replied, while looking out the window at two, thick ass girls walking in our direction.

"Damn, they thicker than a bitch. Shidd, I'm trying to fuck something."

Kamari rubbed his hands together and grinned. "Well, my brother, you can have the one in the dress 'cause the one in the tights belongs to me."

"Shorty bad," I replied.

Kamari's chick walked up to the window and he rolled it down. She was cheesing harder than a bitch. "Hey, bae. Y'all need to pull out the road."

"We ain't staying." Kamari sat his gun down on the floor.

"I'll pull over for a minute." My ass was trying to push up on shorty in the tight dress.

"Step to the side so we can park."

Both girls stepped back, as I parallel parked next to the light post. Killing the lights, I left the car running and got out the car. Shorty in the dress was smiling hard as fuck as she walked towards me. My swag was still on point, even though I was rocking a cab shirt with a big ass Cuban lick and medallion, jeans and Ferragamo sneakers. I leaned up against the car and folded my arms.

"What's up, shorty?"

"My name is Andrea, not shorty." She smiled and rocked on her heels.

Kamari busted out laughing. "Get her ass, bruh. She got a slick ass mouth."

"Be quiet," Andrea giggled.

"Don't worry, I got her, bruh." I stood up and got close enough to her so I could look in her eyes. "Andrea, huh?"

"Yep and you are?"

"A young fly nigga named Skeet. Come step into my office, so we can talk in private." Andrea was behind me as I walked away. "Get in the passenger seat."

Andrea turned around and went to the passenger side. Kamari and his girl stood outside the car while we was inside. It was time for us to get a little acquainted.

"So, where yo man at?" There was no need in beating around the bush about it. Even if she did I wouldn't give a fuck. All I wanted was the pussy.

"I don't have one."

"Quit lying. I know yo fine ass got niggas ringing that phone."

"They ain't nobody."

"After tonight, they won't be."

"You sound confident."

"Oh, I am."

Andrea turned in the seat and crossed her legs. "So, what's a young fly nigga like yourself doing driving a taxi cab? This yo' job or something?"

"Fa sho. That's a problem?"

"No." Andrea folded her arms. "I don't believe you though."

I couldn't help but to laugh. "Why not?"

"You doing more than driving this cab and you hanging with Kamari. We know what he do."

"I got drip for sale, baby."

Andrea and I talked for a little while about nothing in particular. She kept shaking her legs and showing me pussy shots on the sly, so I tried her. Slowly, I leaned close to her and put my hands on her thighs. When she didn't bother to move them, I knew I had the green light. My hands went further up her thigh, all the way to her baldheaded cat. Andrea gasped softly in my ear when I started playing in her twat and grabbing my ear. That told me she wanted to fuck, so I kept on finger fucking her and she was hella wet.

If she was that easy, I knew I could get the pussy right there in the car. All I had to do was bait her up. I unzipped my pants and placed her hand in my lap. "Jack my dick."

With no hesitation Andrea grabbed ahold of it and pulled on him slowly. We were almost to the finish line when the back door opened. Kamari and his chick got in the car.

"What y'all in here doing?" Kamari's girl giggled. "Y'all being nasty?"

"Mind yo business and tend to me," Kamari replied.

The car was back quiet, so I picked up where we left off. Andrea started back jacking my dick and I was fingering her once more. Then out the blue, moaning bounced around in the car. Me and Andrea looked in the back seat and Kamari's girl was in his lap riding him.

That was my chance to go further, because I'd be damned if he was gone be the only one getting some action when I didn't want to come in the first place. "Lift yo dress up."

To my surprise, Andrea raised that muthafucka with no problem and planted one foot on the floor. Reaching inside my pocket, I pulled out a condom and strapped up quick. "Scoot down."

The car was a little spacious, but not big enough to get comfortable. That didn't matter, 'cause I was gone make it work. Sliding my jeans down, I got between her legs and pushed my dick deep down inside her.

"Ssss." She grabbed my waist and held it, while I delivered quick, long strokes.

Due to the lack of space, I couldn't handle her the way I wanted to, so a quickie would have to do. Grabbing the headrest, I rammed her hard and fast until that nut surfaced. Andrea had her hand over her mouth to keep from making noise. My shit was throbbing and on the verge of shooting, when gunshots rang out.

Boc! Boc! Boc! Boc!

Every last one of us in the car jumped up to see what the fuck was going on. "What the fuck, yo?" Kamari yelled and the girls started screaming.

The crowd was hauling ass. The partygoers were jumping in cars and pulling off. It was time for me to do the same. After pulling up my pants, I put the car in drive and the driver door flew open. All I saw was the barrel of a gun in my face.

"Not so fast, playboy. Pop that trunk," the shooter demanded. The girls started screaming again. "Shut the fuck up. Out here fuckin' in cars when y'all need to be in the house."

"What the fuck you doing?" I didn't make any sudden movements because I couldn't go out like this.

"Nigga, you know what this is. Run me that money."

"I ain't got shit."

The nigga pressed the gun against my temple. "Lie again and I'll bust yo' brain all over yo' bitch. Gimme the money you just picked up. Pop that trunk before I start shooting."

"Bruh, just give the shit up," Kamari tried reasoning.

"A'ight! A'ight! You got it." I reached down and hit the release latch.

"Tell that nigga Brick to come see Raheem." The shooter slammed the door and ran to the trunk. From the rearview I could see him taking out the duffle bag and running back to the car.

"Fuck!" I punched the steering wheel hard. "Brick gone lose it when he find out what happened."

"I know, bruh, but ain't no sense in dying behind that shit. He can get that money back. Just hit him up and tell him what happened."

I swiveled my head in his direction. "Yeah, I'm about to."

Picking up my cellphone, I stared at the keypad for countless minutes before I dialed his number. I didn't know where the conversation was headed, but I hoped like hell he was understanding.

Chapter 4
Coop
The next day

From the time I made the conscious decision to leave Danielle, a nigga stress level decreased drastically. It felt good to come and go as I pleased without all the extra shit. One thing about me is I'm a relentless hustler and nobody was stopping that bag. Danielle knew I hustles hard and she was always trying to interfere with that until it was time to spend the shit. *How that work though?* Somebody needed to tell her that money trucks wasn't showing up randomly at front doors. I had to go out and get it, but she wasn't listening to me. Hopefully, she would find her a nigga that punched the clock so he could be in the house by six o'clock.

Don't get me wrong, I loved Danielle and that was why I married her and changed my ways. I wanted to prove to her that I could be the man that she wanted. A lot of times in life you had to love people enough to let them go and love them from a distance.

Presently that was our current situation, because she made my life a living hell. Not to mention, that muthafucka tried to poison me with Fabuloso. One week after I moved out I found an apartment, but it won't be ready for another two weeks. So in the meantime, I was staying with the chick, Tamia. The same chick I was Netflix and chilling with. After hearing an earful of my situation, she insisted I stay with her, instead of wasting money at a hotel. Since I fucked with shorty heavy, I stayed with her.

My first night there we didn't do anything, but that second night it went down. I tried to break her back. She was the first chick I smashed since I got married. Tamia was a younger chick, but she had a good head on her shoulders. She worked and went to school, so I had no problem with breaking her off with five bands when I moved in temporarily.

"Here, bae." Tamia handed me a cold glass of Cognac. My eyes were glued on her ass when she strutted her slim, thick frame in front of the flat screen.

Tamia grabbed her pink throw and covered her legs. Cuddling up underneath me, she rested her head in my lap. "Okay, you can start it now."

The remote was sitting on the arm of the chair, so I grabbed it and pressed play. We were watching *Aquaman* and Tamia was loving every minute of it. That shit was good as fuck, but she was enjoying it for other reasons.

"So, I'm bae now?" I took a sip of the "yak" and cleared my throat.

Tamia blushed every time I said something to her. "You always been bae, so don't act surprised. I just didn't say anything because you were happily married at the time."

"Married. Yes. Happily. Nah."

"Apparently it was something, because when you spent the night, I just knew you were gone try and get in the bed with me. Yo ass surprised me when you slept on the sofa all night."

"I was respecting my vows and you as well, but as you can see, that ain't mean shit. Had I known this would be the result, I would've been cheated. I was faithful and still ended up in the dog house."

"Facts." Tamia crossed her legs. "It's all good though and thanks for respecting me, but you do know that shouldn't have been out overnight like that."

"True, but at the same time, I'm a hustler. My hours vary on a daily basis and besides that, no man wants to be in the house with a female that nags all goddamn day."

"I get what you saying, but you know that comes from lack of trust."

"Dat part. Funny thing is I gave her my phone and all so she can see that I wasn't hiding nothing."

"Yeah. That's how she got my number."

I tapped her on those thick chocolate thighs. "But, check this out though. After she went through my shit and found nothing, she talm 'bout, 'You probably erased the messages.' After that, I was done. Ain't no satisfying that bitch."

"Well, you don't have to worry about me trying to keep you on a leash. You will put yourself on one messing with me." She smiled.

"We'll see about that."

One hour later the Aquaman did his final leap from the water and the movie was over. "Damn, that man fine. That don't make no sense."

"So you gone call another man fine while you laying with me?" I teased, while squeezing her thigh.

Tamia giggled. "Stop. I was just playing, you know I only have eyes for you."

"I'm the only one your eyes better be on."

"Don't worry, bae. I'm Ray Charles when it comes to anybody else after you get a divorce."

"Shiddd, before then. Fuck you mean?"

Tamia turned on her side, so she could face me. "On a serious note, you know I'm fucked up about you."

"If we gone be together, when it's all said and done, you can't pop another pill and I'm serious."

"Bae, I don't pop pills. That wasn't for me. It was for my homegirl. I only smoke."

"Oh, tell me something, shit."

"I want you," she replied.

"Whatchu talm 'bout?"

"You said tell you something and I'm telling you that I want you."

"Oh yeah?" I reached down and slid my hand inside her tights. Slowly, I rubbed her clit in a circular motion.

Tamia grabbed my head and pulled me closer to her. Placing her lips on mine, we kissed passionately. Our tongues wrestled one another's, increasing the sexual tension. Out of the blue, my damn phone starting ringing, interrupting our foreplay. Just as I was about to grab it, Tamia mumbled, "Ignore it." And I did.

Shorty's pussy was so wet when I eased a finger inside and slid it in and out. Tamia rocked her hips back and forth. "Give it to me now."

Anxiously, she used her free hand to try and pull them shits down. When she couldn't get them past her butt, I pushed them down to her ankles.

"Sit up." My damn phone started up again. So, the minute I was free to get up, I grabbed it. "This muthafucka don't quit."

Tamia finished taking off her tights and tossed them on the floor. Then she looked up at me. "Danielle?"

"Yeah."

"Just see what she want. You know she ain't gone stop calling until you answer."

"Fuck her. I'm busy."

"Fine with me." Tamia laid back on the couch and played with her nipples.

Whatever she wanted was gone have to wait. I put my phone on silent, then tossed it on the floor along with the rest of my clothes, and took a condom out my wallet. Tamia watched me as I tore open the wrapper and slipped the rubber over my nine-pack. Climbing on the couch, I pushed her legs back and licked her clit up and down. Gently, I nibbled on it, sucked it and fingered her at the same time.

"Ooh, bae," she moaned, while she continued to play with her nipples. Tamia grabbed her breast and pushed it close to her mouth. I watched as she sucked on the nipple. She was a freak and wasn't afraid to show it.

Now face-to-face, I entered that wet-wet and took several slow, deep strokes. Tamia's body rocked and moved, like she was running from the dick. That stopped when her head made it against the arm of the chair. From there, there was no place else to run. Lifting her leg, I put it on my shoulder and planted one foot on the floor. That ass was in trouble.

Gripping the arm of the sofa, I went deep and pulled out slowly. Then, I did it once more. Tamia's pussy gripped me so tight that I couldn't help going crazy in it. At a fast pace, I beat the box hard with every stroke.

"Sss. Ah! Ah! Ooh! Shit! Bae, wait."

I ignored every plea coming my way and murdered her shit. Mid-stroke, the coochie felt extra wet and good. That was when I realized the damn condom popped.

"Shit." Pulling out, I saw I was right. I pulled off what was left.

"What happened?" Tamia asked.

"The rubber popped."

"Oh. Pass me my phone."

"For what?"

"I wanna record us." I leaned over and picked it from the coffee table.

Tamia pointed the phone in my direction as I eased my semi-stiff wood back inside her snatch. After two strokes my boy was back and in beast mode, so I didn't waste time hammering it down. She tried her best to hold that phone, but I was too deep in the guts. Unable to keep her hand steady, she stuck the phone down on the side of the sofa and put her hand on my stomach.

"Baaaeeee!" she hollered. "You too deep. Slow down."

Tamia's fuck faces were so cute to me. Looking into her eyes, I bit down on my lip and pushed every inch left inside. I wanted to touch an ovary. "Move ya hand."

"I can't," she whimpered.

"Move it," I demanded.

"Coop, it hurt."

"This what you wanted." Pushing her leg back until her toes touched the sofa, I beat it some more. The sounds of our skin colliding sounded like thunder.

"Ouuuuu! Ahhhhhhh! Shiiiittttttt!" Tamia's moaning grew louder and eventually turned into heavy panting and screaming, as I went balls deep. In an effort to muffle the sound, she used both hands to cover her mouth.

Finally, I gave in and dropped her leg. After ten more minutes of hardcore fucking, I raised her leg and busted a nut all up in her. Tamia was breathing hard when I pulled out.

"Make me think you just tried to kill me."

I leaned down and kissed her in the mouth. "Just the pussy baby, not you. Stay right there while I get a rag."

Tamia stretched out on the couch while I went to the bathroom. Standing over the toilet I took a long ass piss, washed my hands and soaped up a rag for her. When I got back into the living room, she opened her legs and I wiped her clean.

"Ouch! Stop wiping me so rough. You got me sore." She pouted. Those pretty pussy lips were swollen.

"Aww. I'm sorry, baby, but I had to mark my territory." I placed a kiss down below and stood up. "You still need a shower."

"After I take a nap, I'll shower. My ass is tieeddd!"

After cleaning myself up, I went back into the living room and scooped Tamia up into my arms. It didn't seem like she was gone get in the bed unless I carried her there. Once she was in bed, I went back to get my cellphone.

My body was tired and I needed some damn rest myself. Tamia laid on my chest as we drifted off into peaceful sleep. Two hours later, my deep sleep was cut short by that damn device of mine. Rubbing my eyes, I leaned over and picked it up. This time it wasn't Danielle, so I was grateful for that.

"Wassup, bruh."

"Get yo' tied ass up, nigga. We got a problem."

Those four words made me get up and focus. "What problem?"

"Somebody hit the shop, so I need you to meet me there like yesterday."

"A'ight. Give me thirty minutes. I'm getting up now."

"Thirty minutes?" Brick repeated.

"Yeah, man. I gotta shower."

"Yeah, do that. I don't need you around me smelling like pussy."

"Yeah whatever, nigga. I'll be there with fresh nuts."

"Bye, dawg." Brick laughed before he hung up the phone.

Careful not to wake Tamia up, I eased from underneath her and stood up. That didn't help 'cause soon as I turned around, those brown eyes of hers were beaming up at me.

"Where you going?"

"To meet my brother. I'll be right back."

"Can I come?"

"Didn't you cum enough?" I smirked.

"Oh, you being cute."

"Get some rest and I'll be back, okay?"

"Okay." Tamia grabbed the pillow that I slept on and wrapped her arms around it. Then I took my happy ass to the shower to prepare for whatever disaster was about to occur.

Chapter 5
Brick

Zuri was sleeping so peacefully that I didn't want to wake her, but I had to because I didn't need her waking up looking for me. The delivery of our son kicked her ass and I knew she was in a lot of pain. Watching her go through childbirth gave me a newfound respect for her. I've always respected her as a woman, but seeing her go through all that pain made me put her on a higher pedestal.

As I stood beside the bed, I watched her sleep a minute longer before shaking her shoulder. "Zuri."

She didn't move, so I attempted to wake her once more. "Baby, wake up."

The medicine they gave her must've had her in the twilight zone because she wasn't moving for shit. Time was ticking and I had to leave so I could check on my investments. Exiting the room, I went to the nurse's station. When I made it to the counter all of the women looked in my direction cheesing. I wanted to say, *dry your panties ladies, I'm taken and no, I don't cheat.* Instead, I opted on the polite route.

"My wife, Zuri Monroe, is down the hall sleeping. When she awakens, please let her know I will be back. I don't want her to panic."

"Yes, sir. I certainly will."

"Thanks."

On my way through the double doors and down the hallway, my phone started to go off. When I pulled it from my pocket, I saw it was Janae calling so I picked up.

"Hello."

"Daddy. Where are you?"

"I'm at the hospital," I replied, while pressing the elevator button.

"Huh?"

"I'm at the hospital."

"I can't hear you."

The elevator doors opened, so I stepped inside and the phone hung up. Janae called back, but I didn't answer. There was no point in doing so since the reception was bad. By the time I made it to the second floor and walked towards the exit, all four bars showed up so I called her back.

"Hello." She picked up.

"Wassup, Nae?"

"Why you at the hospital? Are you okay?" There was heavy concern in her voice.

"Yes. I'm okay. Zuri had the baby early."

"Oh," she exhaled. "I can't afford to lose another parent. Is she and the baby okay?"

"Yeah, they good. He's underweight, so he has to stay here for a while."

"How much did he weigh?"

"Four pounds."

"Aww. I wanna see him."

"I'm leaving now, but you can come up here when I finish running these errands."

"Okay. What's his name?"

"You already know." I chuckled, as I unlocked the doors to my car. "My lil nigga a junior."

"Oh, Lord," Janae laughed. "I should've known."

"It's only right." After I got inside the car and started it, I took a deep breath. Revisiting her pain wasn't what I wanted to do, but I had to make sure my baby was okay. "How you holding up, baby?"

"I'm not." Silence took over the phone call.

"Nae—"

"This is so hard. I don't know how I'm going to do this." Janae starting to sniffle, so I knew she was crying.

"You breaking my heart right now. I don't like hearing you like this. Where are you?"

"I'm at Demarcus house."

"Where is he?"

"At work."

"A'ight. Give me an hour and I'll be there to pick you up."

Janae sniffled again. "Okay."

"Send me your location and I'll see you soon."

"Okay."

Once Janae was off my line, I tossed the phone in the passenger seat. Closing my eyes, I leaned my head against the headrest and took a deep breath. "Damn, I got a full plate. I got this though. God gives his toughest battles to his strongest soldiers."

Breanna's face flashed before my eyes, so I opened them and grabbed my phone. Mehzani's phone rang several times before she picked up.

"Hello."

"Wassup, sis?"

"Hey, brother, you calling to check on Bre?"

"Yeah. How is she?" Finally, I backed out the parking spot.

"Listen here. I don't know where you got this grown lady from. That mouth is something else, but she adorable."

"That's Bre. What she said?"

"She told me she couldn't sleep without a bedtime story. So I attempted to make one up since we don't have books here. She cut me off in the middle and said, 'I never heard of these characters before. Did you make them up?' So I told her yes. That girl told me, 'lying not good. My daddy told me not to trust a liar.' "

Hearing about Breanna's mouth made me laugh and it was well-needed. "I'm sorry, sis. I did tell her that. I'm teaching her to always be honest."

"Well, she got that down pat."

"Yeah, I see."

"Do you want to talk to her?"

"Nah, because she gone want me to pick her up. I'll just see her later on when y'all come to the hospital."

"Hospital for what?"

"That's the main reason I was calling. Zuri had the baby early this morning. She's in recovery and the baby is in NICU."

"Oh, my God! Why so early?" Mehzani shouted into the phone.

"Not listening. You know how your sister is. She stressed herself and the baby, so they had to do an emergency C-section."

"Okay, well we gone go up there as soon as the physical therapist leaves."

"Physical therapist," I repeated.

"Yeah. Gucci has to have extensive therapy if he ever wants to walk again."

"A'ight. I'll see you later."

"Okay."

Quickly, I hung up the phone and mumbled. "That nigga don't need to walk again in life. Limbs are a privilege and he ruined that many years ago. Snake-ass nigga."

***

When I pulled up to the shop, Skeet, Kamari and Chris were standing out front choppin' it up. I got out the car and approached them. "Where's Wayne?"

Skeet shrugged his shoulders. "He said he was on his way an hour ago."

"Okay." I nodded.

These niggas knew that being late to any meeting was my biggest pet peeve, so he better be prepared for what I had in store for him. Just as I was formulating a plan in my head, Coop pulled up behind my car and parked.

"Kamari and Chris!"

"Wassup, boss?" they replied in unison.

"Go inside. We about to start."

"A'ight." Both men started to walk off.

"Chris, hit Wayne up and let him know if his ass ain't here in ten minutes, he'll be selling dinners tomorrow."

"Okay."

Skeet folded his arms, as he stood there waiting on them to get inside. Once they were on the opposite side of the door, he turned back to face me. "What's going on?"

Stroking my beard, I bit down on my lip in frustration. "I need a complete rundown on what the fuck happened, but before that, I need you to get rid of my girl car."

"Shiidd! You know I'll handle that for you."

"Yeah, but I need you to completely destroy it. Don't leave any evidence, fingerprints or nothing behind. I'ma have her to call it in stolen and I don't need that coming back this way."

"I gotchu, Brick. Have I ever let you down?" Skeet gave a disappointing stare like he couldn't believe I said those words and truthfully speaking, I knew I could count on him. Granted, though he was young in age, he still had the heart of a lion.

"Nah."

"Well, I don't plan on starting now." Skeet glanced towards the road, so I swiveled my head in the same direction to see what he was looking at.

"It's so nice to have the old coon to join us."

Coop laughed and dapped us up. "Fuck you, lil nigga. Just pray you live to be my age. Y'all ninety babies dropping like flies."

"Not me." Skeet popped his collar. "I'm the last of a dying breed."

"Let him know, soldier," I replied. "Oh, Zuri had the baby early this morning."

Coop's eyes stretched in their sockets. "Word! How they doing?"

"They good. My lil man underweight, but he gone be alright."

"Congratulations, fool. I guess I'll grab us liquor and cigars." Coop smiled. "I was gone ask you what was up with the hospital band you rocking."

"Congrats, boss." Skeet dapped me up and gave me a G-hug.

"Thanks. Let's get in here so we can start this meeting."

Skeet, Coop and I were strolling up the walkway when we heard a car pulling up with the music blasting. We all stopped and turned around. It was a Chevy Malibu with rims on it.

"Who the fuck is that?" Coop asked.

"Look like Wayne," I replied.

"Yeah, that's him. I saw him driving that car before. That's his girl shit." Skeet turned around and opened the door to go inside. We followed suit.

By the time we walked in and got settled, Wayne came walking in with a dumb-ass look on his face. "Sorry I'm late."

"You know the rules and you also know that apology don't mean shit. I'm running a business, not night school classes. So, fall in line before I dismiss yo ass."

"Damn, bruh, I said I was sorry. It wasn't intentional. My car fucked up and I had to take my girl to work."

"I don't give a fuck what you had to do. You told Skeet you would be here an hour ago and you just strolling yo ass in this muthafucka like you runnin' shit."

Wayne moved his head from side to side. "Come on, bruh, you know it ain't like that. What I gotta pay you for being late?"

Now he was trying me and I was doing my best not to take his whole muthafuckin' head off. He then stuck his hand deep down in his pocket and pulled out a small knot of money. "What I gotta pay?"

"Listen, put that chump change away before I take all of it." I reached down in my pocket and pulled out a fatter knot. "You don't wanna play big bank take little bank. You gone lose."

Wayne put his money back inside his pocket pronto and sat down. "You right. My apologies, boss."

The way he chuckled didn't sit too well with me because now I felt like he thought shit was a game. "Wayne, slide me your car keys."

He did as he was told and pushed them across the table, so I scooped them up and put them in my pocket. Then, I looked over at Coop. "Bruh, grab the supplies for this nigga, 'cause he think shit a game right now."

"Come on, Brick. Don't do this, man," Wayne pleaded, knowing what was coming his way.

Coop walked to the end of the table to where Wayne was sitting and handed him a notebook and pen. He was acting like he was about to get a whooping or some shit by his old girl.

"Bruh, you tried me. Now write five hundred times, I will never challenge Brick and the first two hundred needs to be done before you get these keys back."

"But, I gotta pick up my lady."

"You determine what time you pick her up, so I would advise you to get to writing."

Wayne sucked his teeth and picked up the pen.

"Keep complaining and I'll make it a thousand." Wayne closed his mouth quick and got to writing.

Now that the issue was handled, I was finally able to start the meeting, but first I addressed Kamari, since he appeared to be confused as he watched Wayne. "Kamari, in case you wondering, that's the consequence for being late or kicking slick rap with me. I'm the boss, so I don't tolerate bullshit."

"Thanks, boss, but I already know how to move." Kamari saluted me and dropped his hand back in his lap.

"The youngest and newest member knows better. Take notes, Wayne." Finally, I took a seat after standing for so long and sat my phone on the table. Ten seconds later, it rang. I held one finger in the air.

"Hello."

"Daddy, where are you?" Janae sounded as if she was crying.

"I'm at the shop. What's wrong?"

"I'm on my way up there."

"Okay."

Closing my phone, I sat it down and rubbed my temple. My head was thumping and my body was tired. I was ready to go. I hadn't been to sleep in twenty-four hours and I felt like I would crash at that very moment. All of the stress was taking a toll on my mind, body and soul.

"You good, bruh?" Coop leaned in and spoke so that only I could hear him.

"Yeah. That was Nae," I replied, using the same tone.

"My niece good?"

"Nah. She having a hard time processing it all and it's fucking me up. The whole situation."

"Damn, man!" Coop sighed and sat back in his seat and folded his hands. "Finish the meeting, so we can bounce when she get here."

"A'ight."

Turning back to face my crew, I took a deep breath before I spoke. "Listen, last night Skeet and Kamari got hit up for forty-five stacks by a nigga we beefing with name Raheem."

"How we know it was him?" Chris asked.

Skeet shot him a death stare and gritted his teeth. "Because he sent a message, muthafucka! Fuck you tryna say, a nigga bucked on the cash?"

Chris smirked. "Pipe down, young nigga. I'm just asking a question."

"Nah, you throwing shade like a bitch," Skeet snapped.

"Ain't no bitch in me, boy, so watch that slick rap."

Division amongst the crew in the middle of a war wasn't what we needed, so I nipped that shit in the bud quick. "Both of y'all shut the fuck up."

Skeet looked Chris up and down and smirked. "The boss just saved you, boy."

"The last thing we need right now is beef amongst the crew. This nigga Raheem sent me a message, so that's what we need to be focused on. I know a few of his workers, but I need y'all to bleed the blocks and get locations of his traps. Be clever and don't go around the city shooting shit up."

Leaning forward, I folded my hands and placed them on the table. "We don't need any heat, so take calculated steps when making moves and no more slip-ups. Ain't no telling who he working with, so don't trust nobody. I wouldn't give a fuck if it was a deacon. If that muthafucka ain't sitting at this table, that means they can't be trusted 'cause they ain't one of us. Simple."

"Facts! And I wanna add something to what he just said." Sitting back, I gave Coop the floor while I listened to what he had to say.

***

Mehzani

"I'm coming," I yelled, while walking to the front door and opening it. Mel was standing there with a dumbfounded look on his face and a duffle bag.

"Surprised you called me."

"Don't start that. You still have a job to do, so stick with that and leave the past where it's at."

"Damn!" he sighed. "Just like that, huh?"

"You do know what happened between us was a mistake? I was weak and vulnerable at that time, so delete that from your memory bank. You couldn't possibly think I would continue sleeping with you."

"Humph! Consider it deleted." Mel walked past me and shook his head.

Closing the door and locking it, I went back to Gucci's bedside and grabbed his hand. "Mel is going to stay with you until I get back from the hospital. My sister had the baby, so I'm going to sit with her for a few hours. Okay?"

Gucci nodded his head. The physical therapist that came by five days a week was slowly making progress with him. It would still be a long time before he recovered, but I was happy with the fact that he hadn't given up on life. My eyes then went to Mel.

"If you need me, call me. I fed him and everything, so he should be good until I get back."

"Okay," he replied, while handing up the duffle bag. "This is what I collected for the week, so put it up."

Avoiding all eye contact, I grabbed the bag and tossed it over my shoulder.

"You good, bruh?" he asked, while stepping closer to the bed and giving him dap. Gucci nodded his head. "That's half a mil in that bag. Business is going smooth as usual and everybody has been paying on time. So, you have nothing to worry about. Just focus on getting better and I'll handle the business."

Leaving the two alone, I went into the bedroom and pulled the closet door open. As I dropped the bag on the floor, I punched in the combination to the safe and opened it. Stack by stack, I loaded the money until the bag was empty. Activating the code, I closed the closet door and threw the featherweight bag over my shoulder once more.

Breanna and Legend were in the room watching YouTube when I walked in. "Hey kiddos. It's time to go and see Zuri, so put on y'all shoes."

Neither one of their asses paid me any attention. They kept watching TV like I wasn't standing there. So, being the petty auntie I was, I went and stood directly in front of it, blocking their view.

"Since y'all can't hear me, who wants a whooping?" My arms were folded across my chest.

Bre's head snapped back a little, as she tooted her nose up and grinned. "You do."

"Ohhh, so you a little sassafrass huh?" Deep down I wanted to laugh so bad because that girl was really giving me a run for my money. In fact, I couldn't wait to have a baby of my own.

"What's that?" she questioned.

"A sassy little girl."

"Oh. I guess." Bre hopped down from the bed, grabbed her shoes and started putting them on. "Come on, boy, put your shoes on."

Legend stood up in the bed and jumped down onto the floor, as if he was in the wrestling ring. "You better stop before you hurt yourself," I blurted out.

Bre stood up and grabbed her doll. "You better stop, Legend, before you get a whooping."

All I could do was laugh. "I'm not going to whoop y'all. I was just playing. You don't believe me?"

"Girl, I don't trust you." Bre acted just like an old lady.

"Girl, no you didn't." I smirked. "Let's go, so I can get y'all back to Zuri and Brick."

On our way down the hall, I hear Mel talking to Gucci about some new business moves. Not wanting to interrupt their heavy conversation, I waved my hand in the air to get their attention.

"I'll be back in a few hours."

"A'ight, sis," Mel replied, then went back to talking to Gucci.

Me and the kids walked out the door and headed to the car. After I got them in and strapped down, I got in and did the same. A strange feeling came over me and I felt like I probably should tell Gucci what happened between me and his boy. The timing just seemed all wrong, but with Mel having ill feelings, there was no telling if he would tell him. His aura was all wrong about the situation. My only concern was gaining his forgiveness.

Destiny Skai

Chapter 6
Brick

Half an hour later, the meeting was still going. There was so much we had to strategize to make sure I didn't take another hit. That nigga Raheem didn't know he'd just played with fire and his ass was about to get burnt. The money he stole was chump change, so that wasn't hitting on shit compared to what he was about to lose. My cellphone rang and it was Janae, so I picked up.

"I'm coming out right now."

"Okay," she replied before hanging up.

"Before I end this meeting, Skeet and Chris, do y'all need to duke that shit out in the yard before I leave? I can't have y'all divided right now."

Chris looked over at Skeet and nodded his head. "I'm good. It was just a misunderstanding."

Standing to my feet, I glanced at my protégé. "What about you, Skeet? You good?"

"Yeah. I'm good," he replied.

"Y'all boys shake that shit out before I go."

Chris and Skeet both stood and met each other halfway. The two men dapped it out and G-hugged. "It's all love, man. I ain't mean no harm."

"You good, bruh," Skeet replied before going back to his seat.

"A'ight now, since that's over with, we out. Wayne, finish my assignment before you leave here. Skeet, catch." I tossed the car keys to him. "Give him back his keys once he finishes and not a minute before."

"I gotcha, boss."

"We out. Coop, let's roll."

Coop got up and we all headed for the door, everyone except Chris. "Aye, Brick," Skeet called out.

"'Sup, youngin'?" I opened the front door and stepped onto the porch.

"I got one of my homies looking into Raheem trap spots for me, so I'll have something for you soon. Apparently, his sister fuck with the nigga and before you ask, yes, I trust the nigga."

"You already know where I was going with that." I nodded my head, as I watched Janae get out the car.

"I'm on it. I slipped up and this on me, so I'll make it right."

"I fucks with you, youngin'. Keep moving like this and I'll bump yo rank up."

"A'ight." Skeet smiled, then looked towards the road.

Janae walked towards us, wearing shorts I didn't approve of, exposing her legs and a top that exposed her mid-section and belly ring.

"Damn, shawty thick. Who she here for?"

"Me, nigga," I replied.

"Oh, that's you, bruh? You like 'em young, huh? Ole cheating-ass nigga."

"Nigga, I don't cheat." I gave him the side eye, as Janae stepped onto the porch and hugged me tight. "Hey, baby. It's gone be okay. I'm here for you."

"Shidd, me too," Skeet added.

"Nigga, my niece don't need you," Coop spoke up.

"Niece?" Skeet questioned.

Janae let me go and wiped her eyes with the back of her hand. I then turned towards Skeet. "Yeah, this my daughter. So keep yo' eyes off of this one."

"Ohhh shit! My bad, big dawg."

Coop stepped in and hugged Janae as well. "We gotchu, baby. Whatever you need just let me know."

"Let's go. Get up with me as soon as you hear something." I dapped Skeet up.

Just as we prepared to leave, Danielle appeared out of the blue, rushing towards the house at a high rate of speed. "Here comes that crazy bitch again," Kamari chuckled.

Coop cut his eyes at the young buck. "Easy, bro. That's my wife."

"Oh shit, my bad, dawg. She came here earlier snappin' on us. I meant to tell you, but I forgot."

Coop met her halfway. "What the fuck you doing here? We have no dealings."

"Nigga, we still married. What the fuck you mean?" Danielle huffed with her hands on her hips.

"I'm not doing this with you today and I made that clear earlier. So, take yo' ass home. You love making a scene."

"So. Fucking. What." Danielle clapped her hands together, getting louder.

The stunt she was pulling was too much and I needed to nip that in the bud for him. "Aye, sis." I stepped closer to her. "Don't do this here. You putting everybody in y'all business and that ain't cool."

"Brick, you know I love you like a brother, but this nigga foul as fuck. The shit he pulled earlier was the last straw."

46

"I get that, but this is something that should be handled in private."

Danielle rolled her neck and looked at me. "Do you know he let his bitch call me on the phone while they was fucking? That was so disrespectful, but I guess you don't see nothing wrong with that."

"Stop fuckin' lying. That girl ain't call you."

"Make me think you trying to kill me," Danielle moaned, mimicking Tamia. "Tell me I'm lying, you cheating muthafucka."

Coop paused and his forehead wrinkles appeared like she was telling the truth. "I moved out, so it's not cheating."

"So, fuck the fact that you fucking with a childish-ass bitch playing on your wife phone?"

"Nah. I just don't believe you for the simple fact that you play on our phones on a daily basis. You had me and you blew it, so move on."

Coop turned his back to Danielle and dapped me up. "I'm out, bruh. I'ma slide up on you and the baby later. I have some business to handle first."

"Bet that up, bruh."

***

Zuri

After a much needed nap, I opened my eyes a little and blinked several times. To my surprise, Brick was no longer sitting there, but Mehzani and the kids were seated in the chairs staring at me. A slight smile spread across my lips.

"Good afternoon, sleeping beauty." Mehzani stood up and walked towards me.

"Zuri! Zuri!" Breanna screamed, as she ran past my sister and attempted to climb up on the bed. Legend remained focused on the cellphone he was playing with.

"Careful, baby. I have staples in my stomach." Grabbing Breanna's hand, I helped her up. "Hey LJ."

"Hi." His eyes remained glued to the screen.

"Hey, sis. How are you?"

Mehzani hugged me gently and kissed my cheek. "I'm good, but the question is, how are you and my nephew?"

"We're good. He's in NICU."

"Aww, sis. Why did you have him so early? What happened?"

"It's a long X-rated story, but I'll tell you about it later. In the meantime, just know that stress is the reason behind it all."

Mezhani smirked and shook her head. "I can only imagine. In the meantime, I want to see my nephew."

"Well, if you help me out of this bed, we can go see the prince."

"Please tell me you didn't name him that?" Mehzani's eyebrow shifted downward.

"No." I giggled. "He's named after Brick."

"Okay and what's his name?"

"Brandon Alejandro Riccardo, Jr."

"That's cute, but why the hell does he have three first names? And Spanish at that?" Mehzani helped Breanna down, then assisted me off the bed. "One of his parents Spanish or some shit?"

"Girl, I don't know."

"I need to ask his mama then."

"You won't be doing that, 'cause she's dead and so is his dad."

"Damn," she sighed. "He's an orphan just like us."

"Right." I adjusted my gown and slipped on my bedroom shoes. Taking tiny, slow steps I made my way towards the door. "My stomach hurt so fuckin' bad."

"Do you need a wheelchair?" Mehzani grabbed my arm.

"No. I need to walk on my own if I want to go home soon."

"Bre and LJ, come on."

With each step I took, it felt like my insides wanted to fall right out on the floor. But, for the sake of a quicker recovery, I had to suck it up and keep it pushing. Thank God, the NICU was close so I didn't have that far to go. Once we made it outside the window, I pointed in his direction.

"That's him in the third bed on the right."

"Aww. I'm so happy for you. I want to see him up close." Mehzani placed her hand on the glass and smiled.

"Knock on the window to get the nurse's attention."

She did like I told her and one of the nurses walked to the door and opened it. "Yes, how can I..." she paused once she saw my face. "Hello, mommy. You came to see the baby?"

"My sister wants to see him, is that okay?"

"Sure thing, but no children allowed."

"Yes, I know. They're going to stay out here with me."

From the window, I watched Mehzani interact with my little one. The fact that he was so small and fragile made me feel bad, because it was all my fault. As bad as I hated to admit it, but if I would've listened to Brick and went back to the hotel, we wouldn't be in this predicament.

After spending a few minutes with the baby, Mehzani finally made her exit. "Oh my God!" she cupped her hand over her mouth in excitement. "He's so cute and tiny."

"Thank you. I'm just glad that he doesn't look like a wet-ass rat in distress."

Mezhani burst out in laughter. "Aht! Aht! Don't talk about my nephew like that. Him so cute with that head full of hair."

"Surprisingly, after all he's been through. I figured he'd be stressed out and baldheaded."

"You so stupid."

A throbbing pain at the bottom of my stomach caused me to close my eyes. Mehzani placed her hand on my shoulder. "Are you okay?"

Shaking my head slowly, I leaned against the wall. "I need to go back and lay down."

"Come on."

Mehzani put her arm around my waist and held my arm, as she escorted me back towards my room. Just as we were making our way inside, I could see Brick coming down the hallway with a female in tow. I didn't know who he was with, but I was surely about to find out in the next few minutes.

Sitting down slowly on the bed, Mehzani lifted my legs and helped me get comfortable. "Thanks, sis."

"No problem, babes." Mehzani sat down in her spot. "Girl, we have a lot to catch up on."

"What's going—" Before I could finish my sentence, Brick walked in with the same female who he claimed to be his god-daughter. I had no animosity towards her, but I was curious as to why he felt the need to bring her there.

"Daddy! Daddy!" Breanna shouted while rushing towards Brick. Mehzani swiveled her head around in surprise.

Scooping her up in his arms, he kissed her cheek and hugged her tight. "Daddy missed his baby."

"I missed you too."

Impatiently, I sat in bed with my arms folded, waiting on him to address me. His shadow had me annoyed since she didn't speak when she came in, but sus didn't waste time hugging and kissing Bre.

Chapter 7
Brick

Zuri had the nastiest expression on her face and I peeped that as soon as we walked in. Something told me this conversation had to happen right then and there. Mehzani stood up and looked at me, but her facial expression was a whole lot softer than her sister's mean ass.

"Hey, bro. What's going on?" She reached up to hug me.

"I'm good. Thanks for keeping the babies for us."

"It's no problem." Mehzani took a step back and looked over my shoulder. "Well, who is this?"

"Oh, my bad. This is Janae." I turned to Janae and quickly introduced them. "Janae, this is Mehzani, Zuri's sister."

"Hi, nice to meet you," Janae replied.

"Nice to meet you as well." Mehzani turned to face Zuri. "Well, I'm going to go home now. Call me later, sis."

"I will and thanks for everything," Zuri replied.

As Mehzani stepped away from the bed, I approached Zuri. "Hey, baby. We need to talk."

"You damn right we do," she huffed.

That was confirmation an argument was at bay, but I didn't want my kids to hear it. Reaching into my pocket, I pulled out a stack of bills and pulled off two, twenty-dollar-bills.

"Janae, take the kids downstairs to McDonald's so I can talk to Zuri and when you come back, I'll walk you over to see the baby."

"Okay." She grabbed the money and tucked it into her back pocket. "Come on, kids, let's go."

Bre and Legend followed her out the door. When the coast was clear, I sat down beside Zuri and took a deep breath. But, before I could say anything, she was flying off at the mouth.

"Why did you bring that rude ass girl here?" she pouted.

"Chill out, because that's what I want to talk to you about. That's Janae and y'all met at—"

Zuri cut me off mid-sentence. "I know who she is, but why is she here? That's my question to you."

All I could do was shake my head because she was making shit really difficult. "Zuri, shut up, damn. You love to start shit and right now, you not in a position to be upset, with the bullshit you've been pulling lately."

Rolling her eyes, Zuri sucked her teeth. "I wonder why."

"Save the sarcasm, okay, because you already fucked up everything I had in motion, being hot-headed and shit."

This was not the way I planned on starting this conversation, so I paused and stood up.

"Where are you going?" Zuri snapped.

Ignoring her, I took a minute to regroup by going into the bathroom and washing my face. As I stood in the mirror, I wiped away the water with a napkin and sighed. "Do not let this woman piss you off. You have enough drama and bullshit on your plate to last a lifetime."

After cooling off, I walked back into the room and sat down beside her. To show her I was calm, I grabbed her hand and looked into her eyes.

"Let's start over. How are you feeling?"

"I'm in a little pain, but I'm good."

"Now, like I said previously, I need to talk to you. But, I need you to listen to everything I'm about to say without any interruptions. Can you do that?"

Zuri nodded her head. "Yes."

"Thank you. Now, to answer your question, I brought Janae with me because she wanted to see the baby and I told her it was okay."

"Without asking me first?" Zuri couldn't keep that mouth closed for shit.

"What did I just say about speaking until I was done?"

"Fine. I apologize."

"Now, back to what I was saying. The night you pulled that little stunt with Deja, I received a phone call from Janae. She was crying and asked me to come to the hospital, so I went."

Zuri didn't mumble a word, but I knew she desperately wanted to. The frown on her face said it all, but I ignored that. "When I got there, her mother was lying in bed clinging to life and she asked me to take care of Janae, because she was going to die."

That night replayed in my head and all I could see was her face and hear her voice. Keeping my emotions in check was mandatory, because I didn't want Zuri to feel like something went on with me and Shan while we were together.

"Right before she died that night, she revealed something to me that I never knew." It was hard to look into her eyes, but I had to let her see the sincerity in my eyes. My heartbeat was banging in my chest. Not out fear of what she would say, but because I didn't want to hurt her. So, I hesitated for a brief moment.

"What did she tell you?" Zuri's voice was low, as she looked into my eyes. Not once did she blink.

"She told me that Janae is my daughter."

Zuri continued to stare at me, but she remained silent. Moving closer to her, I rubbed her hand gently. I could see her eyes become glassy and I knew the news hurt her, despite the fact that this happened way before her time. "Baby, say something please?"

Slowly, she pulled her hand away from mine and sat it in her lap. At that point I was expecting her to curse me out, so I prepared myself for that.

"So, you have another child?" She licked her lips and rocked back and forward with her eyes closed.

"Yes, but I just found out about her. So, it's not like I was keeping it a secret."

"So, that's why she was sizing me up in the hospital, because y'all was still fucking before she died?" Zuri opened her eyes and tilted her head to the side waiting on my answer. A few tears slid down her face. I tried to intercept them, but she leaned back to keep me from touching her.

"Zuri, I never cheated on you. Me and Shan haven't slept together since high school, so she didn't have a reason to size you up. She knew I had a girlfriend, but I think seeing you pregnant was bothering her because she was carrying such a deep secret."

Zuri wiped her face with the gown she was wearing. "And you believe that she's your daughter?"

"Yes, I do."

"I'm not trying to be cruel, but you don't think it's a coincidence that she told you this right before she passed away?"

"Shan wasn't that type of girl. I was her first."

"So, how could you not know she was your child? I'm confused."

Rubbing my hand over my face, I sighed deeply. "Shan caught me cheating and broke up with me. She felt I wasn't ready to be a father, so she didn't tell me. When she started to show, I asked her was it my baby and she said no. I let it go because she was dating someone else at that time and before you say anything, she was already pregnant when they starting messing around."

"I wasn't going to say anything, because I don't care. This has nothing to do with me. Nor do I have time for this. I have my own child to worry about now and of course, Bre."

Her response caught me off guard, causing my brow to shift downward. "What the fuck does that supposed to mean?"

"Exactly what I said."

"Damn. So, you want to end this because of something that happened eighteen years ago?"

"This is a lot to take in, Brick, so I don't know what you expect from me."

"I expect you to stand by my side like a woman is supposed to. Don't you think I'm fucked up behind this too? This was just sprung on me a few days ago, and I expected you to sympathize with the situation. We both know how it is to grow up without a mother."

"You right, but this is different. And it's not like you trying to get a DNA test before you bring her into our lives."

Nodding my head, I stood up and looked down at her with great disappointment. "A little FYI, I've been in Janae's life for eighteen years. Sadly, I gave you far more credit than you deserve. Shan looked me dead in my eyes and apologized for disrupting my life and threatening my relationship. I told her don't worry, because I had a good, understanding woman and we would get through this. Obviously, I was wrong about you and you not ready for marriage."

"How do you expect me to feel after hearing you have another child?"

"She's not a fuckin' child. Janae is grown and on her way to college, but you can feel how you want to feel because at this moment, I don't give a fuck. I have a daughter downstairs that lost her mother and she needs me."

"So, what are you saying?"

"I'm done with this. If Janae being in my life is going to be a problem, then I'll step away now. I'm not abandoning my daughter for nobody. None of my kids for that matter. I'll be a father to my son and that's it. So, you can let Jason know you a free agent."

As I turned to leave, I stopped in my tracks when I saw Janae standing at the door with a doleful look on her face. I knew she heard everything that was said, because she had tears running down her face. She stepped closer to me and sat Breanna down in the chair and kissed her cheek.

"Goodbye, Bre."

"Where are you going?" Breanna gave her the saddest puppy dog eyes.

"I can't be here right now, so I'll see you another day." Then, she grabbed Legend's hand. "Bye, cutie."

"Bye, Janae." He smiled.

Grabbing Janae's arm, I pulled her towards me. "You don't have to leave."

"Yes, I do. I don't want to cause you any problems because of something we didn't know about. And, you don't have to take me home. I'll find a ride."

"No, you won't. I'll drop you off after you see the baby. Let's go, Bre." I didn't bother to look at Zuri, as we walked out the door and towards the nursery. I had some choice words for her, but I would save that for another day.

Chapter 8
Coop

Danielle had me hotter than fish grease. One thing I didn't tolerate was disrespect, especially at my place of business. That was the ultimate foul in my playbook. Unlocking the door to my old home, I walked through and slammed the door behind me. The picture that hung next to the door hit the floor and shattered into pieces.

"Danielle," I shouted while storming down the hallway.

When I made it into the room, she was sitting in bed with her phone in her hand. "Don't come in here yelling like you lost the little bit of sense God gave you."

"What I told you about showing your ass and disrespecting me in public? You think that shit was cool?"

"Fuck you and what you stand for. Got me looking stupid while you running around with this young ass thot, who still wiping her pussy from back to front. Embarrassing me and our marriage. You a nasty-ass nigga and I hate your ass."

Before I could blink, the back of my hand was sliding across her face. *Whap!*

Danielle tried to get up out the bed, but I pushed her down and straddled her arms and chest so she couldn't move. Using my left hand, I gripped her throat and slapped her repeatedly.

"Stoopp!" she whined.

"Shut the fuck up, bitch!"

"Please stop," she cried.

Although I felt no remorse for the bitch, I stopped hitting her and climbed out the bed. The impact from my jabs appeared on her face. Danielle had really taken me out of character and I allowed it. She sat on the bed crying and rubbing her stomach.

"You promised you would never hit me. And, you knew what I went through before we got together."

"And, you know how I feel about being disrespected. You blatantly did that shit in front of my squad. After today, don't call me anymore. I'll be in touch once my attorney draws up the divorce papers."

Danielle stood up. "Coop, please don't do this. I know I haven't been the perfect wife, but I promise to work on it. But, you have to promise you'll leave that hoe alone and come back home." She stepped closer to me. "Can we work this out please?"

Standing in place for a few moments, I looked at her and shook my head. "No, there's no point in doing that. You don't trust me and there's no need in wasting more time. My schedule in the streets will never change and neither will this marriage. Goodbye, Danielle."

As I started to walk away from her, she grabbed my arm. "Please don't leave me. I'm pregnant."

Stunned by what she said, I turned back to face her. "What?"

"I'm pregnant. We're going to have a baby."

"Damn," I sighed in disappointment. That was the last thing I needed to hear.

Leaning her head to the side, she whispered, "You're not happy?"

"No. I'm not. Why should I be?"

"This is our first child."

"Are you keeping it?"

Danielle sighed and rolled her neck. "Are you serious right now? Do you expect me to have an abortion from my husband?"

"You can do what you want to do. Just know this situation will not make me change my mind. I'm finally happy now, but you can do whatever you want to do. I don't care."

Danielle sat down on the bed and started to cry. Her tears didn't move me, so I walked away. The last thing I was going to do was allow her to play on my intelligence. It just seemed so convenient that she would pull the pregnancy stunt after I mentioned the divorce. Whatever plan Danielle had up her sleeves, she could save it because I wasn't falling for the okey-doke. She better find a sucker for that fuck shit. As I stepped out into the hallway, I slammed the door behind me. I was exhausted and ready to get back home.

***

When I made it back home, Tamia was lying on the sofa watching television. Whatever she was watching had her zoned out, because she didn't move when the door closed. Walking towards the sofa, I grabbed her phone and sat down. That's what got her attention.

"You lost something in my phone?" Tamia sat up and held her hand out.

"Put your code in."

She took it from my hand. "Oh, that's what we doing now? Checking each other's phones?"

"Nah. That's what I'm doing, checking your phone."

"For what?"

"Put the code in."

"Not until you tell me why." Tamia folded her arms, standing firm on her decision.

"Ughh!" I grunted and I ran my hand across my face, while getting my words together. "Danielle came by the shop today and told me that she heard us having sex."

Tamia rolled her eyes. "And?"

"She said you called her."

"And let me guess. You believe her?"

"I didn't say that, but I wanna see it for myself." Holding my hand out, I reached for the phone because I was slightly irritated. "Just put in the damn code."

"Fine." Tamia put in the code and passed the phone back. "I can see that you don't trust me, since you taking the word of that bitter bitch who couldn't handle her wifely duties."

"Just stop."

Tamia had every right to be pissed, but I didn't care. All I wanted was an honest answer. Scrolling through her phone, the only calls I saw were incoming calls and four of them were from Danielle. Further into my investigation, I checked the length of the calls and I saw that one lasted for damn near five minutes. Closing the phone, I sat it back down on the table.

"Did you answer her call?"

"Weren't you right here with me? Did you see me answer the phone? No. We were too busy fucking, remember?"

Tamia snatched her phone from the table and stood up. "I can't believe you would try me like that. What purpose would that serve for me to let her listen to that? I already have you. Or, so I thought."

She stormed off into the back room. Of course, I gave chase since she didn't do anything. Tamia sat on the edge of the bed with her hand on her forehead. So I sat down beside her and grabbed her hand.

"Listen to me. I'm not accusing you of anything. All I wanted to do was prove Danielle was lying to me and that's what I did. That's what was proven to me."

Tamia looked up at me and cleared her throat. "Are you sure this is what you want? Because it's obvious your wife is going to be a problem."

"Of course this is what I want. I wouldn't be here if I didn't."

I could tell she was affected by everything by her lack of eye contact. In an effort to make her feel secure, I turned her face towards me, so she could look into my eyes.

"Listen to me. I don't want Danielle. My marriage is over and once my divorce has been finalized, you won't have anything to worry about."

Smirking, she sucked her teeth. "And how could I be so sure about that? As far as I know, you might be trying to get back with her on the low."

"What you just said makes no sense whatsoever. If I wanted to be with her, then that's where I would be. No one is making me do anything I don't wanna do."

"I wish I could believe that, but I don't. That psycho bitch has been a problem since you got here, and you keep allowing it to go on. How am I supposed to believe that?"

Looking deep into her eyes I swallowed spit and told her how I really felt. "Because I love you, that's why."

Tamia's eyes expanded in the sockets, as she tried to catch her breath and formulate her words. "W-what?"

Stroking her cheek, I looked directly into her eyes so she would know I was serious. "I said, I love you."

"Are. Are you sure about that? Don't just tell me what you think I want to hear. Be honest with me."

"Tamia. I love you and I'm serious."

"I've fallen in love with you too."

"Good."

Leaning forward, I pulled her closer to me and tongue kissed her slowly. Tamia had a special place in my heart and it had been a while since I felt that way. To be completely honest, I didn't feel like Danielle held that spot. That had me feeling like I only married her to keep her quiet since she put up with so much of my shit in the beginning. I couldn't worry about that dead situation. In front of me was someone special and I needed to prove that to her. Easing her back onto the bed, I placed gentle kisses on her flesh, from her head all the way down to her cute little toes. Tamia shivered as I reached her spot and slurped on her other set of lips.

Chapter 9
Skeet
One week later

The club was still swangin' at damn near four in the morning and I was leaning like a muthafucka. Kamari was leaning against the wall like he was about to pass out.

"Aye, cuzz," his speech was slurred heavily. "How much longer we staying in this bitch? Shidd, I'm ready to go to the crib."

"Damn, nigga, you can't hang? Maybe I should've brought you some breast milk, since you can't handle yo liquor."

"Bro, we been drinking all day and I popped a C-class."

"Apparently you popped more than you can chew."

Kamari's facial expression had me cracking up. "Lame-ass nigga, let's go."

Just as I was about to move from my spot, I spotted something slim and thick headed in my direction. Shorty was wearing a black-lace fitted dress with a bra and panties underneath. My dick jumped inside my boxers, as I salivated over her sex appeal. I waited until she was directly in front of me and grabbed her arm.

"Wassup, sexy?"

Shorty pulled away quickly with a major attitude, but once she looked me up and down, a smile appeared. If I had to take a wild guess I would say my swag changed her attitude with the quickness. Stepping closer to me, she licked her lips.

"Nothing much, what's up with you?"

Checking out the merchandise, I eyed every curve on her body. She looked familiar to me, but I couldn't figure out where I saw her before. At that point it didn't matter, since her response was an open invitation to me, so I decided to shoot my shot. "Shit. What you 'bout to get into?"

"Janae!" a female screamed over the music while approaching us. "Girl, I been looking for you."

"What?" Janae snapped.

"We about to slide with these dudes, so come on."

"No. I told you I'm not going. We don't know them." She folded her arms across her chest. Whatever her girl was trying to get her to do, she wasn't up for it. The two of them continued to exchange words and that was when I remembered Slim Thick. Patiently, I waited on them to stop fussing, but when they didn't I intervened.

"You Brick's daughter, Janae, right?"

Janae rolled her neck in my direction with a bit of confusion on her face. "Um. Yeah. How do you know my daddy?"

"I work for him. That day you came to the shop, I was there."

"Oh, I do remember seeing you there."

The way her friend kept moving from side to side told me she was in a rush before she could even say it. "Girl, what you gone do?"

"I'll take you home. It's not a problem."

"Umm. You sure about that?"

"Yeah. I'll make sure you get home safe. I know how Brick is and I don't want no problems from him about you."

Janae was hesitant at first, but then she gave in. "Go ahead, Kim. I'm going home. Be safe."

Kim giggled. "I promise, I'll use a condom." Then, she walked away in a hurry, ready to be fucked.

All I could do was shake my head, because if Brick knew the type of friends his daughter was hanging with, I'm sure he wouldn't approve. But at the end of the day, it wasn't my business. All I was trying to do was get his daughter home, so she wouldn't be a rape victim.

"You need to find you some better friends," I grilled.

Janae smirked seductively and played with the charm on my Cuban link. Baby was definitely tipsy. "Well, maybe you can be my new friend."

The vibe she was letting off was up my alley, but the way Brick was set up, I knew that wouldn't be a good idea. Ignoring her comment, I placed my hand on her waist. "Come on, let's get out of here."

Kamari was leaning and out his mind, so I tapped him on the shoulder. "Aye bro, let's ride."

Bopping through the crowd, I noticed that Janae was more lit than I thought. She could barely walk a straight line. Wrapping my arm back around her waist, I escorted her out the door and through the parking lot. Opening the car door, I helped Janae into the front seat. The sweet scent of her perfume filled my nostrils. Leaning forward, I inhaled her scent for a few seconds longer. Suddenly, the back door opened and Kamari landed headfirst into the backseat. Dude took wasted to another level. Closing both doors, I stepped over to the passenger seat and got in. If my tolerance for alcohol wasn't so high, we would be fucked up and stranded right about now.

Starting the engine, I put the A/C on max and glanced over at Janae. She was leaning forward, taking off her heels. "You good, ma?"

The longer I stared at her bangin' body, the more I wanted to snatch her up out that dress and put that dick on her. Of course, I wouldn't treat her like a hoe. She was bae material. Janae had this innocence in her eyes and that was something I wasn't used to. It was always the thots and ratchets on my radar.

"Yeah, I'm good. I just had to take these shoes off."

"Just making sure. Where do you live?"

"In Melrose. I'll show you, just drive."

"Got it, boss lady."

Putting the car in drive, I tapped the gas, but then I quickly hit the brake. A group of niggas was walking by and I spotted one dude in particular.

"This pussy-ass nigga walking around town like shit gravy," I mumbled under my breath.

"What you said?" asked Janae.

"Nothing. Just talking to myself."

Raheem was off his square and slipping big time, like he ain't just robbed the craziest nigga in Broward. Fool was too comfortable after pulling a stunt like that. True enough, Brick had hittas, but he would run down on a nigga himself. The killer instinct in me wanted to clap his ass right now, but Janae just bought that nigga a pass to live another day. If she wasn't in my passenger seat, he would've been outlined in chalk. Remaining in the cut, I waited until they piled up in the truck and left the parking lot. Turning up my stereo, I bopped my head to the beat.

"Hey, reach in the back seat and give me that bottle of liquor off the floor."

Janae turned around with her knees in the seat, purposely showing me her ass. That had me thinking of all the different ways I would suck and fuck her from the back. My shit was locked, loaded and pressing hard against my zipper. She caught me looking and giggled.

"You like what you see?"

"I don't think I should answer that." I smirked and shook my head. Janae tried to hand me the bottle, but I didn't take it. "Fix me a cup."

"I hope you don't mind if I have one too."

"Nah." She fixed my cup first, then hers.

Trailing the vehicle, we both got on the interstate and cruised down the highway. Traffic was light that time of morning, so it only took us a few minutes to make it from Pompano back to Lauderdale. They veered off on Broward Boulevard and headed west. I stayed on they ass until they hooked a right in Parkway. The same neighborhood they robbed us in. Keeping my distance and pausing at the corner, I watched them pull up to a brown house on Third Court and get out. Slowly, I cruised by them and took a mental of their location.

"Are you following them?" Janae asked, while staring out the window.

"Nah. Them my homies. I just wanted to make sure they made it in safely."

"Isn't that sweet of you? What, you like a personal bodyguard or something?"

"Nah, I ain't sweet, ma. I'm just doing what I was paid to do."

"Oh." She adjusted herself in the seat and crossed her legs.

"I got y'all bitches now." I mouthed silently and kept it pushing.

Exiting the neighborhood, I shot across the highway and entered The Melrose, where Janae lived. "Point me in the right direction."

Janae gave me directions to her house and we pulled up in no time. She wasn't too far from where Raheem's bitch ass was at. I pulled up and put the car in park. My curiosity made me probe.

"You live here alone?"

"Yeah, now I do." She exhaled deeply. "I was living here with my mom, but she passed away a little over a week ago. So, it's just me now."

That shit hurt my heart when she said that. "Damn, ma. I'm sorry to hear that."

Janae's posture shifted and she went silent. Paying closer to attention to her, I could see tears running down her cheeks. Grabbing her hand, I caressed it a little. "I apologize for bringing that up. Are you going to be okay?"

Shaking her head, she replied, "No. I haven't slept here since she passed away."

"Come on. I'll walk you in." Kamari was still knocked out in the backseat, so I left him there for the moment. There was a slight breeze out, so I turned the car off and took the keys out the ignition.

The inside of the house was dark and the only lighting available was coming from the street lights. Janae stumbled around the house, as if she was a stranger in her own home.

"You good?"

"Yeah. I found the switch." No sooner than she said that, the light lit up the living room.

"Well, I just wanted to make sure you got in okay. I'm about to head out."

"Can you stay for a little bit please?" The sadness in her eyes told me she needed a shoulder to cry on. So I walked over to the sofa and sat down. Kamari would be okay for a few minutes. It wasn't like he never slept in a car before.

"Sure."

"Thank you." Janae sat down beside me, but she didn't look in my direction. There was a lot on her on mind and I could tell by the way she twiddled her thumbs.

"What's going on? You can talk to me," I suggested with sincerity.

At first, she remained silent, but then she turned in my direction and put her legs up on the sofa. "My life will never be the same, now that my mom is gone. She was supposed to be the one dropping me off to college in the fall and now she's not here. She won't see me graduate, have kids or get married. Life is not fair."

"I understand your pain, but at least you still have your dad. He can't take your old girl's place, but at least you're not alone."

"I know, but things are just complicated with him right now. We had a blow-up the other day and I haven't spoken to him yet."

Leaning closer, I played with the strands of her hair. "Whatever it is y'all can through it together. Life is too short to hold grudges against the ones you love. Let that go and have a conversation with him."

"Honestly," she sighed and wiped her eyes. "I don't know what to think. It's not him that has the problem. It's his girlfriend, baby mama or whoever the fuck she is. She don't like me."

"Why wouldn't she like you? And, I don't see Brick allowing a woman to interfere with his relationship with his daughter. I just don't see that."

"That's because we just found out he's my dad. My mom didn't tell us until she was on her dying bed. All my life I was raised thinking he was my god-daddy, but now things have changed."

"Damn! That's a lot to take in, but at the end of the day, he's still your dad. When you get up in the next few hours, call him."

"Okay."

Looking down at my timepiece, I realized the sun would be up soon. "Listen ma, I would love sit and chat with you, but I have to get this drunk-ass nigga home. I'm going to give you my number in case you need to talk."

"Thanks. I appreciate that." Janae handed me her phone and I locked in my number.

I handed her back the phone. "Call me anytime and I'll be here to listen to you vent and give you advice."

Janae leaned forward and wrapped her arms around my neck. Her grip was tight like she didn't want to let go. If I could, I would've held her until the sun came up. Finally, she pulled back just a little and gazed into my eyes. Then, she leaned forward and kissed me on the lips. My first thought was to pull away, but I couldn't control the way she had me feeling. Janae eased onto my lap, straddling me. My hands caressed her ass, while I eased up her dress.

"Don't leave yet," she whispered, while holding my face close to hers. Using her free hand, Janae slid my zipper open and touched my wood. My shit rocked up instantly. "I wanna have sex with you."

Janae stopped our kiss and stood up. I watched closely as she removed her dress and then her bottoms. It was too late to stop now, because I was far too gone. Unbuckling my pants, I slid them down, along with my boxers. Once again, she straddled me and kissed me. Her tight, warm pussy had my dick in a chokehold.

"Fuck!" I smacked her on the ass, as she started to grind on me in a circular motion.

Janae rode me long and hard until I felt myself about to bust. Placing my hand around her throat, I squeezed it and thrusted my hips against her middle. She was moaning like crazy until I let off my round and my boy went limp. After we were done, Janae got up and left the room. When she returned, she was carrying a washcloth. Taking it from her hand, I wiped myself and pulled my clothes back up. We stood face-to-face and kissed once more.

"I hope this won't be the last time I see you."

"Nah, it won't be." I assured her and walked out the door.

By the time I made it outside and to my car, it was a little after six and I could see that the sun would be out shortly. My phone had just stopped ringing, so I picked it up and checked my call log. I had seventeen missed calls from Jenn, so I called her back.

"Yeah."

"Why the fuck you been ignoring my calls?" she yelled into the receiver.

"I was busy."

"Who is the bitch?"

"What bitch?"

"The bitch you just finished fucking. You think I'm so fuckin' stupid, lying-ass dog."

"Listen bruh. It's too early for this shit. I been working and I'm tired. So, I'm not about to argue with you right now. I'll hit you up later after you cool off."

"So, I guess that mean you not coming here?"

"For what? I'm not about to fuss and fight with you. I'm going home so I can go to bed."

"Yeah, whatever. I bet you won't get no sleep today."

"A'ight we'll see about that."

Jenn was on some other shit and I didn't have time for that. She was crazy as fuck if she thought I was coming to her house. Kamari ass was still sleep, so I started the engine and tapped him on the shoulder.

"Aye, bro. Get up." He moved a little, but he didn't get up. "Yo, Kamari, you at the crib. Wake yo ass up."

Finally, this dead-ass nigga raised his head and looked around like he was lost. "Damn, yo."

"Get up and get in the front seat."

Kamari climbed over my seat and sat in the front. "Where the fuck we at?"

"I had to drop somebody off." I was looking at him, trying to see if he was on point.

"You still drunk?"

"Nah. I'm good." His speech was no longer slurred.

"You sure about that?"

"Yeah. I'm just tired as fuck. Bihh, get me to the crib." Kamari stretched and yawned while letting the seat back.

"Boom, check this out." I paused because I knew whenever a muthafucka started a sentence off like that, there was a strong possibility ya asses was going to jail. "A few hours ago, while you was sleeping, I ran into Raheem bitch ass. I know where them niggas at right now. You down for a one-eighty-seven?"

"Hell, yeah! I'm up now, shit. Let's murk them niggas." Kamari grabbed his heat from the under the seat and pulled the hammer back.

"Cool."

As I hit the block, there was no movement, which meant no witnesses. I crept towards the house slowly and to my surprise, two dudes were standing outside on the porch. It looked like they were in the middle of a drug deal. "That's the spot right here."

Pulling up in front of the house, I rolled down the window. "Yo, Raheem in there?"

"Who asking?" The dude put his hand behind his back, which led me to believe he was reaching for his fie.

"I'm a friend of Legend and I got the word on who did that boy in if y'all want it."

"Well, if you a friend, then why you ain't handle that shit yourself?"

"I ain't 'bout that gunplay."

Before he could respond, the front door opened. Lo and behold, Raheem the dream stepped out in the flesh. "Blast that nigga," I demanded. Kamari raised his arm, pointed in their direction and let that bitch bust.

Frakkkk! Frakkkk! Frakkkk!

Raheem, his boy, and the smoker hit the ground. More dudes rushed out the door, but they were met with a bullet to the chest. The windows on the house were exploding left and right. Then, out of nowhere, a slew of bullets hit up my car.

Chapter 10
Zuri

Ever since we had the blow-up at the hospital, things between us were very rocky. Upon my release, Brick surprised me with a new house out west in Sunrise. To say that I was happy was an understatement. The house was beautiful and bigger than my old house. It was a two-story, ranch-style home with five bedrooms and two and a half bathrooms. The master bedroom had a Jacuzzi with his and her toilets and sinks. There was also a two-car garage and swimming pool. The view was breathtaking. Brick took his time and furnished our bedroom, to keep it from looking too feminine. Breanna's room was fit for a princess, while Legend occupied the guest room, until we found his mother. I loved our new place, but it wasn't a home. It was cold and empty. Not what I pictured at all.

Since I've been home, Brick has barely said a word to me. Not once has he slept in bed with me. It was time to end this fiasco right now before it got worse. Walking down the stairs, I set out to locate him and he was right where I expected him to be, in his man cave. At a slow pace, I walked inside and stood beside him. But typical Brick, acted as if I wasn't standing there, so I cleared my throat.

"Excuse me."

He didn't bother to look up. "Yeah."

"Can we talk?"

"I'm busy right now."

"You do know I can see you, right?"

"Then that should tell you that I'm busy," he stated harshly.

All I wanted was for him to talk to me and give me some damn eye contact. "Brick, you've barely said a word to me since I got out the hospital and it's time to fix this."

Brick chuckled, shaking his head slowly. "Now you wanna talk? I'm good love, enjoy."

"Brick, please," I begged.

"Zuri, the shit that's going through my mind will only make this situation worse. Just leave it alone."

"I can't. I need to talk to you," she sighed heavily. "Listen, whatever you have to say, just tell me. I can handle it."

Brick muted the sixty-inch plasma television once he realized I wasn't leaving. "See, that's the problem with your spoiled, selfish, ungrateful ass. You think the world revolves around you and it don't. That's partially my fault, though. I put you on a pedestal too damn high for that big ass head of yours. Maybe if I would've treated you like a random bitch off the street, mistreat you, beat ya ass and cheat on you, you would respect me more than you do."

His words hit me in the chest so hard that I wanted to break down and cry, but I refused to let him see me as being weak, especially since he wasn't moved on tears.

"Brick, that's not fair. You know I respect you. So, stop it."

"Get the fuck out of here, 'cause I don't want to hear this shit. I'm trying to watch the game in peace."

Getting him to talk was harder than expected, but hopefully he would hear my words. And, to make sure he did, I stood in front of the television.

"Zuri, move."

"I'm sorry about everything I said. I was just acting out of anger. But seriously, how did you expect me act after you lay something like that on me? That caught me off guard."

Brick ignored me and moved his head so he could see the screen. I wasn't giving up, so I continued to plead my case.

"That type of information is something that should've been discussed in the presence of us and no one else. That wasn't fair for you to spring that up on me like that. You have to know I would've accepted her, because of the love I have for you."

Finally, his eyes shifted away from the game and landed on me. That made me feel like we were about to make some progress. Making amends with my king was all I wanted. Brick sat up giving me his undivided attention.

"Are you done?"

That response was certainly not what I had in mind. "Are you serious right now? Here I am, trying to make things right and you dismissing me."

"This shit don't happen on your terms. Fuck outta here with that."

"You know what? Brick, you can stay mad at me all you want to. I don't care anymore. All I want to do is apologize to Janae. She didn't deserve that and I'm sorry for making her feel uncomfortable. I should've handled that situation differently and you should've presented it to me in a different way. So yeah, we're both at fault here."

"Yeah, blame me for being honest. But blame yourself for being insensitive in a situation like that." Brick rose to his feet. His frame towered over mine, but his eyes stayed on me.

"How the fuck do you think I felt when she told me this after all these years? I been around this girl her whole fucking life, thinking I was just her god-daddy. That shit fucked me up, but guess what, you didn't bother to ask. If it's not about your personal issues, you don't give a fuck."

Brick was heated and I was doing my best to calm him down, but he was being irrational. Fighting with him wasn't a smart thing to do because he could carry on ridiculously. Reaching out, I grabbed both of his hands so he'll know that I surrender. My ass was already a cry baby and I hated for him to yell at me. And I definitely didn't want him to hit me or rough me up. My man was gentle the majority of the time, but when he snapped, it was scary. He instilled the right amount of fear in me. Therefore, I knew what lines not to cross, what to say and not to say.

"Baby, please stop yelling at me. I can't take this silent treatment anymore. I get it and I'm sorry. At that time, I wasn't thinking. I was already on meds, so of course, my thought process wasn't at its best. Look at how I treat Breanna. I love her like she's my very own daughter and you know that."

Brick didn't open his damn mouth. He just stood there with his eyes glued on me like I had two damn heads. That was all I needed to witness from him. His actions made it very clear that he wasn't hearing shit I had to say. So with that being said, I released his hand and nodded my head.

"Clearly your mind is made up about us. So, I guess that means it's really over between us. I'm moving back in my house." Looking down at my hand, I removed the engagement ring and sat it on the pool table. "You can still be a father to your son. I won't interfere with that."

As I walked away, I felt defeated. Reconciliation was what I set out to do and I failed. It would take some time to get over him, but I would manage. If I could walk away from Daman, I could do the same with Brick.

Upstairs, I pulled out my overnight bag and started to pack a few items. Of course, my emotional ass started crying. That nigga really hurt my feelings. As bad as I wanted to stay, I had to show him I would leave his ass with no problems. The heavy footsteps made the floor tremble, so I knew that he was near me. But, I didn't bother turning around.

"Where are you going?"

My attitude was in full effect, but that didn't stop me from pouting like a baby. "I'm going back to my house. I hate it here."

"Put that bag down. You ain't going nowhere."

"For what? I don't have a reason to be here."

"Fuck you mean, you don't have a reason to be here?" The hair on the back of my neck stood up, as he breathed heavily. However, I wasn't letting up.

"I'm not doing this with you." See, that was his way of trying to get me stay without him saying it, but I wasn't going for that shit. Fuck that. "Keep that same energy you had a few minutes ago. I've been apologizing for days and you've constantly ignored me and shut me down. I'm tired of it."

"Zuri, don't fuckin' play with me."

"Oh, I'm serious right now." Ignoring him, I went to the dresser to gather up my personal items. Brick grabbed my arm and pulled me towards him. "Let me go."

I tried to pull away from him, but his grip was tight as fuck. "I'm telling you right night now, if you ever get the strength to walk up out that door, you can't ever come back and I put that shit on my mama."

"Is that a threat?" Testing his patience was what I did best and I wasn't letting up until he changed his attitude.

"That's a promise."

"Well, too bad, because that's not going to change my mind. You think you can intimidate me to make me stay. Not happening. Not today."

"Zuri, you ain't hard, so cut that shit out. You know how I am, so you know I'm not letting you leave."

We stood face-to-face in silence. His stank ass knew that he could make me stay. My ass was talking all that shit and now look at me, back in his hands like putty. Brick placed his hand on my cheek and kissed me gently. I melted instantly. If I didn't have these damn staples in my stomach or this pad on, my ass would be naked.

"I love you."

"I love you too." Brick's hand slid down my lower back and onto my ass, so I decided to burst his bubble early. "You might as well stop because I'm bleeding."

Quickly, he snatched his hand away. "Ugh! That was a pad I touched?"

"Duh."

"You just fucked my head up. Let me go wash my hands."

Slapping his arm, I giggled. "Really? I want you to keep that same energy when my shit go off."

Brick sat down on the bed and pull me onto his lap. "Seriously, babe. I heard you loud and clear and maybe that wasn't the best time or place to tell you, but you could've been more sensitive. We both know what it feels like to grow up without our mother. You know I would never hurt you intentionally. All I wanted was for you to be understanding about my situation. Maybe I should be apologizing to you as well."

Placing my finger over his lips, I stopped him. "You don't have to apologize. Let's just forget that argument ever happened. And since we can't have make-up sex, I'll just rock the mic for you." Sliding down to the floor, I put my head in his lap and got to work.

***

Brick

After a much-needed nap, I got up and took a piss. It was a little past noon when I finally turned my phone back on. Due to the tension in the house with Zuri, I didn't feel like being bothered. Once it powered on, multiple messages from Skeet popped up. Apparently, there was some type of emergency, so I hit him up.

"Wassup."

"Aye, I been calling you for hours." I could hear the frenzy in his voice.

"My phone was off. What's going on?"

"My car got clapped up last night and Kamari got hit. We at Broward General. This shit don't look good, bro."

"A'ight. Sit tight. I'm on my way."

Zuri was gazing at me with concern in her eyes. "What happened?"

"One of my boys got shot and he in the hospital. I need to get down there and make sure he's okay."

"We're supposed to be going to see our baby."

"It's the same hospital, so come on." Zuri threw the covers off and got out of bed. "And, brush your teeth before you go down there kissing on my baby."

"Be quiet, jerk."

At the hospital, the waiting area was stuffed. However, I recognized my crew when I came in. As I rushed in their direction, Zuri remained behind me. Skeet stood and dapped me up. Frustration was evident on his face, because Kamari was his boy and he was the one that introduced him to the game. Rubbing his hand over his face, he took a deep breath.

"My boy still in surgery, man. This shit fuckin' with me bad. This shit all my fault, bruh. It was me who wanted to run down on them niggas last night."

"This the life we chose and bad shit happens. Stay positive. Lil homie gone pull through. Just stay positive."

A female was walking fast in our direction. Zuri immediately stepped closer to my side. "You the reason he got shot," Kyra shouted.

"Slow yo' muthafuckin' roll and lower your voice when you talking to me."

Skeet stood between us, trying to hold her back like she was gone do something. All that did was make Zuri snap, as she eased towards her. "Kyra, watch how you talk to my nigga, unless you want that ass beat again."

Pulling Zuri back, I held her close in an effort to calm down my little gangstress. "Bae, chill out before we both go to jail. You just had a baby. Let me handle this, 'cause she don't want no smoke."

That bitch was still poppin' off at the mouth. "About Kamari, I want all the smoke. Fuck you mean?"

Skeet tried pushing her away. "See that's what you not go do. Go sit down and wait on the doctor."

Kyra continued to make a scene. "Fuck him. He got Kamari working for him and I know it."

That hoe was truly testing my gangster and I was ready to slap the fuck out of her. Pointing my finger in her direction, I gritted my teeth.

"Listen here, hoe, I'm trying to keep my cool since Kamari is your peeps. I don't hit women, but I'll beat a bitch down, so watch the words that drip from that nut catcher you call a mouth. Now, for the last time, have a muthafuckin' seat befo' I body yo' fat ass."

Kyra locked her teary eyes with Zuri. "That's fucked up, Zuri. You gone let your nigga talk to me like that? My son is laying up in surgery because of this monster."

Confusion was plastered all over Zuri's face. "Kyra, what the fuck are you talking about? You don't have any kids."

Wiping her eyes, she continued. "See that's where you're wrong. Remember when we were in middle school and I went to live with my aunt? Well, my mom sent me away because I was pregnant. Not because she wanted a break."

Zuri folded her arms across her chest. "I don't know anything about that, but whatever."

"Well, let me fill you in on a fifteen-year-old family secret. Your daddy got me pregnant and Kamari is his son, which makes him your brother. Do the math. Better yet, call Daman and he'll tell you." Kyra turned on her heels and walked away.

Zuri placed her hand on my arm. "I'm going to check on the baby. I don't have time for this shit."

"Are you okay?"

"Take me to my baby, please."

"Skeet, I'll be back."

"A'ight. I'll be right here."

Grabbing Zuri's hand, I ushered her away from the drama-filled room, so we could check on our little one.

Destiny Skai

Chapter 11
Mehzani
One month later

Day in and out, had been the same routine. My entire existence revolved around Gucci and his needs. It was hard watching the love of my life suffer. Yes, he was making progress, but he didn't deserve what happened to him. Slowly, I was losing my faith because I felt as if my prayers were falling on deaf ears. Constantly, I was on my knees with a heavy heart, begging my creator to give Gucci a second chance. Maybe he found it hard to answer the prayers coming from an ex-junkie.

My midday errands were over once I picked up his prescriptions and a few items from the grocery store. Unlocking the door, I walked inside the apartment and hung my keys on the holder. Sara, his therapist, was massaging his legs.

"Back so soon, Ms. Monroe?"

"How's it going with him? Is he making progress?"

"He's getting better. Do you massage his legs to keep them from becoming stiff?"

"Yes."

"Good. We have a surprise for you."

"Okay. Let me put these bags down." Heading into the kitchen, I placed them on the counter and went back into the living room. "So, what's the surprise?"

"We're about to show you. Come on, Mr. Williams."

Sara grabbed Gucci by both arms and pulled him up. Pulling his legs around, she eased them to the floor. He grunted through the process. "Come on, you can do this." She gave him a pep talk.

With her assistance, I watched closely as she helped him stand on both feet. Gucci grabbed ahold of his walker and took two steps forward.

"Aww, baby, I'm so proud of you. I-I-I thought he wouldn't walk again." His effort had me so ecstatic that I was stumbling over my words.

"That was a possibility, but with the extensive therapy he's been receiving, I'll have him walking within the next few months."

"Oh, thank you so much." I hugged Sara tight.

"You don't have to thank me. I'm just doing my job."

After the therapist left, I washed him up and put on his pajamas. Once he was lying down comfortably, I fixed myself a shot and downed it. Then, I made a drink. My heart was beginning to feel whole once again, after witnessing my prayers being answered. To see him make progress against the doctor's diagnosis was truly a miracle. As I sat down beside Gucci, I grabbed his hand and kissed it. We locked eyes and I could feel something special happening. Normally, sadness consumed his face, but not tonight. He had a glow.

"This has been a long journey, but I am so proud of the progress you've made. Watching you overcome this battle has been nothing short of amazing, and I'm happy to be by your side. But, I have to be honest with you."

Taking a breath, I sipped my drink to wet my throat.

"There were so many nights I laid in bed, crying all night. So many times I wanted to give up. It wasn't because I didn't love you. I just didn't think that I could take care of you, the way you took care of me. You needed a strong woman and I didn't feel I could fill those shoes."

Taking another sip, I sighed.

"There were times I wanted to start back using just to take the pain away. It's like, the stress was too much for me to handle. The more I watched you fight, it gave me the strength to stay strong for you."

With my emotions running wild, water started to well in my eyes and cascade down my face. "I love you so much, it hurts. You mean the world to me and I can't picture life without you."

Overwhelmed with our entire situation, I broke down and sobbed hysterically. Gucci grabbed the rails and pulled himself up. Gently, he wiped away tears. As he gazed into my eyes, he opened his mouth, but nothing came out. Closing his eyes, he took a deep breath and grunted. Seconds later, his pupils were back on me.

"Stop crying. I love you too." The sound of his robotic voice made me jump out my skin, but as long as he could talk, I didn't give a damn what he sounded like.

Leaping from my seat, I rubbed the side of his face. "Oh, my God!" I screeched. "Baby, you can talk."

"Yes. I've been practicing with the therapist and on my own, when you were sleeping."

"You just don't understand how happy I am right now."

Placing my lips onto his, we kissed long and hard. My baby was finally snapping back and I couldn't wait for him to heal completely. Hope never looked so good in my eyes.

"Mehzani," Gucci spoke slowly. "I want you to know I appreciate everything you've done for me. If it wasn't for you, I don't know where I would be right now."

"I have something for you." Grabbing my purse, I dug my hand inside and pulled out a black satin box.

"I had this day planned out for a while now and the timing is perfect. When I found out you were shot, I thought I lost you forever. It made me realize I never want to spend a single day on earth without you. I also realized life is too short to waste time."

Opening the box, I looked into his eyes. "Marquez Williams, I love you from here to heaven. You've made me a better woman and I owe you the rest of my life. Will you marry me?"

The sockets of his eyes were wide, but he remained silent. Not once did he blink while staring at me. That wasn't the expression I was hoping for.

Gucci took the box from my hand and closed it. "No. I can't do that."

"W-what?" I stuttered. My heart was completely broken at that point and all I wanted to do was leave that apartment quick, fast and in a hurry.

"I'm sorry, but I can't accept your proposal." His response was so nonchalant and suddenly I felt stupid for putting my heart on the front line like that.

"Wow!" I gasped. "After everything we've been through and everything I've done, this is what it all boils down to?"

"No, it's not like that. Mehzani, I do love you. I swear I do, but this is all wrong. The timing. The circumstances."

Before I knew it, I was yelling and crying. "Then, what is it? Why don't you want to marry me? You can't possibly love me. I feel so fuckin' stupid. Don't you worry, because I will be moving out soon."

"Baby, relax and let me explain."

"Don't call me, baby," I screamed like a maniac.

"I'll show you why, but you have to calm down first."

"Oh, I'm calm because if I wasn't, I would've flipped your ass out that bed already."

Gucci shook his head. "Go in the guest bedroom and get that small safe from the top of the closet."

Storming from the living room, I grabbed the safe and returned quickly. Handing it to him, I stood beside the bed with my arms folded. Gucci put in the code and opened it. Then, he looked up at me.

"Before I show you this, I need you to hear me loud and clear. Do you understand that?"

"Whatever." If looks could kill, he would be dead already.

"Yes would suffice. Stop acting like I said it was over."

"Might as well be."

"You didn't have to propose to me to prove your loyalty. I know you're loyal and I trust you with my life. That makes me feel like you did it because you're afraid I will leave you, or have a change of heart once I'm better. And that's not the case. You will never lose me. I promise."

None of that shit made sense to me. It was all foreign. "So, why turn me down?"

"Because." Gucci paused. When he moved his arm, a box holding a shiny ring was in his hand. My ass wanted to pass out right then and there.

"You've been by my side from day-one. You put your entire life on hold, just to take care of me twenty-four-seven. Not once did you complain or turn away from me. You've handled business for me and I could never thank you enough. The love you have for me is more than anyone has shown me. I know this was hard and for that, I will spend the rest of my life making it up to you. I promise."

I was speechless, so I just stood there with my hand cupped over my mouth.

"Also, I want you to know your worth. You not supposed to propose to any man. One thing about men is that we know who deserves that title from jump. Proposing is a man's job. With you proposing to me, you will never know if I chose you or not. So, I'm asking you, Mehzani Monroe, will you be my wife?"

"Yes. I will." I bounced up and down because I had my prize.

"Now, before I put this ring on your finger and make it official, I have to come clean about a few things."

My happiness turned into fear automatically. The beating of my heart increased because I was clueless about what he was going to reveal to me. Whatever it was, I prayed I could accept his secret. Nervously, I bit my nails and prepared myself for his confession.

Chapter 12
Brick

Business was back to normal. My son was finally out of the hospital, healthy and happy. Raheem and his bitch-ass crew was pushing daisies. After that shit went down, me and Coop went and tied up those loose ends. The crew was pushing major weight since the competition had been eliminated. Life was great, so I had no complaints.

The driver pulled up in front of the Hard Knocks boxing gym and put the truck in park. Letting us out, my feet hit the concrete as I adjusted my firearm in my waistband. Checking my surroundings, I walked around to the opposite side of the truck and stood beside Hector.

"We'll be right back," he informed the driver before walking off.

When we made it through the double glass doors, we could hear shouting and boxing gloves putting in work.

"This not a playground. We don't do this shit for fun. You hitting like a fuckin' girl," the trainer shouted.

Hector chuckled, while heading in his direction. "Tell them boys you mean business."

"Hector!" the trainer shouted, as they slapped hands.

"Meet my partner and business associate, Brick." He then looked at me. "Brick, meet Pablo, my baby brother."

"Nice to meet you, Brick." We shook hands.

"Likewise," I replied.

"You boys are in for a show. Sit tight." He turned towards the boxing ring. "Alright, that's enough. Clear my ring, so I can show you what a champion looks like."

The two dudes boxing dipped out like roaches when the lights cut on. Loud clapping and chanting could be heard. Two new faces stepped in the ring, but one of them was quite familiar to me and I couldn't believe I was so lucky to run into this nigga. If the circumstances were different, I would've bodied that nigga the same day. Nodding my head, I smiled because his days of boxing would be over soon.

"You see the dude in the black shorts with all the tattoos?" Hector looked at me.

"Yeah."

"That's my nephew, Marco. That boy is a beast in the ring. He's also a part of the family business, so I'll be introducing y'all, just in case you have to work with him one day."

"Cool."

Hearing that my opponent, Marco, was my plug's nephew definitely threw a monkey wrench in my plans. *Fuck!* I thought. *How in the fuck would I pull this shit off?* My crew wasn't prepared to go up against the damn cartel if they found out I was behind the hit. Now, I would have to reconsider. In the meantime, I would pull the plug on that plan. There was no way I was risking losing my supplier or putting my family in danger.

The bell rang and Marco took off on his opponent. I was tuned in, watching him throw punch after punch to the head and body. There was no doubt that he was good, but I wasn't impressed. A bullet could stop all of that. Not even a minute later, Marco knocked his opponent clean the fuck out. Dude just laid there without moving. That fight was officially over. Hector waved and Marco walked towards us. As he stepped from the ring, he smiled.

"'Sup, Unc?"

"Good job, nephew."

"You know how I do. What's going on?"

"I want to introduce you to someone." Hector looked at me while extending his hand outward. "Marco, this is Brick, my business partner and associate. Brick, this is my nephew, Marco."

Marco extended his hand, so I shook it. "Yeah, I've been hearing your name in the streets."

"Hopefully it was all good," I chuckled.

Marco nodded his head. "Let's just say you're well-respected."

"Well, I'm glad that the two of you are familiar with one another, because you may be working together soon."

"No doubt. I'm looking forward to that." We shook hands one last time before he walked away.

One hour later, Hector and I were sitting inside of a warehouse with his other associates. Our bond had flourished, so he brought me along to important meetings that dealt with the operation. In lieu of his absences, I would be there to fill in when he needed me. Hector did the proper introductions and I could see one of the men was not happy about my position.

"Hmm. Está trayendo matones para ayudar a dirigir la operación ahora?" The heavyset man chuckled, unaware that I knew he just said that Hector was bringing in thugs to help run the operation now.

"Pronto robará. Espera y verás. Entonces necesitará que limpiemos su maldito desastre," his flunky replied.

The moment he let the words, *he'll be stealing soon. Just watch and see. Then he'll need us to clean up his fuckin' mess,* I was ready to up my fie and let him know I spoke Spanish, before peeling his cap back. Knowledge and common sense was a big factor in the game, so I just sat there grinning like I didn't know what was going on. When two fools are talking, no one can attain wisdom. So instead of responding, I allowed them to think I didn't know what was going on.

The flunky tapped his boss's shoulder. "Vamos a matarlo ahora. Sabemos que mató a tu hermano."

Fat Man scratched his chin. "Nos des haremos de ese pedazo de mierda cuando vuelva aquí. Sé que mató a mi hermano. Y cuando terminemos, nos ocuparemos de su hermana."

These muthafuckas were sitting right in my face plotting on Hector's murder, but I wasn't letting that shit go down like that. I already knew that was his brother me and Coop killed when we took that shipment a while ago. Luckily, I was strapped with two firearms, so it was about to get ugly real soon.

The door slammed, so my head swiveled in that direction. Hector came through the door and walked towards me. At this point, I knew my cover was blown, but I wasn't about to let them have the upper hand.

"Alright fellas, let's get down to business." Hector rubbed his hands together.

Fat Man stood up. "I'm sorry, but we won't be doing any business with you or your associate, as you call him."

"Time is money and I don't have time for games," Hector replied.

"Sorry, but this isn't a game." The flunky reached for his gun, but before he could pull it, both of mine were trained on him and his fat-ass boss.

"Keep your hands where I can see them or I'll bust yo' shit open like a melon. And for the record, bitches, I don't steal. I'm a businessman."

"How did you—" Fat Man stopped mid-sentence.

"Brick, what's going on?" Hector asked.

I could see the confusion on everyone's face, so I let them in on a little secret, especially Fat Man. "Don't look surprised, bitch. I understood everything you said. While you were outside, they were plotting on killing you because of what happened to his brother."

"That's not true," Fat Man lied.

"You said, and I quote, 'Nos des haremos de ese pedazo de mierda cuando vuelva aquí. Sé que mató a mi hermano. Y cuando terminemos, nos ocuparemos de su hermana.'" In English, that meant, *we'll get rid of that piece of shit when he gets back in here. I know he killed my brother. And when we're done, we'll take care of his sister next.*

Hector pulled out his Glock 40 and aimed it at Fat Man. "So, you were in here plotting to kill me, you fat fuck?"

The flunky thought he was slick when he reached for his weapon. Not on my watch though, I fired two shots to his dome.

Boc! Boc!

His body hit the table before crashing to the floor. Looking over at Hector, I shouted, "Bust that nigga and let's go. You know he gone come for you."

It was like he squeezed the trigger in slow motion, but when that bullet left the chamber, it ripped through the middle of Fat Man's head. Blood splatter hit the air like fireworks on the Fourth of July.

Loud voices could be heard coming from behind us, so I turned around and saw two more men coming in. Quick on my feet, I pushed Hector down on the floor and fired multiple shots. Both bodies dropped.

"Come on." Grabbing Hector's arm, I pulled him up and escorted him out the building to safety.

Hector removed his jacket as soon as we got inside the truck. He was breathing all hard and shit. "You saved my life. Thank you."

"It's all good. I'm just glad I was here."

"No. I have to repay you. If it wasn't for you, they would've killed me."

"Just keep a mental note in case I ever need something. Other than that, we good. I mean that."

Hector had his eyes trained on me, so I knew he wasn't done talking. "I just have one question for you. So, all this time you understood my language and never said anything?"

I knew that one question was burning his soul. No one ever wanted to be in the dark about you. They had to know every single detail when it came down to money and business. However, I wasn't raised like that. I was taught to never expose my full hand to a single soul. Not even Zuri.

"That's correct. In life, you should never reveal too much. When I walk into a room, I know I'll be judged based on my complexion. No one would ever guess that a nigga like me spoke Spanish fluently. Not that shit they teach you in school. When I hit the dope game, I realized my second language would be beneficial. That I would always be two steps ahead of what was going on."

"Hmm. That makes perfect sense." Hector held his hand over his mouth. "So, where did you learn that?"

"My father."

"Así que entendiste todo lo que he dicho en tu presencia?" He tested me once more.

"Yes, Hector." His reaction to the news made me laugh. "I understood everything you've ever said in my presence," I reiterated his sentence.

Hector sat back in his seat and looked out the window. As I leaned back to relax, my cellphone rang. It was Zuri, so I picked up the phone.

"Yeah."

"Hey, baby. When you coming home?" Ever since the baby came home, she remained on my path about being home whenever I wasn't working.

"I'll be there in about an hour."

"Good. We miss you."

"I bet you do. See you soon." Once I ended the call, I slipped it into my pocket. My mind drifted back to Marco, because he was my intended target, but now there was a change in my plans. After I finished my business with Hector, I was going to round up the crew and pull the plug on that operation. The shit that had just went down was enough for me to change my mind for the time being.

Chapter 13
Skeet

Heavy sliding, I was smoking a blunt and in my zone. My system was bumping. The rims on my Audi truck chopped the streets as I cruised down Federal Highway. The only thing on my mind was Janae. We had been successful at seeing each other on the low for weeks now. Brick would have a fit if he knew about us. It wasn't like I was a bad dude, but I knew he didn't want her dating anyone just like him. I didn't like it, but I understood it.

"Can you take me to get some food now?" Jenn huffed, while turning down my tunes. Shorty had a major attitude.

"You in the wrong vehicle talking shit. Didn't I say I was gone take you? So, chill the fuck out."

"Well, I'm hungry, shit."

"What do you want?" I was doing my best to keep my cool.

"Let's go to Benihana's."

"Nah. I can't sit down nowhere. I'm meeting up with Brick in a few." My ass was lying, but she didn't need to know that. After I got rid of her, I was about to slide up on Janae.

"You never have time for me anymore. And, if I didn't know better, I would think you was cheating on me."

"Well, I guess you know better."

"You think you so slick, but you not. I'm not stupid." She continued to pout.

Ignoring her, I turned the volume back up and hooked a right into the gas station. Jumping out, I went inside to get me a bottle of water and some wraps. When I got back outside, Jenn had a nasty unit on her face.

"What do you want so I can drop you off? You getting on my nerves with all that extra shit."

"Gladly. Take me to Popeye's." Jenn closed her mouth and stared out the window, but that didn't last long. "Who the fuck is Janae?"

Cutting my eyes in her direction, I acted as if I didn't hear what she said. "What?"

Leaning up in the seat, she turned her body towards me. "You heard me so don't play dumb. Who the fuck is Janae?"

"Ion know what you talm 'bout."

"You can stop playing dumb, 'cause you know who the fuck I'm talking about."

This conversation was going nowhere and I didn't feel like arguing about unnecessary bullshit. Before I responded to her, I grabbed my cell and checked the screen. There was a missed call from Janae.

"Why you going through my shit?"

"No, you don't get to ask me that." Jenn started yelling and clapping her hands. "Who the fuck is Janae? That's the bitch you be with when you not with me?"

Popeye's was right on the corner, so I pulled into the drive-thru. The line was too long for my liking, but I stayed put. The ringer on my phone started shouting, so I looked at the screen. After silencing it, I put the phone face down in my lap.

"That's her calling? Answer your phone."

"Nah. That's Kamari."

"Answer the shit on Bluetooth, so I can hear it." Jenn pressed the phone icon on the dash, but I hung up the phone before she could say anything.

"You a lying muthafucka. I know that's her calling your phone." Rocking back and forth, she started snapping. "I gotta be the dumbest bitch in Lauderdale. All you do is cheat. Every time I turn around, a new bitch on your dick."

"Stop turning around then."

Sarcasm was all I could offer, because arguing was out the window. Truthfully speaking, I was tired of Jenn. She was too damn needy, childish and aggravating. It was time for something new. The only reason I kept her around was because we had been together for almost two years.

"Keep being funny and watch I punch yo' ass in the face."

"You ain't gone do shit."

Jenn smirked and nodded her head up and down. "It's all fun and games until I start doing the same thing."

"Yeah, whatever. Do you."

"Oh, that's how you feel?"

"Yup!"

"Good, because I been doing me ever since I first saw her message you. If you can cheat, so can I."

Swiveling my head in her direction, I snapped, "What the fuck you just said?"

"You heard me. Two can play that game."

"A'ight." Tapping the gas, I swerved out the drive-thru and got back into traffic.

"Why you didn't get my food?"

"Fuck you! Whoever putting dick in your stomach need to put food in that muthafucka. I'm not buying you shit. You got me fucked up."

We argued for the next five minutes non-stop. Jenn didn't live too far from where we were, so I got back to the apartment quick. I was ready to put her ass out.

"Get out my shit."

Jenn sat back and folded her arms. "I'm not going nowhere. We going to see that bitch together."

"Bruh, get the fuck out before I beat yo' ass."

"You ain't go do shit."

"Okay. I'll show you."

When I got out the truck, I left the driver's door open just in case she wanted to play games. Snatching the passenger door open, I grabbed her by the arms and pulled her.

"Let me go!" Jenn drew her hand back and slapped me in the face.

That baby ass slap didn't faze me, but I had to show her she had me fucked up once again. Like thunder, my hand collided with her face a good three times.

"Take yo' ass in the house and stop playing with me, bitch."

Holding her face, tears fell from her eyes. "That's how you talk to me? That ho' got you disrespecting me now?"

All that shit she was saying sounded foreign. Hitting on females wasn't my thing, but Jenn had me fucked up. Jumping into the truck, I took off without looking back.

***

Despite the shit I went through hours ago, I was in a good head space, thanks to Janae. She was the definition of peace. The bond we were developing was special to me. Sex had nothing to do with it, although the pussy was a bonus, especially since I was the second nigga to hit that. She was inexperienced in some areas, but I had plans on teaching her how to please me. Tonight was our first official date, so I made it special for her. After all, she was the boss's daughter, so she deserved nothing but the best from me.

We started the evening off with a movie, followed by a seafood dinner right on the ocean. Janae had an appetite to be so small, but I didn't mind. The sun was slowly fading away, leaving footprints across the sky. Our view was amazing. As I sipped my Hennessy on the rocks, I couldn't keep my eyes off of her. Janae was nothing like the girls I was used to dealing with.

"Why do you keep staring at me?" she giggled.

"I think you're beautiful. Something wrong with that?"

"No. Not at all."

Janae finished her margarita and sat the glass down.

"You ready?"

"Yeah."

Reaching into my pocket, I pulled out my money. Peeling off a blue-face hundred, I tucked it away in the black billfold and stood up. Janae slipped from her seat, as I grabbed her hand to escort her out. We ended up walking hand in hand on the beach. In my free hand, I held her shoes.

"Where do you see yourself in five years?"

Janae's tone was soft, but serious. Her question made me stop in place because I couldn't believe what she'd asked me. As we stood face-to-face, I felt a deeper connection once I looked into her eyes.

"Honestly, ma, I don't know. I'm just hoping to be alive in five years."

"Why do you feel like that?"

"Look at the life I live. Every day above ground is a blessing, but I know it's only two ways out this game. Cemetery or prison."

Janae placed her hand on my chest. "You're wrong. You can be so much more than this."

"I appreciate that, but I don't see it."

"I do."

The breeze picked up and her hair started to blow in the wind. Janae rubbed her arms like she was cold. Removing my Ferrari jacket, I draped it over her shoulders.

"Come on, let's go inside."

For the weekend, I booked us a suite at Margaritaville in Hollywood. That bitch came with a hot tub and all. We were about to be locked like crabs until check-out time. Back in the room, Janae filled up the Jacuzzi, while I popped a bottle of bubbly. By the time I made it to her, she was sitting in the water.

"Care to join me?" she smiled.

"Hell, yeah."

Stripping out my clothes and boxers, I stepped in and joined her. Janae filled our champagne glasses and passed me one. "Let's make a toast."

"What are we toasting to?"

"New beginnings."

"I like the sound of that."

Our glasses clinked before we enjoyed the savory taste of the expensive bottle room service provided us. The sound of Makaveli's "Just Like Daddy," started to play. We were tipsy and in our zone. Pulling Janae closer to me, she straddled my lap and kissed me. Our tongues intertwined and moved to the beat. She had me horny as fuck. I could feel my dick attempting to rise to the occasion against the wishes of the water. Licking her ear, I made a trail down to her neck and sucked on her softly. Then I rapped my favorite verse to her.

"Getting hot between the sheets. Make this shit right here discrete. Putting hickeys on ya belly while we fucking on the beach. I love it when ya nut up and grab me. I feel for ya badly, baby girl, just like daddy."

Janae started to grind in my lap and suck on my neck. "Make me cum."

"I got you, ma."

That request sent a signal to my piece. He was almost at attention. Using my hand, I positioned him against her lips and forced my way in. The sound of the water splashing, Tupac, and moans were making one hell of a mixtape and for once, I felt like I was in heaven. If this what our relationship would be like, I would have to figure out a way for us to become exclusive. This was going to be a tough task getting Brick's permission, but she was worth it. All I needed was for him to give me a chance to prove I could be the man he wants for his princess.

For the next few hours, we spent all of our time sipping champagne, and fucking in every position I could get her in. Janae was very limber, so that was an easy task. Right when we linked up, I popped a pill, so I was on it. I lost count at the amount of times I made her cum and yell my name. It was safe to say Janae had me hooked and so was she.

Chapter 14
Brick

"Wassup, bro?"

"Shiidd, I can't call it." We G-hugged. Then, I stepped back and let Coop in the door.

"The castle coming along good, I see."

"Yeah, Zuri been putting her decorating skills to work. She wanted to get an interior decorator, but I put an end to that shit fast. Besides, she need something to do anyway."

"Yeah, that's a good idea." Coop and I walked through the dining area en route to my man cave. "Where's my godson?"

"Upstairs in the nursery. All that lil nigga do is eat, sleep and shit."

"Sounds familiar," Coop chuckled.

"Hell, yeah."

"I had my girl order some stuff online for my lil dude. So, it should be here within the next day or two."

"That's what's up. 'Preciate that, bro."

"Ain't no thang. Just don't have no mo' babies. Between Janae, Breanna and now Bam, y'all gone break my pockets. I ain't gone be able to have kids of my own one day."

"Well, you better get started, 'cause I can't promise you that. As soon as Zuri stop bleeding, I'm busting all up in that. I need at least three more."

"What you trying to start, a football team?" Coop sat down on the sofa and placed his phone beside him.

"Don't forget the cheerleaders too."

"Speaking of which." Coop shook his head and sighed. "Crazy-ass Danielle hit my phone, talking about come over so we can talk. When I get there, she talm 'bout she pregnant."

"Say it ain't so." I stood at the bar and poured us a drink.

"I don't know, but I hope it ain't true."

"Damn, my boy, I been waiting on this day forever."

"Not me. This is not good timing."

Passing him the glass, I sat down in my favorite chair and tried to reason with him. "Maybe this a sign y'all should try and work that shit out. I'm just saying."

"I'm cool on Danielle, bruh. She fucked everything up with her insecurities and I'm not trying to live my life miserable with her ass. That shit for the birds."

"I see." I nodded my head.

"Whatchu see?"

"This new chick putting that young pussy on you. She got yo' ass sprung and you can't tell me different. You and Danielle are made for each other."

"Yeah. A match made in hell. That muthafucka crazy."

Now, I couldn't believe what I was hearing, because he acted like this was new information. "Newsflash, nigga. Where the fuck you been for the last few years? You been knew she was crazy."

"Nah, bruh. This that new crazy. She wasn't like this before we got married."

"Yeah, a'ight. If you say so. We talkin' 'bout the same Danielle. Ain't shit change."

Coop's attention was no longer on me. I could see the shift in his eyes. When I turned around, Zuri was standing at the door, holding the baby.

"Can you watch the baby while I take a shower?"

"Yeah. Bring him here."

Zuri sniffed the air, while holding my junior in her arms. "You not smoking in here, are you?"

"No."

She started to walk towards me. "Don't be smoking around my baby either."

"Give me my young king, 'cause when yo' ass was baking those fake-ass cakes in your Easy Bake Oven, I was fixing bottles of Similac."

"First of all, my cakes came out good and I ate them."

"If you say so. But just know ion play no games. You better tell her, Coop."

"We got baby soldier. This ain't new to us. Look at Nae and Bre. They turned out perfectly fine."

Zuri laughed a little. "Well, I don't know much about Nae, but I know Bre has a mouth on her. So, I guess that explains it all."

She hit the nail on the head with that one, because Breanna was a handful, but that's my baby.

"Yeah, you right about that."

"Well, I just fed him, so he should be good until I get out the shower."

"Bae, I got this. This ain't my first rodeo."

"You right. I'm leaving." Zuri walked off, but stopped in place and looked over her shoulder. "Oh, Bre and Legend are upstairs watching TV."

"A'ight."

Bam was the spitting image of me. It was like I carried my child myself. Those big, brown eyes matched mine, along with his jet black curly hair. He was hella light tho'. My Cuban blood was definitely running through his veins hard. Youngin' sho nuff stole my heart since he was the only boy. All I ever wanted was a junior and my future wife gave him to me. Switching the arm I held him in, I held him up so Coop could see him.

"Look at my baby boy." The excitement in my voice was too high to contain. "This nigga look just like me."

"Hell yeah, he do. His ass look just like that baby picture your mama always pulled out for everyone to see."

Every time I looked into his eyes, he reminded me of someone close to my heart. Someone I wished was still around to see what type of man I turned out to be. Just the thought of him made my heartache. Someone robbed me of the bond we once shared.

"It's so crazy because when I look into his eyes, I see my old boy, bruh."

"Facts. I'm trippin' on this damn onesie he's wearing. Who made that?"

Coop was referring to the big, bold print that said, *straight out of mommy.* "Zuri ordered that from somebody. Shit, you know how these women are."

"Hell, yeah. Give they ass some money and it's over."

The loud chimes from my phone put an end to our conversation. Snatching it up, I accepted the call. "Yeah."

"Let me in. I'm here," Skeet replied.

"A'ight."

Opening the door, Skeet walked in and dapped me up. "Nigga, who white-ass baby you kidnapped?"

"Boy, this all me," I grinned.

"Bullshit," he laughed.

"My father was Cuban."

"G-shit, bruh?"

"Yeah."

"That's why you got that curly-ass hair. I ain't gone lie, he do look like yo' ass, though."

"Already."

We joined Coop back in the cave.

"Now that I got y'all here, let's get down to business. First things first, we have to pull the plug on killing Marco."

Skeet didn't give me a chance to explain before he jumped in with his first question. "Why is that?"

"The other day I was with Hector and he introduced us. Told me we will be working together eventually and he wanted us to be acquainted."

Skeet jumped in again. "Well, the closer you are to him, the better. Shit, that's less work for me to do."

"See, that's where you wrong about this one. That's Hector's nephew. So, that's a double problem. Number one, I can't lose my plug to this shit. Number two, we don't have enough manpower to go up against a damn cartel. We'll be dead before it starts."

Coop chuckled. "Get the fuck outta here. You dead ass. No bullshit?"

"I'm dead-ass serious, bruh. That shit blew me when he said it. I was plotting when I first saw him, but then Hector fucked my plan up with that one."

"Damn. That's fucked up. I guess we can scratch that then."

My phone went off again. Looking down at the screen, I knew it was important. "Hold him." I passed Bam to Coop. "I gotta take this call."

Stepping away, I picked it up. "Hello."

"Hello, Mr. Riccardo. How are you?"

"I'm good and you?"

"I'm wonderful. Thanks for asking. Do you have a moment to talk?"

"Yes."

"Good. My first question is, have you spoken to Breanna's mother?"

"No, I haven't."

"When was the last time you spoke with her?"

Unsure about her line of questioning, I kept it short, sweet and simple. "I don't recall. It's been a while. Why, what's going on?"

"We've been trying to get in contact with her, but she's not reachable by phone or at her address. They even tried to serve her at her mother's address, but no one has seen her."

"I don't know where she could be. She hasn't reached out to me. Not even to check on Breanna."

"Just so you know, her mother has her listed as a missing person. In the meantime, you can maintain custody of Breanna until we locate her."

"Thank you."

"Oh, one other thing. Have the authorities reached out to you about her disappearance?"

"No."

"Well, they may have a few questions, so don't be alarmed. It's just protocol."

"Thanks for the heads up."

"You're quite welcome. Take care of that cutie."

Although I didn't see her face, I knew she was cheesing her ass off. "I will have a good day."

"You as well."

Coop and Skeet were talking about a bunch of nothing as I stood there replaying my voice messages. I skipped through several messages before one in particular sparked my interest. At first, there was a lot of rustling, then I could hear talking and yelling. My ears had to be playing a cruel trick on me, so I put it on speaker.

"Listen to this and tell me what y'all hear."

"The hell if I know. Run it back one mo' time." Coop's ears perked up a bit. "That sounds like Deja and Zuri arguing," he answered correctly.

"This shit about to get real crazy."

"What happened?" Coop asked.

"That was my attorney. She said Deja has been listed as a missing person and the authorities are going to want to talk to me about her disappearance."

"Damn, bruh. That's crazy, but you knew that was coming. You fighting for custody, so of course they gone think you a suspect off top."

"Yeah, I knew that and that's why I told Zuri to mind her fuckin' business and let me handle it. Damn! That muthafucka so goddamn hardheaded."

Bam immediately started crying when he heard me yelling. Cradling him in my arms, I placed his head against my chest. "Ohh, shit. Daddy sorry for yelling, but ya mama don't listen worth a damn."

"What you need me to do?" Skeet was always on ready when it came to me.

"I need you to get rid of Zuri's car. I'm going to get rid of both of our phones. Those cell towers guaranteed to get a bitch cased up."

"A'ight. You want me to torch that bitch tonight?"

"Yeah. The sooner the better. I can't risk them popping up over here and that shit still in our possession. I'll give you the keys, but when you finish, bring them back. If I don't answer, just leave them in the mailbox. I'm going to have her call the car in stolen in the morning."

"I gotchu, big bruh. Me and my dawg will get rid of that shit."

"Who?" Coop gave him the side eye.

"Kamari."

"Nah. That nigga still on medical leave. He can't come back." Coop had a serious expression on his face.

"Medical leave?" Skeet laughed. "This ain't no nine to five, nigga. You wildin', bruh."

"I'm dead-ass. Kamari can't come back yet. I'ma slide with you tonight, so don't worry."

"Cool. I'm with that. Pick me up from the crib at one."

"Yeah." Coop stood up and stretched. "Do you need anything else done before I leave? I promised Tamia we'll go out tonight."

"Nah. I'm good. Thanks."

"A'ight. I'm out."

"Me too," Skeet joined in. "Grab them keys for me though."

After they left, me and Bam went upstairs. Removing my shirt, I laid down on the bed and put him on my bare chest. Zuri climbed into bed with us.

"You gone have him so spoiled."

"Damn right. This my only son."

Zuri scooted closer to me. "That used to be my spot."

"Ohhhh, she jealous-jealous," I laughed. "You hear that, Bam? Ya mama jealous cause you getting all the attention."

"No, I'm not," she giggled. "Okay, maybe a little."

"I got you, baby. As soon as you stop bleeding."

"Damn, it's like that?"

"Just like that."

Skin to skin contact was important, according to the doctor. Since Bam spent his time in ICU, I didn't bond with him the way I wanted to. But, now that he was home, I slept with him on my chest every day.

"Tomorrow your car will not be here, so I need you to call it in stolen. I'll tell you when to do it."

Zuri sat up in the bed. "Why?"

Briefly, I gave her some of the details about my conversation with the attorney. The way her eyes widened in surprise, told me she was afraid. "I'm so sorry."

"This is why I told you to let me handle her. I had her death planned out to perfection. But, don't worry about it. I'm going to fix it. Just keep your mouth shut about that night. If they ask you anything, you don't know shit."

"Okay."

Zuri and I watched television, until it started watching us. And once again, Bam slept peacefully on my chest, while Zuri cuddled close to my body.

Destiny Skai

Chapter 15
Danielle
The next day

Coop still wasn't trying to reconcile and save our marriage, so it was up to me to make sure he changed his mind. If he thought I was about to lose him to a bitch who couldn't wipe her pussy right, he was sadly mistaken. I had to pull out my bag of tricks if I wanted my plan to work.

Sitting at the computer, I clicked print and waited on my papers to come out. Grabbing them, I made sure they looked official. Using a black pen, I filled out the form.

"Okay. Let's see. Dr. Alexander, you're located at 19450 N.W. 76th Avenue."

After I signed the doctor's name, I stood up and picked up my package. Inside was a fake pregnancy belly and test. The stick was already positive, so that was a plus, literally. Laughing out loud, I took a picture of the test and the doctor's note and sent it to Coop. Five minutes later, there was still no response, so I had to try something different.

Danielle: You better respond before I call Tamia's phone
Coop: Gone with the bullshit. WTF do you want?
Danielle: We are about to have a baby, so you can shake that attitude.
Coop: I'm not playing games with you. Just let me know when it's time for you to go in labor.
Danielle: How about this…Get over here now so we can talk or I'm calling your HOE!!!
Coop: Yeah
Danielle: NOW!!!

***

Coop

Danielle was truly testing my patience. She could be such a bitch. Instead of her moving on, she wanted to make my life miserable. That was the main reason I wanted her to have an abortion. I knew this shit was gone get ugly. The shit didn't make no sense. Her ass claim she couldn't trust me, but she didn't want to leave me alone. Some women were so fuckin' indecisive, it didn't make any sense.

As I pulled up into the complex, I dreaded the visit. This was the last place I wanted to be. When I bailed out the crib, I told Tamia I was going to meet up with Brick. She was doing homework, so she was cool with it. Taking two steps at a time, I made it upstairs quickly and banged on the door. Danielle opened the door with a devilish smile on her face.

"Well, well, well. If it isn't my estranged husband. How are you doing, my love? Are you ready to come home?"

Brushing past her, I bumped her shoulder on the way in. "Cut the bullshit, Danielle. What the fuck do you want?"

She walked towards the sofa and sat down. "You know what I want, so stop playing dumb. This shit is getting old so you need to bring your ass back home. I done let you play with that young hoe long enough. Playtime is over."

Clearly she didn't get the memo, or she simply thought this was just a phase I was going through. "This is not a game. I really want a divorce. You and I cannot be together anymore, so get that through your thick ass skull."

"Don't talk to me like that. You've been getting beside yourself lately. I know you didn't get that from Brick, because he would never be disrespectful to his woman like that."

"Guess what?" I sat across from her. "I'm not Brick and you damn sholl ain't his woman."

Danielle rolled her eyes and smirked. "Sadly."

"You are right about one thing. Brick has a woman. You still a little ass girl that's insecure about herself. You ruined this marriage, not me."

"Oh, really? Muthafucka, you been cheating since day one and I stayed with you through it all. Then, you married me and still cheated. You never wanted this. I feel like you married me out of obligation."

This bitch was two seconds from getting her teeth punched down her throat. "Let's make one thing crystal muthafuckin clear." My teeth were grinding hard because I was so damn mad. "I married you because I wanted to and whether you believe it or not, I never cheated after we got married. True enough, I cheated a lot in the beginning, but I changed all of that once we got married. Sadly, I really thought I could spend the rest of my life making it up to you, but I was wrong."

Danielle sat still for a moment without saying a word. When she finally said something, her voice cracked. "I'm sorry. This is not how I envisioned our future, or the way I would have our first child."

Tears started to roll down her cheeks, but she didn't bother cleaning them. "You hurt me so bad. It's like you damaged me and I couldn't trust you anymore. It's not that I didn't want to. Your past wouldn't allow me to do so."

"And that's why this will never work. If you don't trust me, we don't have nothing. It just doesn't work that way."

"I can't live without you."

Hearing the pain in her voice didn't make feel good, so I got up and sat beside her. "Listen, at the end of the day, we have a child on the way. I'm going to be here throughout the whole process, but we can't be together. That part of our life is over with. All I want is for us to have a solid co-parenting situation."

Danielle looked up at me with her dark, red eyes. "After I just sat here and explained to you how your infidelities affected me, that's all you can say to me? This is your fault. You did this to me. To us and you don't give a fuck."

My patience was truly being testing, but I managed to keep my cool. "I'm trying to get you to understand that too much damage has been done. We will never get past this, because you never let go of the hurt. You married me knowing that I cheated in the past. So, that wasn't no damn surprise. You claimed you forgave me, but deep down inside you didn't."

"I did forgive you. I just didn't forget. There's a difference."

"That's your opinion."

"Coop, you were still cheating. That's why you had Brick with you when you stayed out all night. So he can be your alibi."

"Oh, you mean the day you tried to poison me?"

"You deserved it."

"Yeah, okay. I wasn't cheating and that's the truth."

"Fine. I believe you now."

Danielle finally calmed down and spoke with sense, but I wasn't buying it. My mind was already made up. All I wanted was to be a father to my child and move on with my life. Tamia and I were together, but that didn't mean it would last forever. However, I was willing to find out. The only thing left to do was file for divorce, so that could be out the way before the baby is born. My phone vibrated in my pocket. When I pulled it out, Tamia's name flashed across the screen. Ain't no way in hell I was gone answer that, so I sent an automated text that I would call her back.

"Who was that?"

"Stop being nosey."

"Okay." Danielle slid into my lap and tried to kiss me, but I moved my head.

"Danielle, stop."

"Since when can't a wife kiss her husband?"

"Don't go there."

"Come on. I know you miss me. I miss you." Her hands roamed across my chest, as she grinded in my lap.

"You not gone stop?"

"No. This baby has me horny." She licked my ear. "And I know you don't want me to let another man to fuck me while I'm pregnant and feed our baby."

Before I knew it, my hand was around her throat. "Danielle, don't fuckin' play with me. I'll kill yo' ass if you ever try me like that again."

Danielle smiled, unfazed by the pressure surrounding the center of her throat. "Well, fuck me, so I don't have to find dick elsewhere."

She kissed me on my lips and I didn't move. Despite everything I said a while ago, I fell into her hands and kissed her back. I felt her hand on my belt, as she tried to unfasten it. Lifting her up, I carried her into the bedroom and got naked. Lying down on the bed, Danielle straddled my lap and eased down slowly onto my pipe, riding me slowly. I bit down on my lip and squeezed her ass. The pussy was still good. Just like I remembered it. Danielle rode me for a long time from the front and then reverse style. Judging by the way she rode me, I could tell she missed me digging deep in them guts.

Danielle turned back to face me and grabbed me by the arms. Leaning up, she put her legs around my waist and rocked back and forward. She knew that was one of my favorite positions. Putting my back into it, I matched her thrusts and bit down on her neck. We stayed in that position until I busted a nut.

Two hours later, I jumped up after realizing I fell asleep. I had a dozen missed calls from Tamia, so I got dressed quickly. Danielle was still asleep, so I crept out slowly without waking her.

Chapter 16
Brick

When I left the house to meet up with Hector, it was a little after six. Our meeting was at seven, so I wanted to get there on time. As a boss, I knew how important it was to be punctual. Whatever I asked my crew to do, for example be on time. I displayed the same behavior. In my position, you had to lead by example and they will follow. I would never ask them to do something I'm not prepared to do myself.

Unlike the many meetings I attended with Hector, this one was different. He wanted me to come to his house. Ever since that shit went down with his brother-in-law, we've been on a different level. He treated me more like family, versus a business associate. That was cool. It showed me he respected me as a man and trusted me more now than he ever did.

Hector had a dope-ass house in a gated community out in Parkland. Getting out the car, I rang the doorbell and waited. Seconds later, the door opened and he was standing there with a half-smile on his face. He was dressed like Hugh Hefner, rocking a burgundy and gold Versace robe.

"You're early." He stepped back and let me in.

"Punctuality is vital in our daily lives. It shows how serious you are about your business and you know how I feel about mine. If I was late, that would say my time is more valuable than yours."

"Wise man. Come on. Let's go into the kitchen."

Hector's kitchen was huge as fuck and the décor was modern. Just the way I like it. The pots and pans were above the island. That was different. I may have to consider switching mine up.

"Have a seat. I'll fix you a drink."

On the table sat a brown folder with a Ruger SR22 on top of it. My first thought was if he was on some funny shit tonight, I was gone bust his head like a melon. However, my instincts said I had nothing to worry about. Hector had no reason to off me because I've been loyal to him from day one and that hasn't changed. He walked over and slid me a glass of Cognac. Picking it up, I took a swig.

"The day I met you, something within me told me you would be someone that I could trust and keep close by. I've come across many men that wanted to make money, but they failed because their organization was sloppy. They were going to jail and getting raided left and right. In the end, I would have to sever the business because I couldn't afford to take losses. The goal is to make money, not lose it. They were a casualty. Some didn't get the message and though they could run down with a sneak attack, but they failed every time."

As I took another hit of my drink, I paid close attention to what he was saying. Nothing was going over my head, as I read between the lines of the conversation.

"The way you move is different. I've been trying to figure you out, but I couldn't. That task is damn near impossible. Now, I have made some observations about you, so I'm going to share my thoughts with you. You're a silent killer. You don't do that much talking. You do a lot of listening. Just like right now. I remember you made a comment about the difference between a fool and a wise man. You stick to that rule. No bending."

Hector downed his drink and refilled his glass. "You want another?"

"Nah. I'm good for now." I had to be alert because something told me some shit was about to go down.

"Suit yourself." He downed his second drink. "We believe in the same things, Brick, and we are actually more alike than I thought. The way the cartel operates is we never bring outsiders in. We only use them to do our dirty work. But, our relationship is different, so I felt compelled to bring you in and closer to me. A man like you should be kept close at all times. It's better to have you in hindsight instead of on the outside because no one will see when you strike."

The way he spoke in circles was slowly eating away at my patience and I wanted him to get to the point of the meeting. I wasn't slow by a long shot, so I eased my hand under the table and rested my hand on my pistol. One false move and I was gone blow his fuckin' face off. Dental records wouldn't help identify his body.

"So, what are you getting at?" I asked.

"Honesty. That's the next subject."

"What about it?"

Hector leaned his head to the side and drew circles around the rim of his glass. "Why is that you never told me you spoke Spanish?"

"That was on a need-to-know basis. I didn't feel that was something I needed to disclose about myself. Sometimes you have to keep certain things to yourself. My concern was my safety. I didn't know you, so I had to observe you and make sure that I could trust you. My loyalty is one thousand and I've proved that too you. Nor have I lied about anything."

"Is that right?"

"That's a fact."

"Good." He smirked. "Now, I do want to say that I truly appreciate you for saving my life. That is the main reason I brought you here. I'm not on no sneaky shit and I'm not going to kill you, so you can take your hand off of your gun."

Hector caught me off guard with that one, but I didn't say anything.

"I'm learning you, Brick. You're an observant, yet cautious man. So, I know you think I have a hidden agenda for bringing you here."

"At first I did, but I know you don't have a reason to kill me."

I didn't give a fuck what he was saying. My gun was gone stay in my lap. That's how I survived so long in the game, by being observant and going with my gut feeling.

"You're right." Sitting up in his seat, he cut his eyes towards the folder and that heat. "Let me get to the point."

I nodded in agreeance.

"Do you remember what I said when we first met?"

"Yeah."

"Remind me."

"You spoke on loyalty and asked me if I ever heard of your cartel."

Hector nodded his head. "So, does the name Brandon Riccardo ring a bell?"

This muthafucka called me by my government name. That was something I never told him. "How do you know my name?"

"I've been doing my research." Hector moved his arm to the left and on instinct, I drew my gun on him. It happened so fast he didn't know what to expect.

Holding his arms out, he looked at me with no fear in his eyes. Then, he started laughing. "Chill out. I'm not about to do nothing. I want to give you this folder. Put the gun away."

Hector slid the folder across the table and placed his hands in front of him. When he was in position, I sat the gun down directly in front of me.

"You are your father's son." He chuckled and poured some more Cognac in his glass.

"What did you say?"

"I said, you are your father's son."

"How do you know who my father is?"

"Open the folder and you'll see."

Flipping the folder open, I reviewed every piece of paper in it. When I looked up, Hector was staring directly at me. "How did you get this? And why do you have my birth certificate?"

"I have my sources." Hector stood up and paced the floor.

"So, you knew my father."

He paused and put his hands inside his pockets. "He was my brother."

Closing the folder, I stood up and grabbed the bottle of Cognac 'cause now I needed a drink. "Hell, nah."

"It's the truth. Didn't the name Riccardo ring a bell to you?"

"No. It's not like the name isn't pretty common."

"True, but how many muthafuckas are your complexion and speak Spanish fluently?"

"This doesn't make any sense to me."

"Let's take a walk. I'll prove it to you."

Hector and I walked outside and went to the neighbor's house. He used his key to unlock the door. "This your house too?"

"You'll see."

As we walked on the inside, Hector escorted me into the living room where an old man and lady were sitting. "Mama. Papa." He called out. "I want you to meet someone. This is Brandon Riccardo."

Both of them spoke and offered me a seat. Hector sat down beside me. His mother kept looking at me.

"Brick, this is my mother, Nila and father, Delano."

"It's nice to meet you both."

"Brandon Riccardo." Her eyebrow slanted downward. "Is this Fernando's son? My grandson?"

"Sí," he replied.

"You're Brenda's son?"

"Yes ma'am."

"I'm so sorry about what happened to your mom." Nila stood up and walked towards me. "Oh, my Lord. Can I hug you?"

"Yes." I stood up and wrapped my arms around the woman, who was presumed to be my grandmother. Delano got up and hugged me as well.

Ten minutes ago I was skeptical, but after seeing his parents, I knew Hector was telling the truth. After sitting with them for two hours, I learned a lot of things about my father that I didn't know. They also brought up things that occurred in my life only family would know. My grandmother showed me a photo album, as well as my father's birth certificate to ease all doubt that I felt in my heart. If this reunion would've happened when I was younger, the conversation would be different. But, standing in their presence as an adult changed my way of thinking. I never understood why I didn't see my father's side of the family after he died, but now it all made sense. Hopefully, we would be able to develop a strong family bond. Hector and I were already close, so I was optimistic that everything would fall into place.

"You good now?" Hector asked.

"Yeah. I am."

"Good." He patted me on the shoulder. "Now that you're a part of the family, let's get one thing straight."

"What's that?"

"Don't you ever pull a gun out on me again," he chuckled. "I swear, your daddy did the same shit to me when we were younger."

"I guess I got it honest."

"Believe it or not, you act just like him. Wisdom and all."

"That's a good thing."

"Welcome to the family, nephew. I promise, I got you. I can't take the place of my brother, but I'll be here for you the same way he would be if he was here."

"Thanks, Unc. I appreciate that."

"I guess that mean I have to give you the family discount," Hector chuckled.

"I guess so."

For the first time Hector put his arms around me and hugged me tightly. Being here in that moment was the best feeling in the world. Family was important to me and for the first time in a long time, I felt complete. Nothing in the world compared to the genuine love you felt from your relatives. My mama's side was dead to me and all I had after that was Coop and then Zuri. It's funny how things changed for the better.

Before we left, I promised my grandparents that I wouldn't be a stranger. Once I got Zuri and Janae on the same page, I would bring my kids to meet them. This was a special moment for me and I wanted to share that with the ones that mean the world to me. Hector and I went back to his place and had a few more drinks. This time, we left the guns out the equation and chopped it up until a little after midnight. When I left the house, I told Zuri I would be back by one in the morning. It was a respect thing, so I didn't have a problem with that since I wasn't working.

Zuri was up feeding Bam when I made it back home. Taking off my clothes, I dropped them in the middle of the floor. "How was your meeting?"

"It was good. We discussed business and got a little tipsy."

"Yeah, I see that. You about to take a shower?"

"Nope. I can't get no pussy, so I'm going to sleep. Goodnight."
She hated when I did that, but I didn't care. I was tired.

Chapter 17
Zuri
One month later

The waitress took our food and drink order before walking away. Quietly, I sat gathering my thoughts. It wasn't like I didn't know what to say. It was more along the lines of how to say it. After overthinking a simple process, I let it flow naturally.

"Thank you for accepting my lunch invitation. I know it was difficult after everything I said."

Janae was focused on her phone she had clutched tightly in her hand. Seconds later, she sat it face down on the table. Her attention was finally on me. "You're right. It was very difficult for me and honestly I didn't want to come. But, I know how important this is to my dad."

That was the type of response I expected to hear from her, so I didn't take offense to it. "For the record, it's important to me too. I know that I said some pretty hurtful things and I was wrong for that. My intentions were to never hurt your feelings."

Janae sucked her teeth. "Sure as hell felt like it."

"That day at the hospital wasn't about you directly. It was about your dad and the way he told me. He knew I was under a lot of stress and medication after I had your brother. Instead of him telling me when I was in my right mind, he just sprung on me with no explanation of what was truly going on. He only gave me bits and pieces and the way he explained it was crazy. It didn't make any sense to me. It sounded unbelievable.

Janae's attitude was nonchalant as she nodded her head. "Got it."

"From the bottom of my heart, I never meant to hurt you and I'm sorry. If he would've sat me down and explained it, I would've accepted it with no problem. I love your dad and any child of his, is a child of mine. The same way I accepted Breanna into my life and home, I would've did the same thing for you. There was a lot of miscommunication on both sides."

Janae's silence and blank expression told me she wasn't ready to accept my apology or make amends. This would happen on her own terms and I was fine with that. Any progress was better than no progress at all.

"You don't have to accept my apology right now. Just think on it and let it sink in."

She nodded her head. "Okay."

Destiny Skai

The waitress returned with our drinks and placed them in front us. When she left, I continued with the conversation. "Can I share something with you?"

"Sure."

"When I was a little girl I lost my mom, so I know exactly what you're going through. That's why it was so important for me to meet up with you and ask for your forgiveness. That pain is unbearable and you need a strong support system. I want to be that for you."

My mouth was a little dry, so I sipped some of my strawberry lemonade. "The things you're about to experience, I can relate to every situation. You had your mother for eighteen years. Not me. She didn't see me graduate from high school or college. When I first got my period, I thought I was going to die, because I didn't have her to explain to me what a menstrual cycle was. My dad had to do everything on his own, because I wouldn't allow another woman to be in the picture long enough to get comfortable."

Catching my breath, I paused for a few seconds. "It's hard losing a parent and it's like that pain never goes away. I'm an adult and I still cry for my mom. She'll never see me get married or meet my kids. That hurts the most."

Reflecting back on my past caused me to tear up, so I took a minute to get myself together.

"Are you okay?" she asked.

Dabbing my eyes with my napkin, I nodded my head. "Yeah, I'm fine. Sorry about that.'

"It's okay. You don't have to apologize." For the first time I saw compassion in her eyes. "Thank you for sharing that with me. I know it's not easy to open up to someone you don't know. Honestly, I don't know what's worse, your situation or mine. Like, it doesn't seem like it makes a difference what age you are, because it all hurts the same. I guess I thought people who lost their parents at an early age were in a better position mentally."

"Trust me, either way it's hard. Age doesn't matter. It all hurts the same. Just appreciate the amount of time you got to spend with her. Remember what she taught you. The good times you shared."

Tears formed in Janae's eyes. "Out of all the things she taught me, she never taught me how to live without her."

That shit shattered my heart into a billion pieces. I just wanted to comfort her. Sliding out of my seat, I went and sat down beside her.

Hugging her tightly, I rubbed the center of her back. "I'm so sorry you have to go through this. I truly am and I'm sorry for making it worse. Just know that I will always be here for you. I promise."

Janae sobbed softly. "Why did this have to happen to me? Why my mom?"

A few people glanced in our direction, but they looked away quickly. "It doesn't seem like it right now, but I promise everything will be okay. We will get through this together."

Janae's episode lasted for several more minutes, but eventually I was able to get her calm. We then changed the subject and ate our food. Throughout the meal, we shared a few laughs and funny stories about Brick. Things between us were finally going smoothly and I was happy that she gave me a chance. Now, we could take slow steps towards us being a family. Glancing down at my watch time was flying drastically. I knew it wouldn't be long before Brick called to see how we were doing.

"Are you ready?"

"You know I can't leave him with three kids for too long. They'll drive him crazy."

Smiling, Janae laughed. "Yeah, you right. I've had Bre and Legend at one time and whew, chile. They too much for me."

"They are and now I have Bam. We just might need a nanny."

"Make sure she's an old one."

"Who you telling, 'cause I don't play about your daddy."

"Oh, I know."

"Alright, let me pay this bill so we can go free him."

"Umm. Zuri?"

"Yes."

"Thanks for everything and I accept your apology."

"Thank you. I appreciate that."

On our way to the car, Janae stopped in the middle of the parking lot and started throwing up. Standing beside her, I held her hair in place. After her body rejected everything she put in it, she used her hand to wipe her mouth.

"Are you okay?"

"Yeah. I'm fine."

We drove down Flamingo Road in silence, but my mind was not resting. "Can I ask you a personal question?"

"Yeah."

"Are you pregnant?"

She wasn't good at hiding her emotions, so I knew the answer before she said anything. Janae kept her eyes on the floor before she finally looked at me.

"I don't know."

There was a CVS Pharmacy down the street from my house, so we stopped there to get her a pregnancy test. My phone started ringing.

"This might be your dad."

"Please don't tell him," she panicked.

"I'm not." As I took the phone out my purse, I realized it wasn't Brick. "Oh, it's not him."

The number wasn't programmed in my phone, so I didn't know who was calling. All I knew was it better not be Daman. "Hello."

"Hi. Is this Zuri Monroe?"

"Yes, it is. Who is this?"

"This is Officer Bryant and I need you to come out to an active crime scene. It's an emergency."

"Are you joking? What's going on?"

"No, ma'am. I'm not. Please come to Oakland Boulevard by the Turnpike's overpass now."

"Who is this about?"

"Ma'am," he shouted. "I can't discuss any further details over the phone, so please just come. The person is asking for you."

"Okay. I'm on my way."

After I hung up the phone, I stood in place. That whole conversation had me blown. Who in the hell would be calling for me? Then, I thought about Kyra.

"Is everything okay?" Janae asked.

"I don't know." Snapping out of it, I got into the car quickly and pulled off.

Nothing about that phone call sat well with me. My body was filled with this eerie feeling that I couldn't shake. I knew it had to be a bad situation for the officer to call my phone, but what made it worst was the fact that he didn't tell me who it was. That was quite strange to me.

As soon as I crossed over 55th Avenue, I could see that the traffic was extremely thick and one officer was directing the flow of the cars. Thinking fast, I parked at the Checkers on the corner.

"You staying in the car?"

"No. I'm coming with you."

Janae and I jogged up to where we saw a crowd of officers.

114

"Excuse me. I'm Zuri Monroe. I received a call from Officer Bryant to come here."

"Umm. Yes. We have a situation and we are trying to get her to step away from the ledge."

Now, I was confused. "What?"

"There's a woman here threatening to commit suicide and she asked for you. So, we need you to go up and talk to her."

"Okay.

The officer escorted me to the top of the bridge and when I saw what was happening, I damn near passed out myself. The second she locked eyes with me, it all made sense about her disappearance.

"Shakira! Please get down," I begged.

"Zuri, I'm so sorry. I know I was supposed to come back and get Legend, but I can't. I'm not mentally stable to take care of him."

"We can get through this together. I'm hurting just as much as you are. He was my brother and I miss him so much, but this isn't the way to handle this. Legend would never want you to end your life. He would want you to raise his babies and keep his memories alive."

"I can't live without him, Z. Ever since he died, I haven't been right. There is no life without him. I have no life without him."

"You have LJ and he needs you. He misses you." I tried to take a step forward, but the officer held me back.

"He's better off without me."

"That's not true. He asks about you and his dad all the time." My lips started to tremble, as I tried pleading with her.

"Shakira, please. You're pregnant. Please don't do this. I'm begging you. Don't make him live without both of his parents. That's not fair to him. We didn't have a choice with what happened to Legend, but you have one."

"I thought I could do this, but I can't. There is no way I could bring another child into this world. I'm tired of being here. I just want to be with him eternally."

Shakira eased closer to the ledge. "I thought that if I didn't terminate the pregnancy and go through it, it would make me feel better. Truth is it hasn't."

"Just get down and I will help you. You can come live with me, while you get yourself together. I'll even go to counseling with you. I promise."

Shakira cried and rubbed her fully-developed belly. She had to be due any day now. "We were finally going to have the girl he always wanted.

But, someone took my whole life away. I'll never be okay and I don't want to live if he's not here."

"Ma'am, please step away from the ledge," the officer shouted through the bullhorn.

"Shakira. Come on and get down. Let's fix this. Legend will be so happy to know he has a sister. He'll be happy to see you."

Shakira wiped her face. "When you see my baby, tell him mommy loves him. Let him know we will always be with him, just look inside his locket. Zuri, take care of my baby please. Don't let him turn to the streets. It's a dangerous game out here. Protect him like you are going to protect your son."

Shakira removed the necklace she was wearing and tossed it on the ground. "Give that to him."

At that moment, I knew it was over for her. There was no changing her mind, but I couldn't stand there and let her jump. Easing from behind the officer, I ran in her direction.

"Shakira, come with me."

"Goodbye, Zuri. I loved you like a sister, but I love Legend more. My loyalty is to him and I forgive you."

As I rushed towards her, I could hear footsteps behind me, but I refused to stop. There was a chance I could save her. Within arm's reach, I extended my hand to her, but Shakira turned around and jumped off the bridge.

"Noooooo!" I screamed before blacking out.

Chapter 18
Janae

"Is she going to be okay?" I asked sincerely, while standing over Zuri.
"In time, she will be just fine." Brick placed his hand on my shoulder and squeezed it gently.
"Are you okay?"
"Yeah. I think so. It was just a scary situation. I feel so bad for her. She's been through a lot."
"Yeah, but she has me to help her get through whatever comes her way."
"You really love her, don't you?"
"She means the world to me and I'll die protecting her. The same way I would do for my kids."
After she passed out, they transported her to the hospital. I called my dad, so he could meet me there. Watching Zuri go through what she just went through developed a softer spot in my heart for her. There was so much pain that she endured in life, but I had to commend her for remaining strong. The love my dad has for Zuri, made me want to push further to build a relationship with her. At first I thought she was a bad person, but in reality she's not at all. My dad and I had a chance to talk and he explained some things to me that forced me to have a change of heart.
"Come on, so she can get some rest."
"Okay."
"I'm going into my cave if you need me."
Going into the living room, I grabbed my purse from the sofa and went inside the bathroom. Removing the pregnancy test, I sat on the toilet and held the stick against my stream of pee. Sitting it on the counter, I cleaned myself and waited on the longest two of minutes of my life. My heart was racing while I waited to see the results. Once they appeared, I took a deep breath and washed my face.
Skeet was in the man cave when I walked in. It was so funny how he looked at me in the presence of my father. It made me wonder how he would feel if he knew what was going on between us. I didn't expect him to be happy about it, but I did expect him to be understanding. Right now, it didn't matter. We would cross that bridge when we got there, because I had no plans on letting him go any time soon.
"So, what are y'all doing in here?" I asked, while sitting next to my dad.

"Aht! Aht! Get out of here." Brick shook his head no.

"Why? I'm an adult."

"Yeah. An adult with no job," he laughed.

"You said I didn't have to work."

"Speaking of which, when are you leaving for school?"

"January. After Mom died, I told them I needed time to get myself together but in the meantime, I'm taking some online courses."

"Good. I need you out of here as quick as possible." His tone was stern, but he had a smile on his face.

"What school you going to?" Skeet asked.

"None of Your Business University."

Skeet busted out laughing with his sexy ass. I wanted to eat him alive, but I had to keep my composure in front of the old boy.

"Bruh, you trippin' hard."

"My baby can't date nobody like me."

"I'm going to the University of Florida and what's wrong with dating somebody like you? You're a good man."

Brick cut his eyes at me. "Keep dating that nerdy nigga, Demarcus. That's your speed."

When he said that, I almost died because I never told Skeet about Demarcus. Skeet looked at me cross-eyed when Brick put me on the spot, but of course he couldn't say nothing. Technically, we weren't really together because I became distant when me and Skeet starting messing around. I knew I wasn't the only girl he was messing around with, even though he never mentioned being with anyone. His phone blew up too much at night for it to just be about the money.

"I love you, Daddy."

"I love you too."

"Are you going to take me home now?" I asked.

"I will once Zuri wake up. I'm not lugging three kids by myself. So, can you wait?"

"I have homework I need to turn in."

"I'll drop her off for you. I'm about to head out anyway." Skeet stood up and grabbed his keys.

"Hell, no. Drive my car."

"Daddy, stop it. He can drop me off. It's not like he haven't done it before."

Brick's head swiveled in my direction like *The Exorcist*. "What you mean, he dropped you off before?"

"I went to the club one night with my friends and they wanted to leave with these dudes and I didn't want to. He was there and saved me from being in an awkward position. So, you should be thanking him for being a perfect gentleman that night."

He then looked at Skeet. "So, why didn't you tell me about this?"

"I know how you feel about your daughter and I didn't want you to overact. You know how you are."

"True enough. Nonetheless, I appreciate you getting her home safely."

"It's all good. I did it off the strength of you."

He then looked in my direction. "Find you some damn new friends. Anyone who would put you in that type of position don't give a fuck about you."

"Bruh, I told her the same thing."

"Alright, take my baby home for me."

"She in good hands. I promise you that."

"Yeah, I know you a man of your word."

We hugged. Him and Skeet did some funny handshake and then we left.

Skeet opened the door for me. Then, he went around and got in the truck. Before I had the chance to say a single word, he looked at me sideways.

Calmly, he asked, "Who the fuck is Demarcus?"

Chills crawled over my body, hearing him talk to me like that. It kind of turned me on. "Um. He's this guy I used to date before you."

"So, why am I just hearing about him?"

"I didn't think it was important. He's a thing of the past, but I never told my daddy it was over between us. I figured if he thought we were still together, he wouldn't be worried about you and me."

"You sure about that?"

"Yes, baby. I'm sure. You know I don't want anyone but you. Don't you think that if something was going on with me and Demarcus, you would've caught it by now? You've popped up at my house so many times and I was always there alone."

"Nae, don't make me fuck you up. You better not be fuckin' with that nigga and I'm serious. You belong me to now. I just have to find a way to get Brick to understand that I'll never hurt you."

Now, was the time to put it out on the table since we were having a serious conversation. "Well," I sighed. "He may not have too much of a choice depending on what I decide."

"What do you mean?"

"I'm pregnant."

"How do you know?"

"I took a test." Reaching into my purse, I pulled out the test and held it out for him to see.

Skeet was silent for a moment. "Damn. I wasn't expecting to hear that. This nigga gone kill me."

"No, he's not."

"Do you know your daddy?"

"You're upset?"

He shook his head. "Nah. I'm good. What about you?"

"I don't know how to feel. I'm just worried about what he's going to say if I don't go to school."

"Why wouldn't you go to school?"

"That's going to be hard."

"You think I would let that happen? That's what I'm here for." The sincerity in his voice gave me confirmation that he would truly stand by me. I believed he would be a great father. Getting my father to understand was another story.

"This is a lot to think about."

"I don't agree with abortions, but it's your body. Whatever you decide, just let me know first."

"I will. Can we leave now before he comes outside?" Skeet quickly pulled out the driveway.

Back at my house, I couldn't wait to make it to the bedroom. I was so horny. We started kissing as soon we closed the door, up until we hit the room. Shredding our clothes, we tossed our phones on the nightstand and climbed into bed. Our lips connected as we kissed passionately. Skeet was positioned between my legs, rubbing my clit. She was leaking heavily. The tip of his head made an entrance between my lips before his rod penetrated me.

"Sss. Ahh. Ooh."

The whole time we were sitting in my dad's man cave, sex was all I could think about. With my hands on his waist, I rocked my hips to meet each stroke. Holding both legs with his arms, Skeet delivered slow, deep strokes. The dick was big. I felt it all in my tummy.

Moaning my ass off, I mumbled. "Chance, I love you."

"I love you too, baby."

His response sealed the deal because he wasn't going anywhere. We were stuck and no one was going to get in the way of that. Not even my daddy. As soon as that thought popped in my head, Skeet's phone started to ring.

"Shit," he huffed.

"Ignore it."

"Hell, nah. That's Brick. You have to be quiet." Skeet grabbed his phone and cleared his throat before accepting the call. "Wassup, bruh?"

"Did you drop Janae off?"

"Yeah."

"A'ight. Where you at?"

"On my way to check on Kamari."

"Tell that boy I said what's up."

"I will."

"A'ight. I'll get at you later."

"Yeah."

Skeet pushed in and out of me slowly, as he put his phone back on the stand. "My shit almost went limp talking to him."

"Get it back up then."

"Oh, he ain't dead yet."

As soon as we got back into it, my shit went off. "Dammit. That's him. He trying to make sure we're not together."

"Answer it so he'll feel better."

Rolling my eyes, I snatched it up. "I don't know why he trying to keep tabs on me. This my pussy."

"You a lie. This my shit."

"Shh." Sliding the green button, I yawned purposely. "Hey, Pops, what's up?"

"What you doing?"

"Homework."

"You by yourself?"

"Yes, Father. He is not here, if that's what you thinking."

Skeet made faces, while poking me gently.

"Listen, baby. I love Skeet like a son. He's a good dude, but—"

I cut him off. "But what? He's a good dude, but not good enough to date me?"

"He lives the same lifestyle I do. So, I know what comes along with this game and I don't want to see you hurt. That's something I couldn't handle."

"Zuri is somebody's daughter too."

"The difference between me and him is that I'm older. Much wiser. I've settled down with Zuri. Skeet is still young. He's not ready to settle down just yet. He has money and that attracts hoes. I'm not risking him breaking your heart."

"I get it, so don't worry about it. I'm about to finish my homework."

"Janae, I love you and I promised your mother I would take care of you."

"I love you too. I'll talk to you later."

"Alright."

He had me a little upset, but that wasn't about to ruin what I had going on. Skeet kissed my lips. "Relax. It's going to be okay."

"I hope so."

After our session, I fell asleep in his arms. If loving Chance was wrong, I didn't want to be right. The only way to get him to accept our relationship was through Zuri. Little did she know she was about to be in the middle of this love connection. Brick cherished the ground she walked on, so I knew she could get him to change his mind.

Chapter 19
Zuri

For the last hour, I was on the phone with Mehzani, telling her about the situation with Shakira. The entire situation was sad and I still couldn't wrap my head around what she meant by forgiving me. Some nights I would have nightmares and I would wake up in a cold sweat. Through it all, Brick was right there with me, drying my tears.

"So, who's keeping the kids while y'all go up there?" Mehzani asked.

"Janae."

"Who is that?"

"Brick's daughter."

"His daughter? How old is she and where the hell she come from?"

"Eighteen and that's a story for another day."

"Fine. Well, what's going to happen to Legend? Is he going into the system?" Mehzani asked.

"Hell, no. I would never let that happen. He's going to stay here with me and Brick."

"Calm down, sis. I was just asking. You know he's our responsibility now. So, whatever you need me to do, I'm here for it all."

"Thanks, because he's going to need all of the emotional support we can provide." Bam started to get a little cranky, so I put the pacifier in his mouth to calm him down. "How is Gucci?"

"He's doing much better. My baby can talk now and he's trying to walk."

"That's so good. I know you happy about that."

"I am. My prayers have finally been answered." There was so much happiness in her voice. I was genuinely happy that he was making progress.

"Get off that phone and get ready so we can go. The car will be here in one hour," Brick stated while stepping out the bathroom, wearing only a towel.

"That's my cue, sis. We'll catch up when I get back."

"Yes, because we have a lot to catch up on. Have a safe trip."

"Will do."

"Bye."

"Bye-bye," Mehzani replied before hanging up.

"Bae, have you checked on Gucci?"

"Nah," he replied nonchalantly.

"Well, he's talking now and trying to walk."

"That's good news."

"Yeah. It is. You should check on him."

"I will."

Brick stood in front of the dresser putting on lotion. My eyes were locked on his sexy ass body. Those tattoos still did something to me after all this time. We still hadn't engaged in any type of sexual activity and it was killing me. He acted as if it didn't bother him.

"Why you staring at me like that? You look like you wanna eat me up." That man could be so arrogant, until it didn't make any damn sense.

"Are you cheating on me?"

"Is that a real question?"

"Yes. Now answer it." I was trying to keep my voice down since Bam went back to sleep.

"No. I'm not." He held out his right arm. "When the fuck would I have time to cheat? Coop been handling business since the baby came home, so I can spend more time in the house." Brick mumbled, as he went inside the bathroom, "Muthafuckas ain't never satisfied."

The truth did hurt and now I felt bad because he was home a lot. If he did leave, it wasn't for long. My hormones were just crazy and God knows I didn't want to claim having postpartum depression. Even though, that could be an easy factor, considering all of the things that I went through.

When I joined him, he was standing at the sink brushing his pearly white teeth. Stepping close to him from behind, I put my arms around his waist and rubbed his chest.

"I'm sorry. My emotions are getting the best of me and we haven't had sex in a while. To me, it seems like you don't care if we do or don't."

"If I couldn't live without sex, I would've died a long time ago. Zuri, I did six years in the feds, baby. I can do without."

"We sleep in the same bed."

"The only reason I'm not touching you is because you weren't fully healed. I thought I was doing you a favor by waiting. You already know I fuck shit up when I'm in the pussy. I'll fuck around and bust those staples clean out yo' stomach. Have you walking around like you had a botched tummy tuck."

"Brick, it's been a month."

"So, that's the real issue, huh? You want some dick?" He leaned down in the sink and rinsed his mouth out.

"What the hell you think I'm fussing about?"

"Fuck it then. I'm not responsible for what happens." Brick turned around and so did I. "Where you going?"

"In the room."

"Nah. You gone wake up Bam."

Brick grabbed me and pushed me against the sink. Roughly, he hiked up my dress and slapped his dick against my ass. Once it was hard enough, he eased it inside of me. That shit took a bitch breath away when he stretched me open.

"Shit." My hands were flat on the sink, but that wasn't gone work. So, I held onto the countertop.

Brick started off easy to get me comfortable, but that didn't last too long. It escalated quickly to deep, hard thrusts. The head was poking the hell out of the bottom of my stomach. I was doing my best not to scream, but that was damn near impossible.

"Shit. Shit. My stomach."

"You better hold onto it," he warned.

Using my right hand, I clutched the bottom of my stomach right at the bikini line. My muscles gripped his massive piece tight. The friction increased, as I felt him slide in and out of me at a very fast pace. The first scream escaped my lips. It felt like the bottom of my shit was gone fall right on the floor.

"Shhh!"

Brick used his right hand to cover my mouth.

For what felt like an eternity, Brick beat my back in until I tapped all the way out. My legs felt like noodles, so I leaned against the sink to shake it off.

All I could hear was laughter. "You alright?"

"I'm good." My ass was lying. I wanted to pass out right then and there, but I couldn't. He would never let me hear the end of that.

"You ain't fooling me. Yo' ass outta breath. I can hear it."

"I'm about to shower real quick."

He kissed me on the forehead. "You still think I'm cheating?'

"No."

"Hurry up before this car get here." Slowly, I made my way to the shower and stepped in.

***

Brick

Three hours later, we were in Greenville, South Carolina. The first stop I wanted to make was the liquor store, because I knew what lay ahead. Zuri was already an emotional mess and cleaning out this house was only going to make it worse.

"Google the nearest liquor store."

"Okay." Zuri pulled out her phone and started the search. "I found a package store."

"It's the same thing. How far away is it?"

"Sixteen minutes. Take I-85 South."

"Okay."

Twenty-five minutes later, I had my Patrón and we were on our way. It was a white type of day. Besides, I needed something strong. Zuri directed me for the next thirty minutes, until we made it to Hampton Grove at Green Valley. The house was what I expected it to be, lavish. It was two stories, but it looked like it could have an extra floor. Pulling up, I stopped in front of the three-car garage. There was a Bentley truck parked in the driveway. It had to be a good neighborhood for that muthafucka to be still sitting in place after all that time.

Zuri and I got out of the rental and went inside. Legend really moved away and upgraded like a true boss. He was eating fa sho. That was the main reason I wanted to take him out, because he had a lot of territory. Seeing the way everything played out, I wish I could go back and right my wrong. Legend was never an enemy. He was competition and I felt like I had to eliminate him when I touched down.

"Wow, this is beautiful," Zuri gasped, admiring the nine-foot ceilings and fireplace.

Zuri's sandals clinked against the hardwood floors, as she took a tour of the house. I followed behind her closely, sipping on my cup. The house was nice, I couldn't lie about that. There were a total of four bedrooms, three bathrooms, an office, exercise room and living room.

"So, what are you taking?"

"All of LJ's things, important papers and things like that. As far as their clothes, I'll probably just put it in a small storage for now. When I sell the house, they can figure out what they want to do with the furniture."

"Do you think selling it is a good idea?"

"I'll never live here, so it's pointless to keep it."

"You can always rent it out like a vacation home or something. Did you forget that Legend will become an adult? I'm sure he would love to have his father's house."

Zuri bit down on her lip, like she was thinking hard about what I just said. "I guess you're right. I'll look into that. In the meantime, I'm about to tackle this office and get these papers together."

"Let's go."

Legend's office was on the bottom floor. On the wall was a photo of him, Shakira and LJ. Zuri immediately teared up. Holding her in my arms, I rubbed her back.

"I don't think I can do this," her voice cracked, as the emotion poured out.

"Yes, you can. You're so strong and I've witnessed that with my own eyes. I'll be right here with you."

"Okay."

Zuri took a deep breath and sat behind his desk. On the opposite side, I sat there and got my drink on while she sorted through tons of papers. By the time I checked my timepiece, it was little after nine o'clock and I was damn near fucked up. The bottle of Patrón I had was one cup away from being empty. To my surprise, Zuri hadn't shed another tear. So, she was doing better than I thought.

"Come on, let's call it a night. You've been at this for hours."

"This the last box, baby. Give me a minute."

"Yeah." Leaning back, I got comfortable in the dark brown leather chair.

The longer I sat in that seat, the more relaxed I became. My eyes were starting to feel heavy, so I closed them. Sleep wasn't too far away. Zuri's loud sobbing snatched me from a light snooze.

"No! No!"

"What's wrong?"

In her hand was a folder. Her fingers trembled, as she passed it to me. The contents included a handwritten letter from Legend, a discovery packet and a picture of a little girl on the witness stand. I held up the photo.

"Who is this?"

"Mehzani on the witness stand during Daman's trial."

Continuing to flip through the papers, I stumbled across a newspaper clipping. Reading the article, I stopped when I came across a familiar name.

"Who is Zena Hayes?"

"My mother. Daman never told us she was dead. All he said was that she left us. He's been lying to me all my life," Zuri screamed. "I hate that bitch."

"Damn, baby. I'm sorry." Finishing up the article, I handed it back to her. "It says you have a brother. Do you know him?"

"No. The last time I saw my mother she had just given birth to him. She came home from the hospital one day and the next day she was gone. No goodbye or nothing."

My mind went straight to the day I met Marco. He had a very large tattoo on his chest that read, *Zena*. That shit was embedded in my memory bank, like the ink on my skin. In just a short month I've went through some crazy shit, but this one took the cake.

"Does Demarco Riccardo ring a bell for you?" I know what I read, but I needed to see if her head was on right.

"That's my brother's name. Why do you know him?"

"Yeah. That's my cousin."

Zuri's eyes stretched as wide as flying saucers when those words let my lips. Now was the time for me to explain my family tree. Something told me this was about to be a long night. Better yet, a long three days.

128

Chapter 20
Janae

Skeet was knocked out in the guest room after the two doses of loving I put on him. All of the kids were taking a nap, so I was trying to get mine in before they got up. Skeet's phone kept vibrating in his pants pocket on the floor, making that impossible to do. I knew he was a hard sleeper, so I grabbed his phone. The keypad was locked, so I used his thumb to open it. My curiosity was killing me so I scrolled through all of his text messages. There were several unopened messages from a chick named Jenn. It was obvious he was in a relationship with her, based on the shit she was texting. Angrily, I snatched the covers off of him.

"Wake your ass up!"

"Bruh, what you doing?"

"Who the fuck is Jenn?"

Skeet sat up in the bed and rubbed his hand over his face. Blinking several times, he yawned. "What?"

I threw his phone at him to let his ass know he was busted. "I read the messages, so I know you fucking her."

"Man, ain't nobody fucking that girl. She—"

Cutting him off, I shouted in his face, "Stop fuckin' lying."

"If you shut the fuck up and let me finish what I was saying, you will know. You see she mentioned your name."

Wrinkles appeared on his forehead as he tried to explain. "Jenn is somebody I was with before you. We was still together when me and you started talking. But as time went on, I broke things off with her, 'cause I was falling for you. That's why she keep blowing me up."

Sitting down on the bed, I folded my hands and placed them in my lap. It took everything in me to keep from slapping the shit out of him. "When was the last time you fucked that girl? And don't lie to me either."

"A few weeks ago."

"Oh, wow! So, in other words, you was fucking me and her at the same time?"

"That was before we got serious."

"I don't believe you."

"I've been with you damn near every day. When I'm not with you, I'm working." He was calm and it was pissing me off.

"My daddy warned me about you, but no, I didn't want to listen. I thought you would be different. Clearly, I was wrong." Grabbing his clothes off the floor, I threw them at him. You can go home now. I don't want you here."

"Come here, Janae, and stop playing with me. You know I'm not fuckin' nobody but you. I don't want her and you can see that in the messages. Stop playing crazy."

"I'm not playing. Perception is everything and it looks like you and her are still messing around. If that wasn't the case, she wouldn't be blowing you up like that. Obviously, something still going on between y'all."

"I'm where I wanna be. We about to have a baby. Why would I ruin that?"

"I don't know about that anymore."

Skeet sighed and rubbed his hand over his face. I could tell he was aggravated. "You don't know about what? Having my baby?"

"No. I don't know if I want to go through this with you. The cheating and the lies is too much for me. Might as well end that now. You do what you wanna do and I'll do the same."

"Stop fuckin' playin' with me, ma. I'll fuck you up and I'm dead-ass serious."

"No, you won't." My daddy would kill him if he put his hands on me.

"A'ight. Keep thinking that."

"If you telling the truth. Prove it to me. Call her and put it on speaker. I need to hear y'all conversation and if you can't do that, you might as well leave three hundred dollars on the dresser."

Skeet picked up his phone and started pressing buttons. The phone rang as he put it on speaker.

"Why the fuck you ignoring my calls and text messages?" Jenn snapped.

"Why you keep blowing my shit up? I told you I'm not fucking with you."

"Boy, shut up. How many times have you said that?"

"Dead-ass. I'm not fuckin' with you. So, move on and stop calling me."

"I'm not doing shit. Come over here."

"No!" His eyes were on me as he responded.

"So, you wanna leave me for your new bitch, huh?"

"Watch your mouth."

"Oh, he mad-mad," Jenn laughed. "Skeet, stop playing with me. You think you gone just walk out me and my son life like that? It's not happening. I'm telling you right now, if you don't stop messing with that girl, it's gone be a problem."

I couldn't hold my tongue any longer. "Oh, you have a son?"

Skeet shook his head. "No. That's not my son."

"Oh, that's the reason you calling me? To prove something to that hoe, fuck you and her. But, you heard what the fuck I said, though."

Jenn tried me for the last time, so I snatched his phone out his hand. "Bitch, you ain't gone do shit to me. And after he hang up this phone, don't call his shit no more and I mean that. He don't want you, so get that shit through your head."

"Hoe, he don't want you."

"Oh, I already got him. I took him from you, didn't I?"

"He gone be right here in my bed later on, eating this pussy. I will never stop licking and sucking that dick. Don't say I didn't warn you."

"That's what you think. Bitch, go find your son daddy, 'cause he got his own baby on the way."

Skeet took the phone out my hand. "Calm down. She can only do what I allow."

"Fuck her," I spat.

"Skeet, I know muthafuckin' well you don't have a baby on the way."

"Yeah, I do. My girl pregnant. So, stop calling me. It's over between us."

"You lowdown, dirty bitch. I know you didn't get her pregnant," she screamed. After Skeet hung up the phone, he stood up to face me.

"Where are you going?" he asked.

"To shower. I want you gone when I get out."

"Damn, I called the bitch. What else do you want?"

"Time."

"Time for what?"

Leaning against the dresser, I put my hands on my hips. "To figure out what I want to do about this entire situation. I can already see this is going to be a problem. This is too much to deal with."

"Let me handle Jenn. She just talking shit."

"Oh, I'm not worried about her doing nothing to me. My concern is if it's truly over between y'all and if I have to worry about you sleeping with her."

"That's over. I promise. All I want is you. I love you." Leaning forward, he kissed me and my weak ass gave in.

***

Coop

Ever since I went back on my word and doubled back to Danielle, the phone calls from her increased. Day and night, she would call repeatedly with no fucks given. That had Tamia looking at me sideways.

"Why does she keep calling you?"

"Is that a real question? Her behavior is nothing new and you know that."

Tamia paused the movie we were watching and glanced up at me. "This is really getting out of hand. Every time I turn around she's calling you. What are you going to do about it?"

"I don't know."

"There is something going on and you can't tell me it's not. So whatever it is you need to tell me. I don't want to hear about it later."

Silence took over the room, as I debated on telling her about our current situation. One thing I knew for sure was that I want Tamia too catch wind of it. I cared about her feelings, so I didn't want to mess up what we had going on. Tamia turned over on her stomach to face me.

"Listen, you promised to always be honest with me. Don't go back on your word. I don't deserve that from you."

"You right." I placed both hands on my head and grunted. This conversation was not about to go well at all, but I wasn't down with keeping secrets. That shit was a headache and if she wanted to break up, then that's fine too.

"Danielle is pregnant."

The sad expression on her face is exactly what I was trying to avoid. Even though she was aware that I was married, I knew the truth would hurt anyway. Tamia was laying on top of me, but she got up and sat on the edge of the sofa.

"Now it all makes sense. Congratulations on the baby." Tamia stormed out of the living room, so I followed her.

"Please don't allow this to affect us. Her being pregnant doesn't change our relationship."

"I'm not sure I believe that. Who's to say you won't reconcile with her and be a family?"

"Our marriage is over. A baby won't change that."

"That's what you saying now." Tamia looked down at her phone. "What the hell?" she mumbled, never taking her eyes off the screen.

"What's wrong?"

"You fucked her. You liar." Tamia threw her phone at me, hitting me in the face with it.

Rubbing my forehead, I squinted in pain. "What you talm 'bout?"

"Look at the phone." Danielle sent photos of me and her in bed the other day. There was no denying it. I was caught.

"It's not what it looks like."

"Looks like y'all was fuckin' to me." I tried to grab her, but she held her arm out. "Please don't touch me."

"Tamia, please."

"No. Just get away from me."

Granting her wish, I left the apartment. Since I was out, I decided to make my rounds. Kamari wasn't one hundred percent well, so he was only allowed to receive a light load. Once I collected all of the money, I went to drop it off out west. When I pulled up in the driveway, I was confused as fuck.

"What the hell Skeet doing here?" I mumbled.

Using my key, I unlocked the door and stepped inside. The house was extremely quiet, so I was careful not to make a sound. On my way up the winding staircase, I checked both of the kid's rooms and they were knocked out. Even Bam was snoring his lil ass off in his crib. Slight knocking caught my attention, so I went to the opposite wing. The closer I got to the room, the clearer the sound became. Turning the knob, I pushed the door open and had a slight heart attack. Nothing could've prepared me to witness Skeet ramming his dick up in my god-daughter.

"What the fuck y'all in here doing?"

Skeet's eyes were wide like a deer caught in the headlights. That nigga couldn't say shit. Janae covered her body with the blanket and tried to avoid eye contact. Of course, it was embarrassing for her. Shit, it was the same for me too.

"Somebody need to answer me before I get Brick on the phone."

"Uncle Coop, please don't," Janae pleaded.

Ignoring her, I looked at Skeet. "Bruh, this my niece. We told you to stay away from her. This what we doing now?"

"Nah, bruh. It ain't even like that," he replied, while putting his boxers back on.

"Well, tell me what it's like, 'cause I know what my eyes saw. And not only that, you doing it in his house. You know Brick about to snap when he hear about this, right? And I can't promise he won't get rid of you and you know what that means."

"Yeah, he might want to kill me. Bruh, don't say nothing. I need to be the one to tell him."

They had me so damn heated. "Tell him what? That you waited until he left to get at his daughter, after we told you not to?"

Janae was still sitting on the bed crying. "You can't tell him, please."

"So, I'm supposed to keep this a secret? My loyalty not set up that way and y'all know that."

"It's more complicated than that," Janae cried.

"Well, un-complicate it for me."

"I'm pregnant," she blurted out.

"What the fuck? From who, Demarcus?"

Skeet looked me in my eyes. "Me."

"This is not going to end well." Pointing at both of them, I gritted my teeth. "Y'all better figure out a way to tell him before I do."

"We will. I promise," Janae pleaded.

"Damn, I can't believe this shit," I huffed and walked out the door. My day wasn't going good at all. I sho nuff needed a drink and some weed.

Chapter 21
Brick

"How do you feel now since that step is over?" I asked, while holding Zuri's hand as we left the airport. The car service was waiting to pick us up, so we were now on our way home.

"I'm okay. I feel like a huge burden was lifted, but a small one was added. Now that I know my mom is dead, I can grieve properly. All these years I've been grieving over the fact that she up and left us. That's not the case anymore. I know the truth."

"That's true, but at least you have closure and you can move on. We share the same pain, so I know how you feel."

Zuri lay down in my lap. "I'm so grateful to have you. I don't know where I would be without you. You're my lifesaver. I probably would've committed suicide by now."

"I'm glad you saved me that night. I probably would've been dead."

Zuri giggled. "You know, I never told anyone that story."

"Shit, me either. We'll tell them at the wedding."

"I don't know about that one."

"That's our story. It's what created a bond of trust. Speaking of which, I want you to start planning our wedding."

Her eyes lit up. "You sure about that?"

"Of course I am. I can't picture my life without you in it. I'm ready to change your last name and make it official. You gave me my junior, you raising Breanna as your own and you've accepted Janae. That's some shit another female wouldn't do. You're selfless and loyal as fuck. I love that about you. It's what pulled me closer to you. Everything that I'm giving you, you deserve that shit."

"Aww, you're about to make me cry."

"As long as they're happy tears, I'm good with that."

"What did I do to deserve you? I feel so lucky."

"Nah, I'm the lucky one." Leaning down, I kissed her in the mouth. My hand was on her waist, but it didn't stay there long. Slowly, I made a trail down to her thick thighs and caressed them. This would probably be the most action I get once I got home, since we've been gone for days. The kids were not about to give us any privacy. My fingers finally made their way to her sweet spot. Gently, I placed my thumb on her clit and rubbed it in a circular motion. Zuri's moan was only loud enough for me to hear, thanks to the private limo. Inserting two of my fingers, I slipped them in and out. For the next few minutes I repeated the same steps until I felt her cum. Moving my hand, I brought them to my mouth and sucked the juices off.

Zuri was so turned on, she licked my fingers too. Getting on her knees wasn't easy, but she made it happen. My soldier was semi-hard when she freed him and took it into her mouth. The constant slurping and slobbing had me ready to stab something. We was gone have to sneak and handle our business when the kids went to sleep.

For the remainder of the ride, her head stayed in my lap. When I finally opened my eyes, we were around the corner from the house. I knew I wasn't catching a nut. That would have to wait until later.

"Bae, stop. We home."

Zuri didn't get up until she felt the limo come to a complete stop. Wiping her mouth, she sat up and grabbed her purse while I fixed my clothes. The chauffeur opened the back door and we got out. Grabbing our luggage out the back, I tipped the driver and sent him on his way. Zuri stopped dead in her tracks and looked at me. There was a huge smile on her face.

"Is this for me?"

"Yes."

Zuri jumped on me, causing me to drop everything in my hands. While we were away, I ordered her the new all black Jaguar F-Pace truck. I meant everything I said to her earlier. She deserved all I had to offer and I was going to make sure she got it.

"Thank you. Thank you. Thank you," she screeched, while kissing all over my face. "We will finish where we left off when these kids go to bed."

"Oh, I know."

"We have to go for a drive. I'm so excited."

"We will, love."

Janae was in the living room playing with the kids when we walked in. "Yassss! Y'all parents are back. How was the trip?"

Zuri walked up to her and grabbed Bam. "It was okay. I missed my baby though."

"He missed you too."

"We missed you too." Breanna and Legend ran and hugged my leg. "I missed y'all too. Were y'all on your best behavior?"

"A little bit," Breanna smiled, before running to me. "I missed you, Daddy."

136

"I missed you too, princess."

"Did he give you a hard time?" Zuri asked Janae.

"No. He just likes to cuddle a lot. Who's responsible for this damn cuddle bear?" Janae laughed.

"Aye, you see me standing here." She was a little too comfortable cursing in front of me.

"Sorry, Pops."

"That's who's responsible for him being like that. He sleeps with him on his chest." Zuri nodded her head in my direction.

"Really, Daddy? You gone make him soft."

"Ain't nothing soft about this Riccardo blood. That's how we bond with each other."

"I know that's right," Janae agreed. "Zuri, do you like your gift?"

"Girl, I love it."

"I do too. Hint-hint." Janae winked at me.

"Something must be in your eye if you think I'm buying you one of those."

"Really?" she whined. "I see right now I have to get me a dope boy to buy me one."

"Yeah, so I can break you and his neck."

"Zuri, tell him dope boys need love too."

"Nope. I'm staying out of that one. You on your own."

Janae sucked her teeth. "What type of step-mama you supposed to be? You supposed to be on my side."

Zuri laughed and sat down on the sofa. "The type that knows when to be quiet. You know your daddy. I'm not letting you set me up."

"Take notes from Zuri."

"Oh, I am."

"Bae, I'm headed out. I'm about to go meet up with Hector and Marco. So, I'll be back in a few hours."

"Okay. Be safe, please. I love you."

"I love you."

As I walked away, I could hear Janae say that she needed to talk to Zuri about something personal. It made me feel good that she felt comfortable enough to open up to Zuri about whatever she was going through. That was something I prayed on and it finally happened. True enough, she couldn't take Shan's place, but she made a really great substitute, for both of my girls for that matter.

***

"What's up, Unc?"

Hector dapped me up as I walked through the door. "I love the sound of that, nephew. I guess boss is out the window, huh?" he grinned.

"Nah. Only in private. I still respect you as my boss."

"I'm just fuckin' with you. Marco's already here, so we can get to it."

"Cool."

The first faces I saw when I walked into the kitchen were Sparkle and Star's. They both smiled and greeted me as I walked in and stood next to the table. "Hey, Brick."

"Wassup, ladies."

"Marco." I dapped him up before sitting down.

"What's going on, fam?" Marco nodded.

"Shit. I can't call it."

"How is Zuri?"

"She's good."

"One day soon, I want us to get together. It's time to link up with my sisters. I never thought I would ever meet them. When you hit me on FaceTime with her, that shit had me blown."

"Yeah, it was crazy, but we can definitely arrange that."

"Alright, ladies." Hector walked in, tying his robe. "Y'all are dismissed. We have business to handle."

The twins exited the kitchen with the quickness. Once they were out of earshot, Hector joined us. "Brick, I need some new girls. The twins were fun, but it's time for some new toys."

"I can help you with that. Just give me a few days to round them up for you."

"What happened with you opening up the escorting service? You changed your mind?"

"Zuri found a nice building, but there was too much cop activity for me. Then, she had the baby, so that put a damper on the speed of things. I'm not able to run it full-time, but hopefully we can get it started once she feels like she's able to do so."

"I'm telling you, that's a very lucrative business. You can make a killing off of it."

"Oh, I know. I'll speak to her about it and see what she says."

"Marco, are you present?" Hector called him out because he was so deep into his phone.

"I'm ready. What we talkin' 'bout?"

"So, the main reason for the original introduction was because I wanted the two of you to build a business relationship. But, now that we all share the same blood, I don't have to worry too much about y'all getting along. You know the saying, don't mix family and business. Well, I'm not worried about that because our operation consists of family. It's been like that since the beginning of time. But, I do want you to know that there will be no leniency when it comes down to my coke or money. Understood?"

Marco and I both nodded our heads.

"Good. Now, I'll be leaving for Cuba sometime this week and I need for the both of you to handle business while I'm gone. Nobody is in charge. This is a partnership."

For the next hour, Hector broke down everything he needed done in his absence. Things were definitely going up from here. Who would've thought that after I jumped out the feds, I would be heavily connected to the Riccardo Cartel? It was funny how I only heard very little about them. I guess that was because my father was only in my life for six years. It was cool, because it all played out in the end.

Hector broke out a bottle of his favorite Cuban liquor and poured up. We tossed back a few glasses, but I couldn't get too faded because I was still on a mission after the meeting. When it was finally over, we stood up to leave.

"Aye, I need to borrow Star."

Hector chuckled. "Nephew, you tryna hit that?"

"Nah. I have another job for her."

"That's cool. I'll get her for you," he replied.

"I'm out, y'all. My wife waiting on me. Brick, hit me up so we can discuss the details," Marco said, while dapping us up before walking out the door.

"Star! Come down here," Hector shouted.

Seconds later, she walked down the stairs with a smile on her face. "Yes?"

"Brick needs to borrow you for the night."

"Mhmm. Is that right?" She blushed. "Let me go and grab my bag. I'll be right back."

"A'ight."

Star and I rode in silence for a few minutes before she finally opened her mouth. "So, where are we going?"

"You'll see. Just sit tight."

"You not about to kill me, are you?" she said with a nervous grin.

"Chill out, ma. It ain't like that. I got a job for you, that's all. I'll explain everything to you as soon as we get there."

"Okay," Star sighed with relief. "You had me nervous for a minute. We haven't seen you in a while and then you show up out the blue, requesting me."

"I've been busy, that's all." My cell rang through the speakers and wifey popped up. "This my lady, be quiet." I hit the icon on the steering wheel.

"What's up, baby?"

Zuri yawned. "Hey. When you coming home?"

"I'm not sure, but it won't be too late. I have a few stops to make before I head back."

"Oh, I was waiting on you."

"I know. I'm trying to get there as soon as possible. Is Janae still there?"

"No. She went home about an hour ago." Bam's cries boomed through the speakers.

"What's wrong with my dude?"

"You know he used to sleeping on your chest at night. So, he wants to give me a hard time right now, like I'm not sleepy. See what you started?"

"You not treating my dude right, that's all. Tell him Daddy will be home soon to rock him to sleep."

"Yeah, you need to hurry up, so we can finish where we left off earlier."

"Shit, it sounds like you done for the night."

"Then, I guess you have to wake me up when you get here then."

Zuri was saying too much with my company in the car, so I had to cut that conversation short. My personal business was just that.

"Hey, I have to go. But, I'll be home in about an hour. Two hours, tops."

"Be safe. I love you."

"Always. I love you too."

As soon as I hung up the phone, Star turned her body in my direction. "That was sweet. I never pictured you as a family man."

"That's because we only have a business relationship. My personal business is private."

"How old is your son?"

"Two months."

"Oh, you got a fresh baby. I bet he's handsome too, just like his daddy."

Shaking my head, I chuckled. "I have strong genes."

"How many kids do you have?"

"Three."

"Oh, slanging dick-dick?"

All I could do was laugh and shake my head.

"Why you laughing?"

"You crazy."

"I'm just honest and very flirty."

"Yeah, I know."

"I didn't offend you, did I? You still my boss."

"You good. I know how you are."

Finally, we were at our destination. Parking my truck, I killed the ignition and got out. Star walked to the back of the car and looked at me with a seductive smile.

"Hmm. LaQuinta Inn. This my job, huh?"

"Come on."

Stopping at the counter, I checked us into a room. The female at the counter wouldn't stop giving me the googly eyes. When she handed me the key, she held it a little too long for me. Grabbing it, we walked to the elevator and went up to the third floor.

Destiny Skai

Chapter 22
Skeet

Me and Janae was laying in the bed at my apartment, watching movies until it was time for me to bleed the block. My hand was resting on her stomach as I caressed it.

"What we gone do about your daddy? You know we have to come clean with him before it's too late. The last thing I need for him to do is doubt my loyalty to him. Me lying to him will kill our bond for good."

Janae sighed. "I know. I'm just trying to find a good time to tell him. When he came back yesterday, I was intimidated by just looking at him."

"Coop not giving us too much longer to come clean. So, we have to get this over with and deal with the consequences. All he can do is get mad with you, but he'll still love you in the end. I'm a different story."

"He is not going to kill you. Stop thinking like that."

"It's obvious you don't know your daddy."

"If he knows how I feel about you, he won't."

"When it comes to the streets, ma, ain't no code when someone crosses you. All that shit is out the window."

"I hate this. Why does this have to be so difficult for us?"

"I'm not gone lie. If we had a daughter I probably would want the same thing for her either."

"Yeah, jump on his side."

"That's not what I'm saying." Rolling on my side, we were face-to-face, so I pulled her closer. "Let's not argue about this."

"Okay."

Janae's lips were soft and irresistible. We tongue kissed slowly, until we interrupted by my boss' ringtone. "I swear this nigga must smell yo' ass over here. It never fails. He calls every time we about to get busy. Make me think he has a tracker on yo' ass."

"Who knows? He slick like that."

Grabbing my phone, I picked up. "Wassup, boss?"

"I need to holla at you about some business."

"Okay, cool. You want me to slide up on you at the shop or what?"

"Nah. I'm outside."

"Outside where?" My ears had to be playing tricks on me. 'Cause I knew damn well I didn't hear that shit.

"I'm outside your door, so come open it."

"Okay. I'm coming."

"Yeah."

Ending the call quickly, I tossed the phone on the bed and jumped up. "He outside. Put your clothes on."

Janae panicked. "What you mean, he's outside?"

"That's what he just said. The man standing on my porch."

"What are we going to do?" she asked.

"If you don't want him to kill both of us, you have to stay in here until he leaves. Whatever you do, don't come out."

"You know damn well I'm not coming out there. You tried it."

"I'm going to lock this door. Don't unlock it until I tell you too."

"Okay."

Brick was growing impatient, because he started knocking hard on my front door. Securing the bedroom door, I rushed into the living room and let him in. "Damn, nigga. What took so long? You in this bitch getting some pussy, or you jacking off?"

"Neither. I was taking a shit."

"Shitty-ass nigga, I ain't need to know that."

"Shiidd, you asked."

Brick made himself comfortable. Meanwhile, I wasn't too relaxed. It wasn't that I was afraid of him. I loved his daughter and I wanted to be with her. We weren't together that long, but that didn't matter to me. Janae was different. Never in my life had I met a female that had her head on her shoulders and wasn't fuckin' every nigga just because he had a foreign whip and rims. I respected that girl to the upmost and I wanted him to know that. Brick was tough, so I knew that was gone be a hard task.

"What's up, soldier? Something on your mind?"

Deep down, I felt like now was my chance to get at him, man to man with no one around. "Actually, yeah."

"What is it?"

"It's about the other day. The whole situation with Janae." The sound of her name made him shift in his seat, like I was about to say something disrespectful about his daughter. His eyes were on me like he was hunting his prey.

"I don't want you to feel like I was hiding that information from you. My loyalty is with you, one thousand percent. The only reason I didn't say nothing is because I told your daughter I wouldn't. She was in a fucked-up situation, so I did what you would've wanted me to do. Protect her."

Brick rubbed his hands together.

"Listen, I'm not upset with you about that. Nor do I feel like you did anything sneaky. I appreciate you making sure she was good. My problem is that I don't want y'all messing around. In so many ways, you like a younger version of me and that's what I'm not comfortable with. Janae is a bookworm. She don't know nothing about this lifestyle. All she see is the glamorous side to this shit. And if I can shield her from all of this, I am. This game comes with a lot problems from niggas, bitches, cheating and the feds. That's something she ain't built for."

Those were valid points, but I wasn't trying to hear any of that.

"I love my daughter and it's my job to protect her from anything or anyone that's going to hurt her. Janae likes you and I can tell you like her too, but I'm telling you to stay away from her. I'm not saying you're a bad person, because if you were, you wouldn't be around me. I love you like a son and I want to keep it that way."

I was trying my best to keep from telling him that I loved her too, but I kept quiet and changed the subject. "Okay, cool. Now let's talk business. What's going on?"

"We have a loose end that needs to be tied up. If we don't handle this expeditiously, there will be a problem."

Brick certainly had my attention with the new mission. Getting my hands dirty was my specialty. Yeah, I was young, but I was still the muscle and his main shooter.

"Shit, what's the play?"

"It's a kidnapping job and I need it to go smoothly. There is no room for trial and error."

"You know I'm careful when it comes down to shit like this. We both know that if I wasn't qualified to get it done, you wouldn't be here. All I need to know is who to kidnap, where, when and what you want me to do with them."

"A'ight. This is a two-part play for you and a three-man job. It has to be executed properly, so school your helpers. Let 'em know if they fuck up, they will be handled accordingly. In the meantime, this is the game plan."

Brick sat in my living room for over an hour, running down the play. The names he dropped surprised me, because I thought that shit was over with, but I guess not. Janae was in the back growing impatient. The text she sent had me laughing on the inside. *'Tell him you sleepy.'* Janae didn't know what my position with Brick entailed and that was the way I planned on keeping it. To myself. All she needed to know was that I sold dope for her daddy. To her, that was simple and didn't require a lot, but patience was something she would have to maintain in order for our relationship to work.

***

Twenty-four hours later, me and Chris was sitting in the hoopty, lamping. It was darker than a bitch in the parking lot, but the car we was across from sat right next to a light post. The dark tints kept us from being seen.

"What time is it?" Chris asked.

"Why, when you gotta be there? Last I checked you was at work, nigga."

"Damn nigga, I can't turn my phone on, remember?"

"Hell, no you can't. We don't need your signal bouncing off of no cell towers out here." Glancing at my watch, I replied, "It's eight thirty."

"Was that hard?"

"Just be ready to drive after I snatch this bitch up."

"I thought I was doing it."

"You ain't never kidnap nobody before. That's like having a main shooter who never dropped a body. That shit don't make no sense."

"A'ight bruh. You got that."

We sat in silence for like another forty-five minutes, before we finally saw any movement. When I realized it was who I was waiting on, I slipped on my ski mask, black latex gloves and sat back in my seat.

"All you have to do is follow me. That's it."

"Bruh, I gotchu."

"Put those gloves on now so you don't forget."

With caution, I crept out the car with my .380 in hand, as soon as she walked past the car. Her back was turned to me, which made it easier to slide up on her. When she opened the door, I smacked her in the head with the butt of the gun and she slumped instantly. Her purse and folder she was carrying fell from her hands.

Popping the trunk, I tossed her body in the back, grabbed the items from the ground and pulled off. Digging through her purse, I found her wallet and driver's license. Once I had her address, I put it in the GPS on her phone and made my way there.

She lived in Plantation, which was only a thirteen-minute drive all together. Chris trailed behind me until we pulled up in her driveway. The house was completely dark, so I knew we were in the clear to make a move. Backing her car up the door, I popped the trunk and got out. Fumbling through her keys, I finally found the one to open the door. Before I pulled her out the trunk, I checked my surroundings. When the coast was clear, I dragged her inside.

"Tie her up."

Chris pulled out some zip-ties. Restraining her hands and feet, he pulled her next to the sofa. Walking over to where she was, I pulled off her work badge. "Hmm. Sara Hernandez, physical therapist."

"What next?" he asked.

"Grab some shit that's worth money and help me ransack this shit so that it looks like a burglary."

"I'm on it."

After we destroyed the house, I popped her in the skull with a single bullet. On the way out, I locked the door and grabbed the folder she was carrying. Then, we fled the scene. As we rode down Broward Boulevard, I slung her phone out the window into the canal. Once Chris drove us back to our neck of the woods, I powered my phone back on.

Skeet: The liquor store closed. I'm taking it in
Brick: It's cool. I'm drunk anyway

That was my way of letting him know the job was done. After I dropped Chris off, I drove out to the LaQuinta Inn. Stepping off the elevator to the third floor, I found the room I was looking for and knocked three times. The door opened for me to step inside. Pulling the badge out of my pocket, I dropped it on the dresser, along with the folder I was carrying.

"That's for me?" Star asked.

"Yeah. Can you have it done by morning? You need to be able to cover her shift tomorrow afternoon."

"Yeah. I can do that. But, I need a ride. Brick has me out here without a car."

"A'ight."

"Well, come on and make yourself comfortable."

Star walked in front of me and that ass was shaking like an earthquake. I ain't gone lie, but I wanted to take her up through there. No hesitation.

The first time I saw her, I wanted to hit that, but I fell back since I figured her and her sister would be smashing Brick and Coop.

"I see you showing everything."

"Yep."

"You left nothing for my imagination, huh?"

"Nope. Do I ever?"

"That ass fat too." I grinned.

She looked back and smiled. "Boy, you can't handle this. I'm out your league. I know them lil ass girls you entertain don't have an ass like this."

"I'm a grown-ass man."

We kicked back, smoked and filled our systems with liquor. Star was a cool-ass chick. Definitely one I could party with. Star broke the silence.

"Do you pop pills?"

"Sometimes. Do you?"

"Hell, yeah. I got some mollies."

Star took a pill bottle out her purse and dumped two in her hand. Then, she passed me one. With no hesitation, I popped the pill and washed it down with some liquor. She did the same.

"Let the party begin."

Star stood in front of me and did a strip tease. Removing her crop top, she threw it on the floor and played with her nipples. That shit turned me on. Star then pulled her shorts down.

"Damn!"

She definitely had the body of a goddess, so that money was well-spent. My plans were to drop the work and keep it pushing, but there was a change in plans. I was about to hit that all night, so I turned my ringer off. My job was done for the night and I didn't want any interruptions.

Star stood in front of me and licked her lips. Her hands crept up my thigh. "I bet yo' young ass got a big dick too."

"Go down and find out."

Star got down on her knees and sucked me up. All that slurping and spitting was getting me hyped up. Ma was putting in that work, 'cause that was the best head I ever received in my life. Removing my shirt, I tossed it on the floor. It was time for me to show her how my dick game was since she wanted to try me.

"Get on the bed." Star crawled in bed and laid on her back.

"Nah. I need you on all fours."

148

Jacking my dick, I leaned down and took my emergency Magnum out my wallet. Slipping it on, I rubbed it up and down her slit before entering her wetness. Star was drunk and horny, but so was I.

Gripping her ass cheeks, I dug deep in that pussy. I was determined to make her eat them bold-ass words. The tip of my dick needed to feel her heart beating. I wanted her to remember how good a young nigga made her pussy feel.

After I finish fucking her, she was gone be sprung. My back was strong and my dick game was grade-A. I was about to make her a believer. The sound of skin slapping echoed throughout the room. Star's back held a mighty arch, as she tried to throw it back at me.

No ma'am. Not today. She wasn't about to try and fuck me like I was a lil ass boy. Using my hand, I pushed her down so her chest was on the mattress. Switching holes, I slid my dick in her ass and went ham in it. Star was hollering, but I knew she was aroused. I could see her juices dripping. She ain't never met a young nigga like me to give her the best dick she ever had. Now, I just wanted her to say it.

"This dick good to you?"

"Yeahhh!" she moaned. "Ooh! I knew your young ass could fuck."

Star put her hand on her ass, spreading one of her cheeks. Then, she wiggled her butt and started to throw it back. Stopping all movement, I let her do the work.

"Put it back in my pussy and beat it."

Giving her what she wanted, I slapped her hard on the ass. "Say it like you meant it."

"Fuck me hard," she demanded.

Ready to stand up in that ass again, I flipped Star on her stomach and put both legs on my shoulders. Pinning then to the headboard, I beat the pussy down. Star couldn't squirm at all, because I had her locked in place. There would be no mercy on my watch. Star was digging her nails in my back and biting my neck.

"No scratching or biting."

The last thing I needed to explain to Janae was how I had hickies and scratches on my body. That wouldn't go well at all.

Chapter 23
Kamari

Ever since I got shot, I started to really reevaluate my circle. I had been laying low and hustling light. Coop would come by and hit me with a small re-up, so I could get some money in my pockets. For some reason, that shit felt like a set-up to me. It didn't make any sense as to how Skeet was able to escape without a bullet graze or nothing.

Our friendship was questionable because a few months back, Skeet and I had a falling out because of a chick we both used to mess with. True enough, we didn't know this information until we both popped up to her house at the same time. I was feeling shorty, but we agreed to leave to leave her alone. One night, I slid by there and saw his car parked outside. That made me feel like I couldn't trust him at that point, so I started plotting my get-back.

That nigga girl, Jenn, was on my radar, so I started to slide up on her when he was out doing his thing. Skeet always needed me to cover for him when he met up with other females. So, not only did I do that, but I started fuckin' her too. It wasn't like he wanted her anyway.

Opening the front door, I walked in as Jenn laid across the sofa watching TV. Kicking off my shoes, I threw the plastic bag I was carrying beside her.

"You know what to do with that."

She picked up the bag and peeked inside. "Why are you giving me this?"

"Just go take the test."

Jenn got up and went into the bathroom and I followed her. I was curious to know because she had been sick lately. Jenn removed the contents from the package and sat down on the toilet. Closely I watched her every move until she sat the stick on the side of the tub.

"You nervous?" I asked.

"No. You?"

"It is what it is."

Finally, Jenn picked up the stick and stared closely at the results. Silence lingered in the air for a few seconds.

"What does it say?"

Jenn handed me the test and put her head down. Pregnant is what it read and I couldn't believe what was happening right in front of me. True enough, we stopped using condoms, but I wasn't expecting a positive test result. The situation that I created was about to get a tad bit messier. Deep down, I was a little happy, but a small part of me was upset. I always wanted a baby, but I never wanted it to be with Jenn. *What was I supposed to do once Skeet found out?* For a fact, I knew there were about to be repercussions, just because we were still boys. And see, he was about that gunplay, so I knew what was coming next. Me, on the other hand, I wasn't a killer.

My mind was running away from me and I needed to stay calm and focus. "Are you okay?" Jenn asked.

"Yeah, I'm good."

"Okay." Jenn placed her arms around my waist and I could hear her sniffling.

"I know you not crying." Jenn nodded her head and that shit made me snap. "What the fuck you crying for? That nigga don't want you. He got a baby on the way. Did you forget he left you for somebody else?"

"Don't you think I know that?"

"Well, act like it and stop trippin', ma. Let me handle Skeet." She was so damn sensitive, so I had to calm her down. "Go shower and I'll be in there in a minute."

After I sent Jenn off, there was someone I needed to speak to and it was urgent. I dialed her number to get to the bottom of the rumors I had been hearing.

"Hello."

"It's been hard trying to catch up with you, girl. That nigga done snatched you up and locked you down, huh?"

"Who the fuck is this?" Janae snapped.

"Kamari. Are you surprised? Or did you think I was going to forget about our deal?"

"What fuckin' deal are you talking about? I didn't make shit with you, so you need to stop calling my damn phone."

"Damn! It's like that? I thought we were cool."

"Nah, you ain't think that."

"That's what I will tell Skeet."

"There is nothing to tell, because I don't know what the fuck you talking about."

"Oh, really? How do you think he will feel when his best friend tells him about our little plan to take his money and position from right up under him?"

152

"You can do whatever you want to because I never had a conversation with you about shit."

Looking over my shoulder, I took a step back to make sure I heard the shower running. "So, you fell for the nigga, huh?"

"Listen, I suggest you don't call this number anymore, before we really have a problem."

"We'll see about that when I hit up Kim."

"Who?"

"Your homegirl, Kim. She told me you was down with it."

"I didn't tell her shit."

Janae may have hung the phone up on me, but we weren't finished just yet. She was going to help me whether she wanted to or not. Skeet thought he was untouchable and he needed to be handled. If Janae wasn't on board with this plan, everything I worked hard on would be in vain. For now, I would just sit back and wait for the opportunity to present itself.

***

Janae

Skeet wasn't answering any of my calls and it had me worried. The day prior, I overheard him and my dad talking about some kidnapping job he wanted him to do. Now, the only thing that kept popping up in my mind was whether something bad happened to him. Pacing the floor, I dialed his number a few more times before sending him a text.

Not only was I dealing with my issues, but now I had to deal with this dumb-ass nigga. Kamari had a lot of fuckin' nerves calling my phone with that bullshit. Making threats like he was gone do something to me. Dialing Kim's number, I put the phone to my ear.

"Hello."

"Why would you give Kamari my number?" I snapped.

"He called you?"

"What do you think? Clearly I'm asking why you gave him my damn number."

"That stupid muthafucka!" she shouted. "I'm sorry. It wasn't supposed to happen like that."

"What are you talking about?" Her reaction had me curious.

"First, let me just say that I didn't give him your number. He must've went in my phone and got it."

All that talking in circles was getting on my damn nerves and I didn't have time for riddles. "Just tell me what he's talking about."

"Okay," she sighed. "Do you remember the night when we went to the after-hour spot?"

"Yeah."

"Think back to that night."

The wheels in my head started to turn as I reminisced on everything that unfolded that night.

"Janae!" Kim screamed over the music while approaching us. "Girl, I been looking for you."

"What?" I snapped.

"We about to slide with these dudes, so come on."

"No. I told you I'm not going. We don't know them." I folded my arms across my chest. We continued to exchange words.

Skeet stepped in. "You Brick's daughter, Janae, right?"

I rolled my neck in his direction with a bit of confusion on my face. "Um. Yeah. How do you know my daddy?"

"I work for him. That day you came to the shop, I was there."

"Oh, I do remember seeing you there."

Kim was impatient, by the way she kept moving from side to side. "Girl, what you gone do?" she asked.

"I'll take you home. It's not a problem," Skeet offered.

"Umm. You sure about that?"

"Yeah. I'll make sure you get home safe. I know how Brick is and I don't want no problems from him about you."

I was hesitant at first, but then I gave in. "Go ahead, Kim. I'm going home. Be safe."

Kim giggled. "I promise, I'll use a condom." Then, she walked away in a hurry, ready to be fucked.

Snapping out of it, none of that shit made sense. "I remember, so just tell me what the hell you talking about."

"That whole thing was a set-up. Kamari is trying to set Skeet up about some foul shit he pulled. He knew Skeet would offer to take you home if you were in an awkward position. After that, the plan was to get you on board, so you can help him."

"You know we are together and you would try to help him? That's fucked-up, Kim. You really letting dick make you do some fuck shit."

154

"I know and I'm sorry. But, when you said your daddy was against y'all talking, I kind of told him I could get you to do it."

"Why would you tell him that? Now, he talking about he gone tell Skeet that I had something to do with it, if I don't help him."

"I'm sorry. I'll fix it since it's all my fault."

"Yeah, you do that."

Kim had me hot when I hung up on her. After she fixed the mess she made, I was gone fuck her ass up. I tried calling Skeet, but he wasn't answering his phone. It was late, so I took a shower and got in bed. All I could do was sleep at that point. I was in my early stages of my pregnancy and this baby was beating my ass already.

Chapter 24
Mehzani

Today, I was meeting up with Zuri, so I could see my nephews. I hadn't seen them since she got out the hospital. Our lives were so busy that we didn't get to speak on a daily basis or hang out. The only time I was able to get out the house briefly was when Gucci's therapist showed up. Now that he was moving around, it wasn't so bad, because I didn't have to be permanently at his side.

Slowly but surely, he was now moving around and using the bathroom on his own. Gucci was sitting on the edge of the bed when I walked out. He was just as handsome as the day we met. His dreads were freshly twisted and he had a fresh line-up by some mobile barber I found on social media.

"How are you feeling?"

"Like I gained some of my independence back."

"That's good. I'm so proud of you."

Standing in front of him, I leaned down and gave my baby a long, wet and sloppy kiss. Gucci's hands caressed my backside and I almost had an orgasm from his touch. It had been so long since I was penetrated that I didn't remember what his dick felt like.

"Whew! Stop." I stepped back. "You can't tease me like that. My body can't handle that."

"Why not?"

"You know why."

"We both been out of commission for a long time. Don't you think it's time we try it?"

The offer sounded tempting, but I didn't want to pressure him about sex, just in case he couldn't get up. That would only bruise his ego and I didn't want that to happen.

"Honestly, I don't know. Do you think you ready for that? I believe we should be patient and give it some more time."

Gucci rubbed his hands up and down his thighs. "Are you sure it's been that long for you?"

"What are you asking me?" I played dumb.

"You know what I mean. Have you been sleeping with someone?"

Gucci's voice was so calm it was scary. A part of me wanted to tell the truth, but the smarter version of me told me not to be dumb. "No."

"Are you sure about that? You can tell the truth. I've been out in this position for a long time and I'm sure you got tired of waiting. I get it. Women have needs just like men. So, tell me."

It was harder to confess because he had some strength now and I was scared about what he would do to me. That nigga might try to kill me in my sleep. In my mind I felt like he was trying to use reverse psychology on me, but I wasn't confessing.

"Are you serious right now? I've been here waiting on you hand and foot all this time and you would ask me that? I have no social life. I don't go anywhere. I have no friends. Zuri is too busy being a wife and mother, so she doesn't have time for me."

"Why you yelling? I asked you a question. If you didn't cheat all you had to say was you didn't. That loud outburst makes you look guilty."

"I'm frustrated because I've given up my life to take care of you and you want to accuse me of cheating. The only time I leave this house is when I'm running errands for you. That's it. Who do I have time for?"

Gucci buried his head in his hands.

"Mehzani, you getting all hostile for nothing. I know what you did for me and I appreciate all of it. This is what I'm saying to you."

He grabbed my hands and pulled me close to him.

"I've been confined to this bed for damn near a year and I'm finally making progress. I've gained my feeling back and I can talk again. When I mention that I want to attempt sex with my woman, she denies me. How do you think that makes me feel?"

Tears formed in my eyes. "I'm sorry. I don't want you to feel that way. My only concern is you. What if," I hesitated, because I didn't want what I truly wanted to say, to come out wrong.

"What if what?"

"Umm."

He finished my sentence for me. "What if I can't perform?"

"Yes."

"Then, I'll deal with it."

Ding! Dong!

Saved by the bell. Sara was right on time, as usual. Speed walking towards the door, I pulled it open and was greeted by a stranger.

"How can help you?"

"Hi. I'm looking for Marquez Williams."

My hands were on my hips because I had a problem with an unknown female asking to speak with my nigga. If she was on any bullshit, I was gone flip her ass. "And, you are?"

"Oh, I'm sorry. I'm Tracy Smith from the Wellness Institute. I'm covering for Sara. She called out sick today."

"No one called me."

"Here is my badge." She pulled it from around her neck so I could see it. "And, I can call my superior, if you need to confirm." Tracy pulled out her cellphone, but I was just relieved that someone was here to rescue me from the uncomfortable conversation we were having.

"That's okay. Come in." Tracy followed me over to the bed. She looked a little hood. Especially with all that light-ass makeup, looking like she stepped fresh out the casket. But I ignored it and introduced them.

"Tracy, this is my fiancée, Marquez. Bae, this is Tracy. She's filling for Sara today."

"It's nice to meet you Mr. Williams."

"Same here."

Leaning in, I pop kissed him on the mouth. "I'm gone, baby. I'll be back in a few hours."

"I need you to do something for me while you out."

"Sure, what you need me to do?" Tracy was standing there looking directly at us.

Gucci looked at her from the corner of his eye. "Can you excuse us for a minute?"

"Sure. I left something in the car. I'll be right back." When the door closed, he pulled me close to him and whispered in my ear.

"Go in the room and get my gun out the closet."

"For what?" His request had me perplexed.

"I don't know this chick."

"You watch too much *Lifetime*. She showed me her badge."

"I still don't know her."

"If it makes you feel better I will get it for you."

"Thank you."

Quickly, I rushed into the bedroom to grab it and return before the therapist came back. "When I come back, you need to tell me what's going on and why you so damn paranoid."

"I will."

"I'll stay if you want me too."

"I'm good. Go enjoy yourself. I love you."

"I love you too."

***

Gucci

"Well, Mr. Williams, it's just you and me." She smiled.

"Apparently so."

After Mehzani left, I sat back on the bed and covered my legs with the blanket. My gun rested beside me underneath my pillow. A strong feeling within me kept saying that something wasn't right with this girl. I just couldn't put my finger on it.

Tracy stood beside me with the folder in her hand. "How are you feeling today? Do you feel any pain?"

"No pain."

"Okay. Umm. How about we start with your daily exercises?"

"My legs are stiff right now and I can't move them. So, can you just work on that for now?"

"Sure thing. Whatever you like."

Tracy moved the blanket and started to rub my legs with no moisture on them. This girl had no clue to what she was doing.

"Are you new?"

"Yes. Why do you ask?"

"Just curious. Can you do me a favor?"

"Of course."

"Can you massage my legs with the Biofreeze that's on the shelf next to me?"

"Sure."

Tracy squeezed the cold gel on my leg and got to work. That time around, it felt better. She actually put some muscle into my massage. It relaxed me completely, but I was still on high alert with her. After she spent an hour doing that, Tracy took her time and stretched out both of my legs.

"I can give you something for the pain if you need it."

"I'm good."

See, there she goes, offering me pain medicine again. It was like she was determined to get me to sleep. It took everything in me to keep from saying, *bitch, you supposed to be helping me walk, not sleep, hoe.* Instead I kept my cool. After she left today, I was gone call the agency and tell them never to send me an inexperienced therapist. How the fuck was I supposed to make progress, if she was trying to dope me up?

Another hour passed and she was out of shit to do. Tracy was raggedy as hell. I had to keep telling her what needed to be done and she was starting to get on my nerves.

"Tracy."

"Yes."

"You can leave now. I don't need anything else done. Thank you."

That came out better than I expected it to. Tracy stood up and gathered up her things. "May I use your bathroom before I leave?"

"Yeah."

When Tracy went inside the bathroom, I muted the TV. Carefully, I listened for the water, but I didn't hear anything. Slipping my hand underneath the pillow, I gripped my heat and pulled it out. Slowly, I eased my legs from the bed and placed them on the floor. Using all of my strength, I stood up and stretched before taking my first step. At a steady pace, I took baby steps until I was standing directly in front of the door. Tracy was on the phone whispering, but I could hear everything she was saying.

"I don't know what to do. He doesn't want anything for pain and he's not as immobile as y'all thought. He is alert as fuck."

Silence occurred, so that meant whoever she was on the phone with was telling her what to do. Patiently, I stood there so I could hear the rest of her conversation.

"I can't, he wants me to leave. He said he doesn't need anything else. So, what do you want me to do?" Tracy paused. "I'm in the bathroom."

That was all I needed to hear at that point. Pushing in the door, Tracy froze and dropped her phone. Fear was in her eyes, when she looked down and saw the gun.

"W-what are you doing?" she stuttered.

"Don't play with me, bitch. Who the fuck were you on the phone with?"

"What are you talking about?"

Aiming my gun in her face, I pulled the hammer back. "You sure you wanna play that game right now? Pick that phone up and give it to me."

Tracy did as she was told. Snatching the phone, I checked her call log and shook my head. "Brick, sent you here, huh?"

Nodding her head, she busted out crying. "Please don't kill me," she begged. "I'll do anything."

Those tears didn't mean shit to me. "Bitch, you was about to kill me with no remorse. You think I give a fuck about you or your tears. Fuck outta here with that."

"I'm sorry please."

"Get down on your knees."

Using her phone, I FaceTimed Brick, the first time we've seen each other since he came to my place with Zuri. "So, you sent this hoe to take me out? Paralyzing me wasn't enough, huh?"

"This between me and you, leave her out of this."

That shit was hilarious to me. It actually made me laugh.

"You should've thought about that before you sent her over here. Now, you get to watch her die. Her blood is on your hands."

Adjusting the camera, I put it on Tracy. "What's your real name? I know it's not Tracy."

"Star." Her face was completely soaked with tears.

"Brick, tell Star goodbye."

"Gucci, don't do this, man."

"Too late."

Pew! Star's body fell backwards and hit the tub.

The look on Brick's face was priceless when he saw Star's lifeless body on my bathroom floor. Turning the camera back on me, I smiled.

"That silencer works like a charm. Now, before you hang up, I hear that congratulations is in order. I heard y'all over there living as one big, happy family. Living your best life, while I was over here confined to a bed. Unable to wipe my own ass. Now, my question to you is, have you told Zuri that you killed Legend?"

Brick didn't say anything the second I mentioned Zuri's name.

"I guess that means no. So, how do you think she would feel when she finds out?"

"Leave her out of this."

"Nah, I think she deserves to know she's been sleeping with the enemy all this time. What's sad about it is that I heard she had a mental breakdown after his death. Hmm. This is not going to end well with you at all."

"You don't wanna do that. What you wanna do, meet up? I heard you walking now. Don't you want them to keep working?"

"My trigger finger works too, but you knew that already. You saw what I just did to your bitch." I waved the gun in front of the screen. "I'll pass on the scheduled meet-up. The last time you coincidentally popped up, you shot me in the back. I will tell you this, though. Keep your eyes open and watch your surroundings. You will be seeing me soon."

Right when I hung up the phone, Mehzani walked through the door. Approaching me, she looked down at the gun.

"What did you do?"

"I killed her."

Mehzani panicked instantly. "What happened?"

"She was hired to kill me."

"What? By who?"

"I'll explain it to you in a minute. In the meantime, call Mel and tell him to get here now. After that, go and pack us up some clothes. We can't stay here."

Brick really got some shit started now. This was the second attempt he made on my life and I wasn't gone rest until he was laying in the cemetery with his mama and daddy. He started the war, but I was gone end that muthafucka.

Chapter 25
Brick

Watching Star get killed really fucked me up. That shit wasn't supposed to go down like that. If she couldn't do it, she should've left. Now, all the guilt was on me. There was no way I could look Sparkle in the eyes and tell her I was responsible for her death.

Falling back onto the bed, my eyes were glued to the ceiling. This was supposed to be an easy target, but I guess I waited too long. I should've offed that nigga when I first saw him. It was about to be an all-out war between us. I wasn't worried about it. My soldiers were already on deck and if need be, so was the cartel.

My mind then drifted to Zuri. That nigga definitely had to die talking about exposing me. I knew for a fact that he was going to make sure she knew I was behind it. Not only does Gucci want blood, he wants to ruin my relationship in the process. If Zuri caught wind of this before I told her, I knew for a fact she would leave me. There was no question about that. The only way I could keep my wife was by coming clean. At least, I could give her my version on the way shit really went down.

My mind was so caught up in my thoughts that I didn't feel Zuri sit down beside me. "Bae, can you hear me?"

"We need to talk." There was no need in beating around the bush about it. Might as well get it over with.

"I need to talk to you first. This is really, really urgent and I need your undivided attention. I also need you to have an open mind about everything."

That certainly had my attention. "What's wrong?"

"Remember when Janae said she had something personal to talk to me about?"

"Yeah."

"Before I tell you this, I need you to promise me that you will stay calm and not overreact."

"I can't make a promise on something I know nothing about."

"I need you to be a little more understanding, please."

"Fine. I'll stay calm."

"Janae is two months pregnant."

All that calm shit was out the window when I heard that. Jumping up from the bed, I shouted, "What the fuck you mean, she's pregnant?"

"That's what she wanted to talk to me about."

"And you just now telling me?"

Zuri stood in front of me. "I promised her that I wouldn't say anything until she was ready."

"That's not some shit you keep a secret."

"Yes, it is. She confided in me and I wasn't about to break her trust. Brick, having a baby is not the end of the world and legally, she's an adult."

"Janae is still a child."

"No, she's not and the sooner you accept, that the better off you'll be. It's not like you didn't know she had a boyfriend and she lives alone. I'm sorry, but I don't know what you expected."

"I expected her to make better decisions."

"You need to calm down."

"I'ma break that nigga neck when I catch his ass." Grabbing my gun, I shoved it into my back pocket.

"Where are you going?" she asked.

"To talk to Janae."

"She's here."

"Where?"

"Downstairs in the living room."

Zuri was on my heels, as I rushed downstairs. "Baby, please calm down. You can't solve anything acting like this."

When I made it to the final step, my front door swung open and Skeet walked in.

"This is a bad time, bruh. I'm having family issues right now. I'll get at you later about that."

Business had to wait. I had more important shit to worry about. Janae was sitting down on the sofa when I walked in. "You have something you need to tell me?"

When she looked up at me, she nodded her head. "I'm sorry."

"Sorry for what? For throwing your whole fucking life away? I can't believe I'm having this conversation with you. How could you be so stupid?"

"Brick, stop!" Zuri shouted.

"Where the fuck is punk-ass Demarcus? Why he not here with you to face me?"

Janae looked towards Zuri and broke down. "It's not his baby."

"What the fuck you mean, it's not his baby?"

"It's not."

"Then who baby is it?" I turned to face Zuri, but instead I was face-to-face with Skeet. She was standing beside him.

"It's mine, bruh. I've been trying to find a way to tell you, but I just couldn't find the right time to tell you."

"To tell me what? That you was fuckin' my daughter after I told you to stay away from her?" Janae wasn't getting off easy. "And I told you to stay away from him. Now look at you."

Something came over me and I snapped. My gun was pointed directly in his face. Zuri and Janae's screams filled my eardrums.

"Give me one reason why I shouldn't blow yo' shit off?"

"Baby, please put that gun away." Zuri placed her hand on my chest while standing in between us.

Skeet stood his ground. He didn't flinch at all. "Bruh, I know you mad, but believe me when I say that I love your daughter. It shouldn't have happened this way, but it did and for that, I'm sorry."

"Daddy, please." I felt a hand on my shoulder.

When I turned around, Janae was standing there with a face full of tears. "Please don't. I love him."

Seeing Janae cry broke my heart and it took me back to that night Zuri found out about Legend. Slowly, I lowered my gun to my side.

"Daddy, I'm sorry. Please forgive me." Janae reached out to me and I couldn't help but to embrace her.

"I love you, Nae."

"I love you too."

Everything that unraveled was too much for me to deal with, so I left the house without saying another word.

***

Coop

Brick hit my phone right on time, with the perfect escape plan. Between Tamia and Danielle, I didn't know who was working my nerves the most. That was confirmation I needed to hurry up and find me a house. My realtor was taking too long, so I was gone reach out to the person that Brick went through.

Hector's spot was always packed with people. Sliding through the front door, I walked around until I found him chillin' in the VIP section.

Normally, we would be posted in Hector's booth, but he wasn't there. He took a trip out to Cuba for a few.

"What's going on, bruh? You look like shit."

"I feel like it."

Grabbing the bottle, I poured me a cup of Rémy. "I'm sure it's no worse than the bullshit I been going through."

"Wanna bet on it?"

"What you got?"

"Five hundred." Brick took a shot and down his glass.

"Bet. Let's hear it." I pulled the money from my stash and placed it on the table.

Brick took another shot. "Bruh, I fucked up big time. All this shit so fucked up, I don't even know where to start."

"Start with the one that hurts the most."

The darkness in his eyes told me that it was much deeper than Janae being pregnant from Skeet. Taking a deep breath, he sighed and leaned back.

"I'm about to lose my family for good. I can feel that shit."

"For what? I thought everything was cool with you and sis. You just told me y'all moving forward with the wedding."

"That was before the hit with Gucci failed. After today, all this shit is about to hit the fan and I know she gone take my kids away from me."

"Ahh, shit! What happened with that?"

"Star called me from the nigga bathroom, telling me how she couldn't drug him, because he wouldn't take the medicine she was trying to give him. The nigga busted in on her, took her phone and called me on FaceTime, so I can watch him kill her."

"Damn, bruh. Star dead?"

"Yeah, man. He shot her in the head."

"Sparkle gone have a fit when she hear this shit."

"I know and that's why we can't tell her what happened. So then this tough ass nigga was like, 'Congrats on the baby. I heard y'all living y'all best life while I was over here confined to a bed, unable to wipe my own ass for a year.'"

Cutting him off, I replied, "That nigga must've forgot that he started all this shit when he shot up yo' car and killed Mariah."

"Facts! This shit takes the cake though. He was like, 'I wonder how Zuri gone feel when she finds out that you killed Legend.'"

Sliding the money across the table, I shook my head. "Here, bruh, you won. That shit worse than everything I'm going through with Danielle and Tamia."

"This fuck-ass nigga talm 'bout he gone tell her, since I didn't."

"That's fucked up. He playing with fire now. That nigga better count his last muthafuckin' days 'cause if I catch him, it's lights out for good."

"But, check this out. Him and Zuri's sister, Mehzani are together. That's who been taking care of him all this time."

"He didn't think this through at all."

"Yeah, he did. All he has to say is that he just found out and the heat off of him."

The bottle girl walked up and smiled. "How are you guys doing over here?"

"Bring us another bottle, please," I replied.

"Coming right up." She sashayed away quickly.

"My advice to you is to come clean. You have to tell her before he gets in her ear cause if you don't he gone spin the story and she gone believe him. You want to give her your version on what happened. She'll appreciate the truth if it comes from you."

"I just have to figure out a way to tell her."

"The situation is above you now and it's too late for strategies. All you can do is go home and tell the truth. That's it."

"She gone leave me. I know it." Brick dropped his head into his hands. I felt bad for my brother from another mother.

"Y'all just had a baby, so she can't go too far. Whatever happens, bruh, I'll be right here going through it with you."

He held his head up. "I appreciate that, bruh."

The bottle girl returned with the liquor and the turn-up continued. We tossed back a few shots and vibed to the music for a few minutes. That was short-lived though.

"Janae pregnant from Skeet, dawg." When I didn't express any emotion, he looked at me sideways. "You knew, didn't you?"

"Yeah."

"Damn, so everybody knew but me?"

"Trust me, I found out on accident."

"How did you find out?" He looked me in dead in the eyes and waited on me to respond. It took a minute for me to give him the watered-down version.

"I walked in on them."

Brick shook his head and frowned. "You walked in on this nigga fuckin' yo' niece and he still alive?"

"When I confronted them about it, Janae was crying and begging me not to tell. So, I told her they both needed to sit you down and come clean before I told it myself."

"Well, they did that with the help of Zuri. It was like I snapped. Just hearing he been fuckin' my baby, man, sent me over the edge."

"What did you do?" I knew him like I knew the Bible, so he definitely did something.

"I pulled my gun out on him."

"Where was Janae and Zuri?"

"Standing right there. Zuri was standing in the middle of us. Janae crying, talking about she love the nigga."

"Come on, bruh, you know that wasn't right. I know you pissed off, but Skeet a good nigga and he loyal to you. Do you really think he'll fuck over your daughter?"

My words hit him hard and I could tell by the way he shifted in his seat. Brick poured himself a cup this time. "Fuck that! We told that nigga to stay away from her."

"Well, what did Skeet have to say about all of this?"

"He claims he love her and he not gone hurt her and all this other bullshit."

"Whether you want to accept it or not, the damage is already done. You gone have to accept the fact they love each other. If you get in the way of that, you gone lose your daughter and yo' most certified and loyal soldier."

"That nigga ain't loyal if he got my daughter pregnant behind my back."

"Why don't you sit them down and have a conversation with them? See how it started and how long it's been going on. You have to be receptive about this. Trust me, it's hard. It was hard for me when I found out, but I didn't react off of emotion. That's how you fuck up."

Brick was so drunk by the time we finished the bottle, I refused to let him drive home alone. The way he carried on in the car would make a grown man cry. He was really going through the motions. Zuri was blowing up his phone and he ignored every call. I knew she was worried about him.

When I finally got him home, I helped him upstairs to the master bedroom. Zuri was sitting on the bed with Bam in her arms. She looked up and shook her head with a frown plastered on her face.

"I should've known he was drunk. Where did you find him at? Or, was he with you?"

Ignoring her questions, I helped him onto the bed. "Listen, he going through a lot right. He fucked up and you need to talk to him. I need you to listen to him and give him a chance to explain before you make an irrational decision based on emotion."

"What did he do?"

"He'll tell you. Give me the baby. I'm going to stay here tonight in the guest room and make sure y'all get through this."

"His ass must've cheated or some shit." Zuri handed me the baby.

"Wash his face, so he can pull himself together." I stood there and waited until she did what I told her. Brick tried to shake it off, so I walked out the room to give them their privacy.

Chapter 26
Zuri

Coop had me nervous to talk to him. In my heart, I truly felt like he was about to ruin our relationship. Heartbreak wasn't what I wanted, but I felt it coming. Brick was sitting on the bed with tears in his eyes. That hurt me because he wasn't an emotional person. Therefore, I knew for a fact that whatever he had to say could potentially ruin us.

Kneeling down in front of him, I wiped his face. My heart was beating fast. "Baby, what's wrong?"

He grabbed my left hand. "I'm sorry for what I did and I need you to forgive me."

"What did you do?" Just watching him become so emotional had me about to cry before he confessed.

"Will you forgive me?"

There was no doubt in my mind that we couldn't get through what it was. Even if he slept with another woman, I loved Brick with everything in me. He made me whole and I couldn't picture my life without him in it.

"We've been through a lot and we can through whatever it is you need to tell me. But, we can't work through it if you don't tell me."

Brick just sat there and said nothing.

"Did you cheat?"

"This is far worse than cheating." Brick paused and stared at me for a few seconds. "What I'm about to say is going to break your heart and I'm sorry. Just know that it wasn't intentional because I would never hurt you purposely."

"Brick, what did you do?" I whispered.

"I killed Legend."

My heart dropped to the pit of my stomach and I could feel myself become light-headed. I know I didn't hear him correctly, so I had to be sure that what he said was true.

"W-what did you say?"

"It was me that killed Legend," he repeated.

His words sent me flying off the handle and straight into fight mode. My fists were flying as I hit him in the face repeatedly. Brick used his arms as a shield, but he didn't move.

"You killed my brother." I continued to hit him.

Fighting him wasn't enough for me. He took my flesh and blood from me. Allowed me to continue this relationship built on lies and deception.

The death of Legend took a toll on me. Day in and out, I've had nightmares and mental breakdowns because of it. When all along, he was the very person that caused me all that pain. There wasn't that much love in the world to make me get over what he did to me and my sister.

Backing away from him slowly, I opened the nightstand drawer and pulled out the .380 handgun that he gave me. Walking close up on him, I placed it at his temple. Brick turned his head slightly towards me.

"Killing me won't bring your brother back, but if it makes you feel better, do it. I've done so much fucked-up shit in my life. I knew this day would come. I just never thought that it would be the woman that I love."

"And not once did I ever think that the man that I love more than life itself could betray me. All this time I've been sleeping with the enemy."

"I'm not the enemy. It's the drug game. Me and Legend were in a game where death is the ultimate price to pay. We were competitors, not friends. We were fighting over territory. It was never personal. His crew robbed me and tried to take me out. I retaliated and killed him."

His explanation wasn't enough to make me change my mind. "I don't believe you. Legend wasn't like that."

"It's the drug game, baby. Everybody is like that. Ask yourself this, do you truly believe I would've killed him if I knew he was your brother?"

"I can't answer that."

"I'll answer it for you. On me and my kids' lives, if I knew that Legend was your brother, I would've handled that situation totally different. I would've tried to reach a resolution that didn't involve anyone getting hurt."

"You didn't hurt him. You killed him."

"Zuri, I'm sorry. I truly am. But, I can't erase the past."

"I'm sorry too."

When I cocked the gun back, Brick closed his eyes. "Before you pull that trigger, I love you and the only reason I didn't tell you is because I didn't want to lose you."

Tears covered his face and slid down, wetting his beard.

"Please take care of my girls for me. Neither one of them have mothers. Chanel is dead and you killed Deja. Tell Bam how much I loved him and the way I slept with him on my chest every night after he came home from the hospital. Let him know that I died because of the life I chose. Don't tell him that you killed me."

I was crying right along with him. Just thinking about raising these kids on my own hurt because I never thought this would be my reality.

"I love you, Zuri, and I've made my peace."

"I loved you too." My finger gripped the trigger and the sound of an explosion filled the room.

***

Skeet

"Are you okay?"

Janae was laying in the bed crying. "I don't know."

Sitting down beside her, I rubbed her back. "Listen to me. Everything is going to work itself out. We just have to give him time to accept our decision."

"I don't think so. He wants to kill you. And I don't understand how you can be so calm when he shoved a gun in your face? Why do you still want to be with me? He'll never accept us," Janae rambled.

"Tonight wasn't my first time having a gun in my face and I'm sure it won't be the last. There are some things you don't know about Brick. He's a killer and if he wanted me dead, I would be on a cold slab right now."

"You sound so sure about that."

"Brick was just upset. No one can stop him from pulling the trigger when his mind is made up. Not you. Not Zuri. He knows deep down that I'm a solid dude and I would take care of you. If he thought otherwise, he would've killed me in front of y'all with no remorse."

"He's that bad?"

"It's not that he's a bad person. He just don't care. Brick stands on principle and if you break any of those, that's what you get. Except, it ends in fatality."

"I'm worried about you. Promise me you'll stay away from him until I speak with him first."

"Don't be worried. He loves you too much to kill me. Just lay back and relax."

Pulling out my wrap, I rolled me a fat ass blunt and blazed it up. Brick's reaction was exactly what I expected, so it didn't surprise me when he pulled his heat on me. Janae sat up in the bed and sat Indian style.

"I need to tell you something."

"Wassup, love?"

"Your so-called friend Kamari called my phone."

My brow shifted when she said that. I was confused as fuck at that point. "He called your phone?"

"Yes."

"How the fuck did he get your number?"

"My friend, Kim."

"What the fuck he wanted?"

"Saying that I need to help him set you up and if I don't, he's going to tell you I was in on it from the jump. We got into it and I told him don't call my phone anymore."

Kamari calling her phone was crazy as hell to me. "That's not making any sense to me. So, help me understand."

"Kamari is trying to set you up. The night we met at the club was planned out. He told Kim that if you felt like my safety was in danger, you would save me. They are trying to use me to get to you. They know how you feel about me."

"Keep going." I needed all the details and not a half-ass story, because Kamari was about to feel me real soon.

"After I hung up with Kamari, I called Kim to ask her what he was talking about. She told him that my daddy was against us being together and that I would help him rob you and take your spot, so he could get close to my daddy. He's jealous of you."

I didn't want to believe he was trying to use my girl to get to me after all I did to help him. But, I also knew he still felt some type of way about the chick that me and him was smashing. I didn't give a fuck about the broad and I left her alone after it came out in the open. Pac said it best, keep your enemies close and watch your homies. That was the greatest quote of all time.

"Yeah, I see that now. I'ma handle Kamari in due time, so don't worry about that. And if that nigga call your phone again, you let me know."

"What are you gonna do?" she asked sadly.

"I'ma handle him the way I see fit."

"Chance, I don't like the sound of that. I don't need you doing anything to jeopardize your freedom. What am I going to do if I lose you? I'm not trying to raise this baby on my own."

"You won't have to, because I'm not getting caught. My steps are too calculated."

"See, that's exactly what I'm talking about." She rocked back and forth with her eyes closed.

"What you want me to do? Wait until he runs down on me, so you can bury me instead? Nah, this shit don't work like that. I'm not letting no nigga have the ups on me. This nigga know where me and you sleep. I'm not risking it."

"Fine, I get it."

Taking a pull from the blunt, I let the air fill my lungs before exhaling. "You get it, but do you understand it?"

"Yes. I'm just scared."

Lifting her chin up, I kissed her lips. "Don't be. Protecting you is my number-one priority and I'll always make sure you safe."

"Thank you."

"That's my job. I love you."

"I love you too."

Over the next few days, I did a little investigating on my own. If it wasn't for a specific disloyal-ass bitch, I would've never gotten the run down about Kamari and trifling-ass Jenn. From day one, I knew her best friend, Tonya, had a thing for me but I never smashed her or came on to her. After Janae gave me an earful, I slid up on Tonya to see what I could find out. Of course, that didn't come without a fee.

Tonya's kids were sitting in the living room when I arrived, so we went into her bedroom and closed the door. "So, what can I help you with? It sounded urgent over the phone."

"It is. What's going on with your girl and my boy, Kamari? And, don't lie, 'cause she tell you everything."

"I'm not gone lie. Besides, I'm not feeling Jenn too much these days. But, my question for you is what do I get in return for spilling all this good-ass tea?"

"How much you want?"

"Not money." Tonya moved closer to me. She grabbed my hand and placed it between her legs. "I want you to fuck me."

That wasn't what I expected to hear. "Why?"

"I just want some bragging rights. She fuckin' your boy, so why not fuck her girl?"

She had a point and I couldn't lie, Tonya was finer than a bitch. I wasn't losing points for fucking her and I knew Janae would never find out, so I did it. Technically, it wasn't cheating because I wasn't doing it for pleasure. I only did it for information. Tonya got the dick for a good twenty minutes. No kissing. No hugging. No touching. Just straight fucking. After we were done, she sung like a bird, spilling Jenn's deepest, darkest secrets.

It was a little after midnight when I pulled up to the duplex where Jenn lived. As expected, Kamari's car was parked outside. Pulling the hoodie over my head, I grabbed the strap and snuck inside. The living room was dark, but the bedroom light was on. I could also hear the shower running. Stepping inside the room, I could see clothes on the floor. Kamari's gun was on the dresser, so I grabbed that and waited.

There was plenty of moaning going on, but I didn't interrupt because that was the last nut he would ever catch, and the last dick Jenn would ever feel in that friendly-ass pussy. Ten minutes passed and the water stopped. I could hear Jenn giggling. It was all fun and games until they walked in the bedroom and saw me standing in the corner with my back against the wall.

Jenn screamed, "What are you doing here?"

"I know muthafuckin' well you ain't fuckin' this nigga in my apartment, bitch."

"You see me, don't you? It ain't like you live here. You don't even want her."

"So, y'all been fucking all this time, huh?"

"Skeet, please. I'm sorry. It's not what it looks like."

Kamari looked at Jenn cross-eyed. "What the fuck you mean, it ain't what it look like? That ain't what you was just saying in that shower a few minutes ago."

"Kamari, be quiet," she snapped. "Can you please put the gun away, so we can talk like adults?"

"Fuck a talk. I don't give a fuck about you or this nigga."

"So, why you here then, nigga?"

Kamari had some big nuts while he was standing beside Jenn. He moved his arm behind her back and grabbed the dresser. So, I held up his pistol.

"You looking for this?" I laughed.

"Come on, Skeet, let's talk about this," Kamari pleaded once he realized he had no protection.

"Oh, you wanna talk now. What happened to the gangster that was just talking to me sideways a minute ago?"

Then, I looked at Jenn. "This the pussy you chose to get pregnant from?"

Jenn's eyes stretched wide.

"Don't be surprised, love. I know everything."

"Who told you that?"

"Your best friend, Tonya. Or as you say, your best bitch. It's funny how your girl spilled all the tea, just so she can fuck me and get braggin' rights."

Jenn grabbed the dresser like she was out of breath. "You fucked Tonya?"

"Yep and I can't lie, she got some good pussy too. You should've got your clit pierced." That painful look on her face was everything to me. "That shit get real wet when you touch it."

Kamari was pissed. "And this the nigga you love?"

His slick rap was getting on my nerves and I couldn't hold it in any longer. Reaching out, I touched his ass with a solid punch to the nose. "Shut the fuck up."

Kamari grabbed the towel he was wearing to stop the bleeding. As I waved my gun in Jenn's direction, she flinched. "Please."

"Get on the bed." Then, I pointed it back at Kamari. "Put your clothes on."

"For what?"

Clearly, he didn't learn his lesson, so I hit him in the face with the gun twice. Kamari's body dropped to the floor. He squirmed like a fish out of water. My blood was boiling. Raising my foot, I stomped him repeatedly in his ribs and face. Blood was flying from his mouth and onto the tile. Jenn was crying her eyes out.

"Skeet, please stop!" she yelled. "You gone kill him."

"That's my plan and when I'm done with him, you next."

Jenn hated the sight of blood. Unable to take the sight of Kamari's bloody face, she started throwing up.

"Skeet, please don't do this," she begged.

"Shut up!" Kicking him once more, I yelled, "Get yo' punk ass up."

Kamari stood up slowly and looked me dead in the face. Right into the eyes of a deranged killer. The man he knew all too well, a man that would pull the trigger without hesitation. Kamari knew it was over. He slipped up and there was nothing he could do about it.

"Come on, bruh. Don't do this. We've known each other too long for it to go down like this."

"You know I never thought it would come to this between us either, but I was wrong about that."

"It doesn't have to. Not behind a female."

"You think this is about Jenn? I don't give a fuck about that. A hoe gone be a hoe regardless and a disloyal bitch can't be on my team point blank period. You were supposed to be my brother and my number two. We supposed to be taking over the drug game right about now, but you let pussy get in the way of that."

"This shit wasn't supposed to go down like this." He looked over at Jenn.

"Oh, this was definitely on purpose. I know how it all started and why. You mad because we was fuckin' the same hoe. I left the bitch alone and it still wasn't enough for you."

"No, you didn't, bruh. I slid over there a few days later and I saw your car out there."

"Yeah you did, but I didn't fuck. I left my shit over there and I had to get it. She can tell you that. It's all good though. You got me back by fuckin' my old bitch and getting her pregnant."

No one said a word. You could hear a pin drop. Taking a step back, I made sure to have them both in my eyesight.

"Jenn, you love this nigga? Don't look surprised. That is what you told Tonya, right?

She didn't respond. "Well, I'ma fill you in on a little secret. While you so busy fucking him, thinking you found something better, he running around chasing Kim. My baby mama's conniving ass friend."

My laugh was a wicked one and Kamari looked uncomfortable.

"Kamari, sit down with Jenn, so we can end this and get back to my lady."

After he sat down, he held Jenn's hand.

"For the record, I know all about the phone call you made to my girl. There's no need for me to go into detail about it, because you know what you said to her. That was your first mistake. Your second mistake was not killing me when you had the chance. Instead of you attempting to set me up, all you had to do was pull the trigger and get it over with. Brick probably would've gave you a promotion, but no, you was too pussy to do it on your own. You sought out the help of a messy-ass female that couldn't hold muthafuckin water."

Raising my arm in their direction, I aimed Kamari's pistol at Jenn first. Her deception is what had us in that moment.

"Don't kill her. Kill me."

"Sorry, big dawg. She gotta go and I want you to witness it. I'm sorry you won't get to see your firstborn child, but then again, no I'm not. I may come by and piss on your grave."

With my finger on the trigger, I fired one shot into Jenn's chest. That was where a heartless bitch deserved to be hit. Then, I fired two to Kamari's dome. That was his punishment for not thinking about the fuck shit he was trying to pull.

Chapter 27
Brick
Two weeks later

Life that I've known it to be was completely over. As I drowned myself in alcohol, I had Anthony Hamilton's, "I'm a Mess," on repeat. The pain that I was feeling in my heart was worse than death. Zuri should've killed me and taken me out of my misery. That's what life without her and my kids felt like. I no longer had a purpose. That night I lost everything and now I was suffering terribly. All I could do was reflect back to what happened.

"Killing me won't bring your brother back, but if it makes you feel better, do it. I've done so much fucked up shit in my life. I knew this day would come. I just never thought it would be the woman I love."

"And not once did I ever think the man I love more than life itself could betray me. All this time, I've been sleeping with the enemy."

"I'm not the enemy. It's the drug game. Me and Legend were in a game where death is the ultimate price to pay. We were competitors, not friends. We were fighting over territory. It was never personal. His crew robbed me and tried to take me out. I retaliated and killed him."

My explanation wasn't enough to make her change her mind. *"I don't believe you. Legend wasn't like that."*

"It's the drug game, baby. Everybody is like that. Ask yourself this, do you truly believe I would've killed him if I knew he was your brother."

"I can't answer that."

"I'll answer it for you. On me and my kids' lives, if I knew Legend was your brother, I would've handled that situation totally different. I would've tried to reach a resolution that didn't involve anyone getting hurt."

"You didn't hurt him. You killed him."

"Zuri, I'm sorry. I truly am. But, I can't erase the past."

"I'm sorry too."

When she cocked the gun back, I closed my eyes. *"Before you pull that trigger, I love you and the only reason I didn't tell you is because I didn't want to lose you."*

Tears covered my face and slid down, wetting my beard.

"Please take care of my girls for me. Neither one of them have mothers. Chanel is dead and you killed Deja. Tell Bam how much I loved him and the way I slept with him on my chest every night after he came

home from the hospital. Let him know I died because of the life I chose. Don't tell him you killed me."

She was crying right along with me. I guess reminding her about the kids made reality sink in, and she realized that killing me would have her raising these kids on her own. "I love you, Zuri, and I've made my peace."

"I loved you too." Her finger gripped the trigger and the sound of an explosion filled the room.

The sound of the gun going off made my ears pop and eardrums shake. I just knew I was about to bleed out and die at any moment. When I checked my shirt, I didn't see any blood. Zuri was screaming hysterically and shouting obscenities.

Coop busted through the door and rushed towards her. "I heard a gunshot. What happened?"

"He deserves to die for what he did to me." The gun was still clutched tightly in her hand.

"You don't mean that." With extreme caution, Coop removed the gun from her hand.

"He destroyed my life. He killed my brother and didn't bother to tell me."

"That's a difficult situation, sis. Y'all have kids in here and you can't be firing this gun like that. I understand that you're upset, but this is not the way to handle this."

"That's easy for you to say. He didn't kill the one you loved."

"Y'all need to talk about this. Think about the kids. They don't need to see or hear about this."

"I am thinking about the kids and I want him out of here."

"Zuri, baby. Let's talk about this, please." Standing to my feet, I walked towards her, but she took a step back and stood in a defensive stance.

"Please don't touch me. There is nothing to talk about. Ain't shit you can say to make me forgive you, I hate you."

"Don't say that. You hate what I did, but you don't hate me. You can't un-love me just like that. I hurt you. I get it and I'm sorry for that, but you have to believe me. I didn't know he was your brother. I didn't even know you had a brother, for that matter. Our relationship was still fresh."

Zuri's eyes were blazing with fire. Tears covered her face, as her voice trembled. "How could you sleep beside me every fucking night, knowing what you did? Are you that fucked up and without a conscience that you were able to sleep peacefully. I've cried in your arms. You've dried my tears on several occasions and it didn't bother you one bit. You don't carry an ounce of compassion in that cold ass heart of yours."

"That's not true. I've tried to come clean on more than one occasion, but every time I opened my mouth, I couldn't do it. It hurt me to my soul to watch you grieve like that. I wanted to tell you so bad, but I couldn't bring myself to break your heart again."

"Well, you did that. Thank you."

Zuri removed her engagement ring from her finger and placed it on the dresser. "You really damaged me with this. Just when I thought I found the love of my life, the truth comes out. All I ever wanted was to be your wife and have your babies. I didn't care about what you had. I don't care about this house, the cars or the money. If I had to give it all up just to love you forever, I would've done that."

Zuri wiped her tears with her hand. "I loved you with everything I had left in me and now, I have nothing left. Breanna can stay here because I love her like she's my daughter, but you have to go. When I wake up in the morning please be gone."

For the past two weeks, I've been staying at the hotel. Zuri won't answer my calls, so I haven't seen or heard from my kids. That was painful for me. I even went by the house, but she changed the locks on me. The distance she put between us was killing me slowly. I would rather drink acid than to be inside this room dying. My phone was blowing up, but none of the calls came from the person I wanted to talk to.

Standing in the mirror, I looked rugged and raggedy. I didn't bother getting a haircut, shave, or nothing of that nature. All I did was drink and smoke until I lost all consciousness. Turning up the bottle of hot Hennessy, I swallowed half of its remaining contents. Grabbing the same kit I used to kill Tone, I took out the needle and sat it on the sink. It was time to end my life once and for all. Picking up my phone, I created a group text for my loved ones, Zuri, Coop, Janae and Skeet.

(All): This will be the last time that y'all hear from me. I have made a conscious decision to take my own life. I have caused nothing but pain and heartache to the ones I love the most. ZURI, my queen, the love of my life. I love you more than life itself. I will never get over the pain I caused you. Not even in death. My soul will burn forever for all the shit I did. Check the safe and go to the safe deposit box. I left you everything I have so you and the kids will be financially stable. JANAE baby, I love you beyond the earth and I'm sorry I couldn't succeed at completing your mother's request to protect you and keep you safe. When you have your baby, protect him or her until you leave this earth. Love that child unconditionally, despite their mistakes. Something I failed to do when I found out you were pregnant.

SKEET, I know you think I hate you, but I don't. I love you like a son and I respect you as a man for not backing down and displaying your love for my daughter. Any other dude would've folded and left after that stunt I pulled. I'm sorry for putting that gun in your face like that. Please take care of my baby and grandbaby. Be the man she needs you to be and never leave her side. She's your responsibility now. I'm leaving her in your hands. COOP, my number one. My brother. Take care of my queens and king. Make sure they're safe at all times. I made a mess in these streets and ain't no telling who watching. Keep my legacy alive and I love you forever, man. See y'all on the other side.

Several minutes after I pressed send, my phone was blowing up from everyone in that chat. There was nothing to discuss. My mind was already made up and things would be better that way. Now that all of my loose ends were tied up, I got back to drinking and getting high. It was my last night on earth and I wanted to go out high as a kite.

Two hours later, I was stuck and ready to check out. Heading back to the bathroom, I sat down on the toilet and tied the tourniquet around my arm. Staring at the ceiling, tears cascaded down my face, as I gripped the needle with the little bit of strength I had left.

"God, forgive me for all of the destruction that I caused here on earth. All of the heartbreak that caused my family to suffer and other families when I took their loved ones away. I know there's not a snowball's chance in hell that I will make it to heaven. A man like me don't deserve a second chance. Just watch over my wife and kids and keep them strong as they deal with my death."

Slowly, I pushed the needle into my arm to end my suffering for good.

***

Hector

After three strong kicks, the door went flying open with great force. When I rushed into the room, everything was still. A chill came over my body. Liquor bottles were scattered all over the room, so I ran into the bathroom. Brick was sitting on the toilet with a syringe hanging from his arm. Quickly, I pulled it from his arm and threw it on the floor. Slapping his face repeatedly, I shouted, "Brick! Brick! Wake up."

Fast on my feet, I stuck my finger down his throat until he gagged. His body jerked and vomit poured from his mouth. Leaning him forward, I patted him in his back until he stopped and gasped for air. His eyes were big and empty.

"I need you to get up and get in this shower. On the count of three, I'm going to lift you and I need your help. One, two, three." Brick wasn't much help with me getting him up, but I managed to get him in the shower.

Turning the water on, I made sure it was warm. Cold water would've sent him into shock. While I made him sit there, I stepped out to call Coop.

"Did you find him?" his voice was shaky.

"Yes. He's alive."

Coop breathed heavily into the phone. "Whew! Thank God. He got Zuri and Janae over here losing it."

"You too."

"I know. I'm glad you found him. Where is he?"

"I got him sitting in the shower."

"What happened?"

"When I got here, he wasn't answering, so I kicked down the door. I found him in the bathroom with a needle hanging in his arm. He could've overdosed, but since he doesn't do drugs a small amount hit his system and knocked him out."

"Damn, where y'all at? I need to see my brother."

"I'm taking him someplace safe for now and when he snaps out of it, I'll have him to call you."

"Take care of my dude."

"I got him. Let them know he's okay."

"A'ight."

"Coop."

"Yeah."

"Thanks for calling."

"Thank you for finding him."

Brick was sitting in the shower looking around confused when I walked in. "How you feeling?"

"How did I get in this shower?"

"I put you in there."

"What you doing here?" He tried standing, so I helped him to his feet.

"I came to save you."

"For what?"

"Let's start with that suicide text you sent your family and the fact that you didn't send it to me."

Brick dropped his head to avoid eye contact. "I fucked up and I didn't send it to you because I knew you were the only person that could find me."

"You're right. I have a lot of connections. So, finding you was easy and I'm glad I found you. I've spoken with Coop, so I told him to let your family know that you're alive."

"I don't have a family anymore."

"Yes, you do. I'm standing right here or did you forget that?"

"Nah, I didn't forget."

"Take a shower. I'll be out here waiting."

While Brick showered, I closed the door and sat down on the bed. Altogether, I counted fourteen empty bottles of Patrón and Hennessy and four new bottles. He was truly going through it and I didn't know the extent of it. The situation at hand could've played out completely different if I didn't have friends in law enforcement to trace his number.

Brick stepped into the room wearing a towel, so I turned my back to him in order for him to get dressed. Once he was done, he walked over and sat in the chair next to the A/C.

"You hot?"

"Yeah." He had sweat beads on his forehead.

"That's what coke does to you and you know that. I'm just curious to know why the hell you thought this was the answer to your problems."

"I just wanted to end it all."

"Suicide is a coward's death. Real men don't go out like that and neither does a Riccardo that shares the same blood as me. I understand that a lot is going through your mind right now, so I'm not going to push the envelope just yet. But understand that we will revisit this conversation."

Brick nodded his head. "I appreciate you showing up."

"When I found out who you were, didn't I tell you I would be here for you no matter what?"

"Yeah."

There was something deeper going on with him and it was something I couldn't fix. However, there was someone that could help him mend that cold, broken heart inside his chest.

"Get your things and come on."

"Where are we going?"

"Some place I should've taken you a long time ago." Brick packed up his belongings and we were on our way. Hopefully, this visit would bring closure.

Chapter 28
Zuri

The frightening text I received from Brick almost had me in the emergency room. Yes, I hated him for what he did, but I didn't want him to kill himself. We still shared kids and eventually, I was going to let them see him, but I guess it was too late. Janae and Skeet rushed over here to make sure I was okay since I was alone.

Janae walked into the living room where I was sitting and watching Bam sleep. She sat down beside Skeet and put her leg across his lap.

"He looks so much like Dad."

"He does."

My poor baby was never going to remember his father and I somewhat felt like I was to blame. I was trying my best to keep from breaking down. Breanna didn't know what was happening and I wanted to keep it like that.

"Where is my daddy anyway?" Breanna asked.

"He's at work, Bre," Janae lied.

"Well, how long he gone be there? Y'all keep saying that, but he never come home. He must have a new family."

"No, Bre. He only has this one," Janae assured her.

Just hearing her talk made me shed a few tears. Breanna looked at me and wiped them away. "Don't cry, Zuri. Daddy will be back."

There was no way I could formulate a response for that child, so I looked away. It was killing me on the inside. "Bre, go upstairs and play with Legend."

"Okay."

"I couldn't say this in front of her, but I just got off the phone with Coop. Dad is alive, but he doesn't know where he is."

"Well, how does he know he's alive?" Skeet asked.

"He said Hector found Dad in time to save him and to tell us that he will be okay. I guess he was in bad shape. Who the hell is Hector?"

"Our Cuban connect."

"His uncle," Skeet and I replied simultaneously.

"Which is it?" Janae questioned.

"Both," I replied. "It's a long story. I'll tell you about it another day. I'm not mentally available right now."

The doorbell rang. Janae hopped up. "I'll get it."

Skeet pulled her back in her seat. "I'll get it." Then he disappeared.

From the living room I could hear a familiar voice yelling. Right after that, Mehzani hit the corner. Her hair was disheveled and her face was wet. Standing to my feet, I stepped away from the baby's car seat.

"What's wrong, Mehzani?"

"What's wrong?" she repeated. "I'll tell you what's wrong. How could you have me sitting around this pussy-ass nigga, knowing what he did to Gucci and Legend?"

Before I could respond, Janae was getting out of her seat and walking towards us. "Bitch, you better watch your mouth talking about my muthafuckin' daddy, pussy-ass hoe."

Skeet held her back to keep them from fighting. "Bae, chill. We got this." All of the commotion woke Bam out of his sleep. He was screaming at the top of his lungs. "Get the baby," Skeet yelled.

"Mehzani, you need to chill out running up in my house like that when you don't know what you talking about."

"Gucci told me everything, so I know what the fuck I'm talking about. You that dick whipped you can't leave that bitch alone?"

She was talking mighty reckless and putting her hand in my face. "I'm telling you right now to get your hand out my face, 'cause you being real disrespectful right now."

"What you gone do?"

Skeet stepped in between us in the nick of time and pushed Mehzani out the way. That bitch was two seconds away from getting her ass beat the fuck up.

"You better leave before I flip yo' ass, hoe."

"Hoe? I know you ain't call me no hoe. You the one that was laid up fuckin' Daddy at night."

I lost every piece of patience I had left in me and rushed that hoe, knocking her to the floor. Straddling her, I punched her repeatedly in the face. Mehzani dug her nails in my face, but that didn't stop me from busting her lip, nose and blackening her eye. Skeet grabbed me from behind when I started banging her head against the floor.

"Zuri, stop!" He pushed me towards the sofa and pulled out his gun.

"Fuck that flakka-smoking bitch. Go suck on a glass dick and overdose, hoe."

Skeet aimed it at Mehzani. "Get the fuck outta here and I'm not repeating myself.

Mehzani pulled herself from the floor. "Oh, you gone shoot me?"

"Shut up and get out," he replied.

"Bitch, you better get your black dress ready, 'cause when Gucci kill that fuck nigga, you gone need it." Mehzani hawked and spit blood out on the floor.

"Nah, you get yo' black dress and tell pussy-ass Gucci to run up on me so I can dump all my bullets in his ass.'

Skeet escorted Mehzani out the house. Janae looked at me and smirked. "Remind me to never piss you off."

The way Mehzani put me on blast, disclosing my personal business took things to another level. There was no coming back from that. I confided in her about that situation and jumped at the chance to throw it in my face. Sister or not, I wasn't fucking with that bitch ever again in life. That was below the belt and because of her actions she was now dead in my eyes, along with Daman.

***

Hector

After we left the hotel, I took Brick by an after-hour clinic to have him checked out. I wanted to be on the safe side and make sure he was okay. The doctor placed an IV in his arm, so he wouldn't be dehydrated. Once he was cleared to fly, we boarded my private jet and took off. The medicine in his system had him drowsy, so it didn't take long for him to fall asleep.

An hour and a half later, we were landing at a commercial airport. Walking to the back, I shook Brick's shoulder. "Brick, wake up."

He stirred around in his sleep before rubbing his face and sitting up. "I'm up."

"Come on."

A black Tahoe was waiting on us when stepped off the jet. Brick checked his surroundings as usual. "Where are we?"

"Cuba."

"What the hell we doing here?"

"You'll see."

During the forty-five-minute ride, Brick was silent as he looked out the window. I knew he had a lot on his mind. Silently, I prayed that whatever demon was riding his back would disappear and he would make peace with the decisions he made. Pulling up to a black iron gate, I rolled down my window and hit the intercom button.

"Quién?" he asked, "who is it?"

"Héctor."

The gate opened, giving us access. Pulling up to the mansion, Brick looked around. "This is a big-ass mansion. Shit look like Tony Montana crib."

"You want to move in?"

"Nah. This too far away from home. Who shit this is, anyway?"

"This is where I grew up. It's the family house. So, whenever you want to visit, you can stay here."

"That's what's up."

Before I could knock on the door, it opened on its own and I was greeted by Maria, the maid. "Hola."

Brick and I greeted her and walked inside.

"Damn! We don't have shit like this in the states."

"Not even close."

As we made it to the family room, my brother stood up and walked towards us. Brick stood there in silence with a strange look on his face and his mouth slightly open. The awkward behavior and looks had the room in complete silence.

Chapter 29
Brick

The drugs and alcohol had to still be in my system, because for a split second, I thought I was standing in front of a mirror. And the image was an older version of me with a lighter complexion. He hugged Hector, then stepped in front of me.

"Thank you for bringing him to me."

"You're welcome."

"Brandon." He smiled.

"Yeah. I go by Brick now."

"¿Todavía hablas español?"

"Yeah, I still speak Spanish, but I prefer English."

"Okay. Do you know who I am?"

"Yeah. Not to be rude, but my question to you is, how the fuck you standing here when I have my mom buried next to you in the cemetery?"

Ain't this a bitch? Fernando Riccardo was standing right here in my face and not six feet under where his headstone clearly states his muthafuckin' name.

"That's a long story," he replied.

"I have nothing but time."

"Well, we need something strong for this occasion." Fernando reached into his pocket and pulled out a small walkie talkie.

"Maria."

"Yes, sir."

"Bring me a bottle of Havana Club 7 Años, a Coke and some glasses."

"Yes, sir."

"Follow me."

Hector and I followed behind Fernando to what I assumed to be the family room. The décor was antique, yet unique. The colors were burgundy and gold. It had a nice touch to it. When he extended his hand, I sat down on the sofa beside him. Fernando was looking me up and down like he was in awe of how much we looked alike.

"This is amazing. I thought I would never see you again in life."

"That's funny, 'cause I thought the same thing," I replied.

My sarcasm was on point, locked and loaded. This nigga had a lot to explaining to do, especially since my mama committed suicide because of his ass.

"I know you're upset with me. I don't blame you, but once you hear what happened, I hope you can forgive me."

"A little, but I'm confused more than anything."

Maria walked in carrying a gold tray. She sat it down on the coffee table and excused herself. Fernando poured up three glasses and passed them off. Taking a sip, he cleared his throat and started telling his side of the story.

'Fernando's Story'

There was a territory war going on between some of the cartel members and a local kingpin. Things were violent and bodies were dropping left and right. The feds swooped in and started to pick up anyone's name that came across their desk. One of them happened to be an alliance of the cartel, and when he was in the water he couldn't swim, so he started to snitch.

Word got back to the camp that the feds were hot on my trail and that I needed to get my family and flee. Walking through the front door of my home, I called out my wife's name.

"Brenda." She walked out the kitchen and greeted me with a kiss.

"Hey, baby. What's wrong?"

"We need to talk. Where is Brandon?"

"In the room reading a book."

Before I could surprise my son with another gift, he came running towards me. "Daddy! Daddy!"

Brandon jumped into my arms and hugged my neck tight. I held him tighter than I normally would and kissed his cheek. He had the biggest smile on his face.

"Guess what I did today, Daddy?"

"What's that, son?"

"I finished the Spanish Heritage book you bought me."

"Good job."

"So, when are we going to Cuba?"

"Sooner than I expected." Kneeling down in front of him, I ran my hand through his jet black curly hair. "Brandon, I need for you to go in the room for a little bit while I talk to your mom."

"Okay."

196

When Brandon closed his bedroom door, I grabbed Brenda's hand and walked her over to the sofa. "Tonight is the night that we have to get out of here."

"But—"

I cut her off. "No buts. If we not out of here by sunrise, I'll be in custody before the sun rises."

"Okay."

"Pack up whatever clothes and personal items you and Brandon need and put them by the door. When I get back, we're leaving."

"Okay," she agreed. "Where are you going?"

"I have to pick up the money from the warehouse and I'll be back."

Changing my clothes, I put on my bulletproof vest, grabbed both of my guns and headed out the door. My twin brother, Ferdinand, was standing beside the car waiting on me. As soon as I made it to the sidewalk, a van pulled up on us and multiple shots rang out. I fired back, but there were too many shooters.

"Ferdinand, run," I shouted.

He took off behind me or so I thought, but when I turned around, he was on the ground. I couldn't stop, so I kept going. My main concern was staying alive so I could get back to my family.

Once I made it out the area, I called my right-hand man to pick me up. The first place we went was back to my house, but when we got there the place was swarming with cops and the feds. We parked up the street and walked, careful to stay within a safe distance. The closer we got to the crime, I heard a woman screaming and crying. It was Brenda.

"I have to get up there."

"For what? And go to prison for life?"

"My wife and kid think I'm dead."

"Exactly. Let them think that for now. At least, that way they will throw out the case and it's all over. After a few months, we come back and get them. Problem solved."

At that moment, it sounded like a good idea, so we left. I fled to Cuba that night. Three months later, I was arrested in Cuba and sentenced to prison for three years. My right-hand man was killed and I had no one to seek out my wife and kid. When I got out, I couldn't leave the country or I would go back to prison. That was when I knew that I lost my wife and son forever.

Fernando was teary eyed when he finished his story. My expression was blank. It sounded legitimate, but the verdict was still out on that in my eyes.

"I heard about your mother and I'm sorry. She was the love of my life and the reason I could never marry again. No one was ever good enough for me. When I lost y'all, I lost everything. I was never the same again."

"She was my everything too."

"I still miss her and I carry her with me every day. That will never change."

"How so?" I was curious to know the depth of his love for my mother or was it all an act.

Fernando stood up and removed his shirt. When he turned his back towards me, there was a face portrait of me and my mom with our names, Brenda and Brandon, written in cursive. That touched me in a place I haven't felt in a long time. He turned back to face me.

"As you can see, I carry you with me also." Fernando put his shirt back on. "I just want to hug you. Is that okay?"

Standing to my feet, Fernando hugged me tight. "You were six years old the last time I hugged you. I'm sorry. Please forgive me for my absence and forcing you to grow up without your parents."

His words had me a little teary eyed, but I did my best not to show it. That was a hard thing to do when you always wanted the love of your father.

"Aww. That's so sweet," Hector laughed. "Can I get some too?"

When we let go, I wiped my face and sat down. "I need another drink."

"Yeah!" Hector shouted. "Enough of that mushy shit. We are back together and it's time to celebrate."

In the middle of us drinking, talking and laughing, a woman walked into the family room, wearing a long silk nightgown.

"Hello. I didn't know we had company." She smiled.

My first thought was how beautiful she looked and secondly, did she belong to Fernando. "Hello." I smiled.

The chocolate bombshell walked towards me and extended her hand. "You are handsome, just like your father."

Fernando stood up. "Brick, this is—"

"Zena," she replied.

That name rang bells in my head like crazy. I was in a daze, as she continued to hold my hand. "How is my daughter, Zuri?"

Chapter 30
Zuri
Seven months later

So much time had passed since Brick left and I couldn't lie, I missed him. I missed his presence. His personality. The sex. My hormones were raging like crazy and I couldn't do anything to fix it. More times than I cared to admit, I found myself lying in bed at night, crying and staring at our pictures. He had me completely damaged on the inside. My heart was torn. If it wasn't for Janae moving in, I don't know how I would've coped with anything or handled these kids on my own. Marco and I even became close over time and that was a good feeling.

"Who are you thinking about?" Janae smiled, while rubbing her full-sized belly.

"No one," I lied.

"You're lying and I know it."

"You don't know nothing."

"I know I'm tired of being pregnant. This shit is for the birds. I don't see how you can do it. After this, I'm getting my tubes tied."

Laughing, I replied, "You're too young. They won't do it."

"Well, I'm getting on birth control. He won't trick me again."

Drifting off into my thoughts once again, Brick crossed my mind. I wanted to call him, but he hurt me too badly. Janae's eyes were stuck to my skin and I felt it.

"What?"

"You're thinking about Dad, aren't you?"

"No."

"Yes, you are. Whenever you think about him, you drift off into space and your eyes get glassy. She was right, but I couldn't admit that to her.

"You still haven't spoken to him?"

"No."

"Still ignoring his calls, huh?"

"I'm not ready to talk to him yet."

"Zuri, it's been seven months. Eventually, you have to talk him. You can't keep this a secret that much longer."

"You're right, but now isn't the time."

Janae moved closer to me. "I get it. You hate what he did, but deep down, you still love him and he loves you too. Every time we FaceTime so he can see the kids, he asks about you. He's hurting. I can't count the amount of times he's cried to me about making that terrible mistake."

My emotions wouldn't act right at all and I hated the fact that I was crying over him again. Janae knew how to trigger me. That was a fact and she knew it.

"One day, you have to forgive him. You can't expect forgiveness if you won't give it. I don't go to church and I know that much. You go to church every Sunday and that still hasn't registered in your heart yet."

Janae wiped her own eyes. Then she wiped mine.

"Now you have me crying, so stop. I know for a fact that you still love my dad. It takes a special type of woman to raise someone else's kids and treat them like they are hers. You have been the best stepmom to me and Bre and he couldn't have picked a better you. I love you and I won't stop doing this until you forgive him."

The doorbell interrupted our bonding session.

"I'll get it." She leaned forward.

"I got it. You should be resting."

"Girl, I'm pregnant. Not handicap." Janae got up and wobbled towards the door.

Sleep was calling me, but I was too hungry to lay down. Leaning my head down on the sofa, I closed my eyes. Janae's heavy footsteps alerted me that she was back.

"Who was that?"

When I opened my eyes I saw a pair of Nike Air Max's in front of me. Raising my head, I came in contact with my estranged fiancée. Brick looked refreshed, happy and better than ever.

"Hey, Zuri."

"Hi."

"God, I've missed you so much." Brick got down on his knees and placed his hand on my stomach. "Why didn't you tell me you were pregnant?"

"I didn't want you to know."

"Your stomach is so big. What are you having?"

"Twin boys."

Brick's eyes lit up, as he rubbed my stomach. "Damn. So, that's why you've been avoiding me all this time."

"How long are staying?"

"I don't know. That depends."

"On what?" I was curious to know what he was talking about, although I already knew the answer to that question.

"You." Brick stood up and grabbed my arms. "Stand up so I can see you. It's been so long."

Pulling me up, he hugged me tight and rubbed my stomach again. "It's Daddy."

The scent of his cologne tickled my nose. It was so intriguing. As he continued to play with my stomach and talk, the twins started to kick. "Oh, they excited. I wish y'all mama was happy to see me."

"Don't do that."

Janae was sitting over there smiling. Brick looked over at her and nodded his head. "I need to talk to Zuri."

"I guess that's my cue to leave."

"Yeah, wobble up outta here," he joked.

My legs were hurting from standing, so I sat back down. Brick kneeled down in front of me.

"I've had a lot of time to sit, think and meditate with no interruptions. During that time, I did a lot of reading. I've read the Bible and a lot of spiritual books, so my mind is on another level right now. My thought process is clearer. These past several months have been a real learning experience for me. Before I left, I was in a really dark place and I wanted to die because you left me. Now that I think back to that night that was a selfish move I tried to pull. My mama did the same thing to and there I was attempting to do the same thing to my kids."

Brick's eyes were glassy, but he didn't shed a tear.

"I don't know if they told you, but I tried to overdose on coke by shooting it into my vein. That was the lowest point in my life and I never want to experience that again."

That came to me as a surprise. Brick never used drugs, so for him to do that meant he was just as damaged as me. "I'm sorry. I didn't know."

"Yeah. That's how you had me feeling. I didn't believe I had a reason to live if you didn't want me."

"But why would you want to do something like that? Regardless of what I chose for us, that doesn't dismiss the fact that we have kids that need you."

"Don't you get it? There is no life without you. I love you and I'm not giving up. So, if it takes hours, days or months, I'll be right here until you change your mind. Until you forgive me for what I did."

"I don't know if I can forgive you."

"Have you ever heard this quote? The weak can never forgive. Forgiveness is the attribute of the strong."

"No."

"I've never viewed you as weak because that's a trait that you don't possess. It's in you to forgive me. You just don't want to. Who are you trying to prove yourself to by not forgiving me and giving our family a second chance?"

"Nobody and that's not fair for you to think that someone has that much power over me."

"I gave you the whole truth. You know I didn't know about him, because you never told me. So, why is it so hard for you to believe that it wasn't intentional? Nothing personal."

"I believe it wasn't intentional."

"Just answer this last question for me. This will determine my next move because you have your mind made up."

Brick and I locked eyes for what felt like an eternity.

"Do you still love me?"

That was the one question I wished he would've avoided. Love made you do stupid shit and I didn't want to be put in that category. Sighing, I looked into his eyes and nodded my head.

"Yes."

"That's all I need to know. I'll be right back."

"Where are you going?"

"I have a surprise for you."

Anxiously, I sat and waited for him to return. Brick came back into the living room where I was sitting and stood in front of me.

"I need you to stand up. Give me your hands." When I was on my feet, he instructed me to close my eyes. Taking a few steps, he turned me in the opposite direction.

"Open them."

Standing in front of me was my mother. She looked the same way she did when she left. Her smile was the last thing I saw before I passed out.

A few hours later, I tossed and turned in my bed. When I opened my eyes, Brick was there. "That was the craziest dream I just had. I dreamed that you came back from Cuba and you had my mother with you."

"That wasn't a dream, baby. I'm right here." Zena moved closer to the bed.

Seeing her face for the first time in years sent me back in time to that little girl that desperately needed her mother's love. Rubbing my eyes to make sure it wasn't a dream, I blinked several times. When I stopped, she was still there.

"Mommy, is that really you?" my tone was hella whiny.

"I'm going to leave so y'all can talk." Brick left the room expeditiously.

Zena sat down and rubbed the top of my head. "Yes, baby. It's really me."

There were so many questions I had for her and so many things I wanted to tell her. I missed having her in my life and had she been there, I wouldn't be fucked up on the inside. Zena placed her hand on my belly.

"Girl, you are huge. I know this not one baby." She smiled.

"No. It's two boys."

"Wow! Twins do run in his family." Zena looked so youthful. "I always wondered what you would look like when I saw you again. You're beautiful."

That made my heart smile. "I look like you."

"That you do."

"Why did you leave us?"

"Is that what your father told you?"

I nodded my head yes.

"He's always been a lying-ass man. I didn't leave my kids. I left him. After I had Demarco and realized it wasn't Daman's son, I decided to make it work with his father. He didn't like the fact that I wanted to leave because Pablo was his distributor. When I came home from the hospital, he waited until all of you were asleep to put me out. That was when he told me that I could never see my kids again, since I chose another man."

Their lives were a twisted one and of this blood shared between strangers. All of it sounded crazy to me and I needed clarification.

"So, you were having an affair with Daddy's distributor and got pregnant?"

"Yes. They set us up in a safe house when Daman went to Cuba. He was gone for a long time and I got lonely. Pablo was there a lot and we got close. That's how Demarco came along."

"Where have you been all this time and how did Brick find you?"

"I've been in Cuba all this time. Demarco's father moved me to Gainesville. They expanded their clientele and needed someone there, so we left. He became abusive. He even tried to kill me. Hector showed up and found me on the floor bleeding. Pablo knocked out a few of my teeth, broke my ribs, jaw and blacked both of my eyes. Hector agreed to help me escape. Pablo had another woman living in the house with us. She told Hector that if he took me, she would tell, so he killed her and put her in a cement tank with my teeth. Then he paid a detective to release information that it was me in the tank. Hector then took me to Cuba and that's how I met Brick's father, Fernando. I never came back to the states because I couldn't risk being seen by Pablo or Daman. I knew if that happened, one of them would kill me."

"Legend had that newspaper clipping about your death."

"It had to look real."

Sadness appeared in my eyes whenever I talked about him.

"Legend's dead."

"I know. Brick told me."

"Did he tell you what happened?"

"Brick explained everything to me while he was there."

"And you're okay with that? The fact that he killed your son."

Zena hesitated and rolled her neck. "I am. One thing that you have to realize in this type of business is that death is inevitable. You live by the sword, you die by the sword. When you are on the opposing team, there will always be beef. He didn't do it to hurt you because he didn't know anything about a connection between you and Legend."

"Yeah, that's what he said."

"Do you believe him?"

"I never told him about any of my siblings. Things happened so weird and fast between us that we didn't know that much about our backgrounds."

Zena giggled. "So I heard."

"He told you?"

"About how y'all met? Yeah he did and I must say that is a crazy-ass story."

"You think I'm crazy, don't you?"

"You're human. We can't help who we fall in love with." She had a point. "Do you still love him?"

"More than he knows," I admitted.

"He loves you and I know it. I saw it in his eyes when he told me about the night he tried to commit suicide. Men like Brick don't do that. He's a killer. They don't have remorse when they take a life. I can't just pop up in your life and tell you what to do, but give him a chance. Forgive him, because I did." All of that came from the woman who gave birth to Legend.

"I'm trying."

Zena stood up. "How is your relationship with his daughter, Breanna?"

"I love her like she's my own child."

"Let me give you something to think about. How would you feel if she found out you killed her mother when she gets older? Would you want her forgiveness? Could you live with the fact that she hated you? You're no different from him. The only difference between you and Brick is that you knew she was the mother of his child. You took her life with no remorse and he's not holding a grudge against you for that. I'm sure at one point in time he was in love with her and I'm sure he had love for her because she birthed his child. Think about those questions when you make your decision."

Zena leaned down and kissed my forehead. "I love you."

My mind was all over the place when she left that room. All I could imagine was Breanna crying. That gave me a lot to think about, but in the meantime I was going back to sleep. The twins were kicking my ass.

Chapter 31
Brick

My impromptu visit was going better than I anticipated. It felt good to reunite with my babies and make amends with my wifey. Zuri wasn't all the way on board with it, but she was halfway there. It was going to take a little more effort before she dived in. Coop was the first person I saw upon my arrival, so he had been scratched off my list of people to see. However, there was still one more person that I needed to slide up on.

Pulling the address up on my phone, I put it in my GPS. The neighborhood was quiet, just how I liked it. Tapping on the door with my knuckles, I stood back and waited for someone to answer. No one came to the door. Nor did I hear any movement. Using my fist this time, I hit the door three more times. The door finally swung open and there stood Skeet. He was wiping the sleep from his eyes.

"Wake yo' ass up, nigga."

Skeet chuckled and we G-hugged. "Damn, bruh. It's good to see you. Come in. Who the fuck let you back in the states?"

"It was time for the return."

His spot was laced with a black sofa set, a big flat screen, silver and white vases with a splash of gray. "This a nice bachelor pad you got here."

"Bachelor pad?" he replied, in his Souljah Boy voice. "Don't let your daughter hear that. Janae ain't having that, period. She the one that decorated in here. If it was up to me the only things that would be in this bitch is a bed, my flat screen and PlayStation."

"Shit, that's all we need."

The photo on the table caught my attention, so I walked over and picked it up. A smile spread across my lips. It was a picture of Janae in a bra, exposing her painted belly. Skeet was shirtless on one knee, kissing her stomach.

"Damn! My baby having a baby." Sitting it back down, I turned to Skeet and chuckled. "She changing you, huh? Got you taking maternity pictures and shit."

"Yep. I'll do whatever she ask me to do." He flopped down on the sofa. "I'm still a gangsta though."

"That I know." It was time for me to get down to the nature of my visit, so I sat down in the chair and folded my hands.

"First, I owe you an apology for the way I snapped on you. My emotions got in the way and I shouldn't have pulled my strap on you. That was wrong."

"It's all good, bruh. Janae means a lot to you and I understand that. That's your responsibility as her father. My wild ways made you think that I would do her dirty."

"Yeah, you right. Apparently, I was wrong about that 'cause from the looks of things, she looks happy."

"We are happy. I love her to death and that's why I couldn't leave her alone. The day you came to my apartment, I tried to tell you about us, but you wasn't having it. You chomped me off first quarter."

Thinking back to that day raised a brow. "She was there, wasn't she?"

"Yeah."

"Y'all was like fuck what he talking about."

"Nah!" He smirked. "Nae was scared when she found out she was pregnant. She kept saying, 'My daddy gone kill you.'"

"If I would've killed you, she would've never forgave me. All she kept saying was Zuri's somebody daughter and you just like Chance."

He laughed. "I hate when she call me that and she hate calling me Skeet."

"That's a half-nut baby name."

"Whatever, nigga. Did you see yo' wifey?"

"Yeah."

"She big as fuck, dawg."

"I didn't even know she was pregnant until today."

"Yeah. Nae told me Zuri didn't want you to know. Y'all gotta work that shit out. I need my lady home with me. I'm tired of sleeping in this bitch alone."

"You ain't alone every night."

"I'll never bring a bitch in here. Shit, I'm not even cheating."

"You sho' 'bout that?"

"Nah. I'm a one-woman man." Skeet leaned forward and started to roll up. "Remember when you told me that I'll stop when I find the one I want?"

"Yeah."

"I found that and I'm not trying to fuck that up."

"Good. I don't want to fuck you up."

"I'm not giving you a reason to do that."

For the next couple of hours, we kicked back like old times. He filled me on Gucci and his sudden disappearance. The fight between Zuri and Mehzani pissed me off because I didn't like how she put my wife's business on blast like that.

Skeet's eyes were low like he was Chinese and he kept grinning and shit. "On the real, bruh, I'm glad you back. These women wearing my ass out. That's why I was in this bitch sleep. For these past months, I been the driver, security guard, errand boy and the goddamn babysitter. I'm exhausted, so it's your turn."

"I appreciate you looking out for my family while I was away. That means a lot to me."

"I'm in the family now." Skeet jumped up and left the room. When he came back, he had something in his hand. "I been waiting on you to get back so I can ask you something."

"What's that?"

"What you think about this?" He opened his hand and showed me a diamond ring.

"I know you not asking me to marry you?" We both laughed.

"Hell, no. Is it okay if I propose to her? I needed your blessing first."

"Let me think about it."

Skeet put the ring on the table. "You fuckin' with me, right?"

"Yeah, I am."

"You ain't shit. My whole heart dropped."

"I know it did. You should've saw your face."

Skeet's phone rang. "Speaking of the devil."

Janae called him on FaceTime. "Where are you?"

"Home. Where you at?" he asked.

"Ahh! Shit."

The sound of her voice made me get up and see what was going on with her. Janae's face was balled up and she appeared to be in pain. I knew that look all too well.

"Bae, what's wrong?" Now his voice was laced with worry.

"I'm having contractions. This shit hurt."

"That's what you get. I told you not to have sex in the first place," I teased.

"That's not funny. This shit hurt."

"Stop all that cursing, girl."

"I'm in fucking pain. Get here." She ignored everything I said.

"Where are you?" he repeated.

"On my way to the hospital to meet my doctor."

"I'm coming. Hold out until I get there."

"Hurry up," she screamed.

Skeet hung up the phone and walked in circles. He was mumbling shit I couldn't understand.

"What you doing? Let's go."

"This shit got me nervous."

"Go put on some clothes and let's go."

"A'ight."

Later on that night, Janae finally gave birth to my first grandson and Skeet's junior with no complications. She did a lot of crying, being that it was her first child. It was a very sentimental moment, because Shan would never get to see her grandson. I stayed at the hospital until she fell asleep. As I pulled out the parking garage, Zuri called my phone.

"Wassup, love?"

"Where are you?"

"Just leaving the hospital. Janae had the baby."

"She called before she went to the hospital."

"So, what's going on?" There had to be a reason for her call.

"Where are you staying? A hotel?"

"Yeah." That wasn't my plan, but I had a feeling she didn't want me to come home.

"Come home so we can talk."

"I'm on my way." There was a God.

When I made it back to the house, everyone was asleep. Zuri was in bed when I walked in. "Close the door." She sat up and put her back against the headboard.

After I closed the door, I put my gun on the dresser and removed my shirt. Zuri's eyes beamed directly on me. The bed was as comfortable as I remembered when I laid beside her.

"What you wanna talk about?"

"Us."

"What about us?" The riddle game was in full effect and it seemed like I would have to pull teeth. "Talk to me."

"I'm trying, but it's so hard to express my feelings to you."

"It's not hard. Just say what you feel."

Just like clockwork, those tears appeared. I used my thumb to wipe them away.

"Tell me how you feel without the tears. We're beyond the crying stages. Everything that happened is in the past. It's time to move forward. We either gone be together or we not. If you want me out, I'll take Breanna and go back to Cuba. I'll fly back to the states twice a month to see the other kids."

The expression on her face was a Kodak moment. What I knew about Zuri was that a strong Alpha male turned her on. As long as I was weak in her eyes and crying over her, she felt superior. She felt like she had control, but that was over with. Tonight she was gone make a decision and she was gone do it now.

"I don't want you or Bre to leave. I'm too attached to her. She's my child."

"So what do you want, Zuri? I'm exhausted. It's been seven long-ass months and you still don't know what you want. It seems like you want to string me along so I won't move on. You'll die before you see me with another woman, because you know I'm a good man."

"I'll kill you first," she replied.

"What are you saying?"

Zuri took a deep breath. "I forgive you and I want you back home. Together as a family. I don't want you to go back to Cuba. These past few months have been hell without you. I missed you so much that it hurt. I love you and I never want to be without you again."

That was what I needed to hear. Getting up, I walked to her side of the bed and kissed her passionately. "I love you too. Does that mean the wedding is back on?"

"Yes. We'll get there eventually. Let's work on rebuilding what we lost." That answer was good enough for me.

Zuri was on top of me, riding the shit out of me. She was wild with it. Her sex drive was through the roof. Gripping her waist, my thrusts met hers simultaneously. It felt good to experience sex with the one I've been missing. My dick was so dry. I knew he was happy. We moaned together and loudly at that, without a worry that anyone would hear us. I wanted to feel her lips on mine, but that mission was impossible with the twins sitting directly on my chest.

Eventually, we switched positions. Zuri laid on her side, so I could slide in easily. Surprisingly, she was still limber. Placing her leg on my shoulder, I slid in and out. Her muscles clenched me tighter and I could feel them contract. Seconds later, her juices released and covered every inch of my dick. When it was all over, Zuri fell asleep, holding me tight. Once again, I was complete. I had my family back and that was all that mattered at that point.

Chapter 32
Daman
One year later

I was finally walking through those barbed wire gates as a free muthafuckin' man, after serving eight years. The last two years of my sentence were the absolute worst. Zuri left me for that nigga, Brick. Word got back to me that he moved her out west and dropped three babies in her. I guess he was trying to hide her from me. That was impossible, because I had eyes and ears everywhere. If he wanted to hide her he had to move her out of Florida. Word also got back that he was the one that killed my son, Legend. On my mama, I swear to God, I couldn't wait to run into that nigga. Right hand to the sky, I was gone murder his ass for taking what belonged to me.

Zuri was gone pay too for fuckin' that nigga while I was on the phone. I'll never forget those moans that corroded my ears. Of course, I wasn't gone kill her, but I planned on causing damage. My heart was still with her and I couldn't let go. Even though she was acting just like her cheating-ass mama.

A small part of me hated her, but the majority of me wanted her desperately. Zuri hurt me bad. She abandoned me when I needed her the most and I wanted her to pay for that pain she caused.

My vendetta list was longer than I-95. There were a few lame-ass niggas on my list too and let's not forget about the bitches that forgot about me along the way. There was one in particular that I had a special agenda for, and that was Kyra.

It was that hoe's fault Zuri met Brick in the first place. If she wasn't pressuring my baby to go out, she would've been right here waiting on me at the gate. I should've known Kyra wasn't shit when Zuri started bringing her around the house. She met Kyra back in middle school and she was fast as fuck. I told my daughter that I didn't want her hanging out with a girl like that. Kyra's mama used to have card parties all the time, so she kept a house full of niggas. The apple didn't fall too far from the tree. Matter of fact, that bitch didn't fall at all. Kyra happened because she needed somewhere to stay and she had to contribute something. A few months later, she got pregnant and her mama moved her away. Upon her return, there was no baby in tow. Meanwhile, she was trying to convince me that it was mine. I didn't believe that. She wasn't a virgin and I wasn't the only nigga she was giving the pussy to.

"Come on and get your ass out the van, so I can make it back before count," the C.O. hollered, as he opened the door.

I was so caught up in my thoughts that I didn't realize we were at the Greyhound station. I stepped down, pulled my pants up and stretched. I was a fairly big nigga, so I had to duck on the way out. I inhaled the sweet taste of freedom, as the cool breeze slapped me in the face. The weather was lovely and I was in a great mood.

"I'm a free man," I shouted. "Damn this shit feels good." I glanced at this Pee-Wee Herman looking ass nigga. "Glad I don't have to see your ugly ass face no mo."

"Fuck you, inmate."

"Pussy-ass cracka, that's Mr. Monroe to you and I'm free now." I grabbed the crotch of my pants and yelled, "Suck my dick, bitch!"

The ride back to the 'Dale was long and mad boring. There wasn't a decent bitch on this muhfucka to look at. You would've thought that after eight years, I wouldn't be so picky, but the devil was a lie. These hoes looked like ass in the face. I was hoping for a farewell quickie from freaky ass Tate before I left the compound, but they had shit on lock this morning.

Four hours later, I was pulling up at the Fort Lauderdale bus station. I couldn't wait to get to Kyra's house and dig in them guts. I was ready to manhandle some pussy. Every time I fucked Officer Tate, it was like we were in a marathon. Not tonight though, tonight I was gone hit that ass until the sun came up. I hopped into the first cab I saw and gave him the directions.

"Step on it, bruh, I'm on a mission."

Halfway to her crib, I stopped at the corner store to pick up some Magnums. There was no way I was hitting that raw. When we pulled up I paid my fare and hopped out. I stepped onto the front porch and knocked on the door.

"Who is it?" She flicked on the porch light.

"Daman."

Kyra swung the door open fast. She stood there in a pair of boy shorts and a tank top looking me up and down. "Oh, my God, why didn't you tell me you were getting out today?"

"I wanted to see if you was lying in those letters you was sending." My head dropped and my eyes were focused on her print. "Damn, that pussy fat! That's a pad?"

"Hell no, this is all pussy."

"Let me see." I grabbed a handful and she wasn't lying. "I guess that's all you."

"You want something to drink?"

"Hell yeah, some liquor." She led me into the kitchen. My dick was jumping as I watched her ass bounce. "Damn."

She turned around and giggled. "What?"

"I'm just admiring the view."

"Do you want chaser?"

"Nope." She handed me the cup and I downed it in one gulp.

"Damn, slow down."

"Hell nah. I'm ready to fuck. I suggest you down yours too, 'cause you gone need it. It's been a long time for me."

My ass was lying like a motherfucker. Kyra was trying to waste time and drink slow, but I wasn't going for that. I walked up on her and stuck my hand in those shorts and played with that clit.

"Yeah, you ready. That pussy dripping."

As soon as we got in the room, I got naked. Shiidd, wasn't no time for pump faking. I was horny. I put that condom on quick.

"Take that shit off!" I was aggressive. Climbing on top of her, I slid that pole right up in that twat. *Ain't no foreplay, bihhh, just straight pressure!* She inhaled quickly, but released it slow. Her juices were flowing heavy. With every thrust, her wet box made that gushy sound. Roughly, I pounded on her harder and harder. I could tell she was holding her breath. She couldn't take this dick.

"I thought you could handle this dick. That's what you said in your letters and on the phone."

"I can."

"Well, breathe then. I don't need you passing out in here. Let that noise out."

I grabbed her ankles and pinned them over her head, so they were touching the headboard. I was determined to hear some screaming and I wasn't stopping until I was satisfied. I hammered that pussy until she felt it in her stomach.

"Ah. Um." She grabbed my waist.

"Unh-unh," I grunted. "Move your hands. Give me that noise."

I hit that G-spot and she hollered like a hit dog. "That's what I'm talking about." I kept going until I could feel the nut build up in the tip of my head. Pulling out, I dropped them legs and straddled her chest. My dick slipped right in her mouth and down her throat. Tate turned me into a

215

bigger freak and that was the type of shit I was into. Kyra got her warning every time we spoke. Apparently, she was a freak too since she didn't stop me. My dick was pulsating in her mouth, with every stroke and she gagged. I kept going until I busted my first nut. My plan was to lay low at Kyra's spot for a few days. After that, I was gone slide up on Mehzani. My grand finale was Zuri. She didn't know I was out, but she was gone find out. Lauderdale was about to become the murder capital when my feet officially hit the streets.

Chapter 33
Brick

Zuri stood in front of me with a face full of tears, makeup smearing and all, crying in front of our closest friends and family members. The day was a good one, yet filled with so much emotion. Looking into the eyes of the woman that saved my life, I couldn't help but to tear up myself. She could've turned me in that night, but she didn't. After rebuilding our foundation for one long-ass year, we finally tied the knot. The road wasn't easy, but it was well worth it in the end. The trials and tribulations made us stronger and made me a better man. Holding her hand, I continued to express my deepest feelings to her in a song, during our first dance. With my own vocals at that.

"Girl you had me from the moment I looked into your eyes. And I knew you were an angel, but you were in disguise. Tell me how can I be so lucky. That you'd fall down from heaven for me. Ooh baby! Some people search a lifetime and never find the true love, ooh wee. Heaven cared enough for me to give me you. And now our heart can beat together. Standing strong, girl, here forever. You and I. You and I. I just want you to know you are. The reason I love. The reason I trust. God sent me an angel."

By the time the song came to an end, we were both an emotional mess. Fortunately, they were happy tears. Our family was stronger than ever. She had her mother, I had my father and we had our kids to share this special moment with. And of course, Hector and Demarco were amongst the crowd. Zuri and I shared another kiss.

"I love you," she said with conviction.

"I love you too, Mrs. Riccardo."

Zuri giggled. "I like the sound of that."

"I do too."

After the dance was over, the DJ played "Before I Let Go" by Frankie Beverly & Maze. Our guests got up and joined us on the dance floor. Everyone was having a ball and I couldn't be happier. Bam, who was about to turn two, was being chased by Breanna. The twins, Braylin and Bryce, were being held by the grandparents. Legend was doing his own thing on the dance floor.

From the corner of my eye, I could see my best man slowly approaching us. Kissing Zuri on the cheek, he smiled. "You look beautiful, sis."

"You really do." Tamia smiled, while giving Zuri a hug.

"Thank you."

"Can I steal my brother for a second please?" Coop asked.

"Enjoy him now, because for the next week you will not see or hear from him." Zuri giggled, before walking off with Tamia in tow.

"Wassup, my brother?" We shook hands and hugged.

"Yo, I'm so happy for you, man. Real spill."

"Thanks, man. We wouldn't be here if it wasn't for you."

"You know it's all love." Coop sipped on the drink he was holding.

"Tamia really pregnant, huh?"

"Yeah. I had to make sure, 'cause I wasn't going through that fake ass shit Danielle took me through."

"That muthafucka faked a pregnancy for months, like you wasn't gone find out."

"It's cool though. My divorce is final and I'm a free man."

"You gone marry Tamia next?"

"Hell nah. Marriage change these crazy-ass heffas. I'm straight. You can have that. Sis a keeper, though."

"I owe her my life."

"Facts."

The crowd began to fade away slowly as it got later in time. Janae and Skeet walked up to me and Zuri while we were saying goodbye to our guests.

"Parents, we about to head out. I'm tired and so are the kids." Janae gave us both a hug.

"Thanks, Nae. We appreciate you keeping the kids while we're gone."

"Don't thank me yet, Pops, 'cause you owe me big time. Y'all kids are bad."

"No, they're not," Zuri defended. "They just busy."

"Have you met y'all kids?" she joked.

We both nodded.

"Well, have fun on your honeymoon and Zuri, please don't come back pregnant."

"I can't promise you that," I stated matter-of-factly.

"I'm happy for the both of you. The two of you are meant to be."

"Thanks, baby. I'm happy for y'all too. I mean, I would've preferred a wedding so I can walk my firstborn down the aisle."

"You'll get the chance to do that once we're situated. I just thought it was more important for Chance to start his business first. He has to be legit, so he can remain free and help me raise our kids."

Zuri tilted her head to the side. "Y'all only have one child."

"Not anymore. We have another one on the way."

That caught me off guard. "What the hell you got going on?" My eyes were on Skeet.

"Shiiidd, we trying to catch up with you two," Skeet chuckled.

"No comment." I shook my head. "Take care of our babies until we get back."

"A'ight."

The hall was finally empty and it was time to leave the premises. Zena and Coop were still there with us. The sky was dark pink with blue traces and the moon was full. As we stood beside the black Cadillac Escalade I rented, a small figure stepped from an unknown car and proceeded in our direction.

"Who the fuck is that?" Coop stated while stepping to the truck and pulling out his heat.

"Shit, I don't know. But get ready, in case you need to bust this bitch."

"I been ready."

As the figure got closer, I recognized the female as Mehzani. She wasn't invited, so I was confused as to why she was there. Stepping closer, I moved Zuri out the way.

"You might as well go back where you came from. Nobody invited yo' ass here."

"I only came here to apologize to my sister. Is that okay with you?"

"You have a lot of nerves showing up here after you was bumping them gums sideways."

Zuri grabbed my arm. "It's okay, baby. Let her say what she needs to say so she can leave."

"Can we talk in private?"

"No. I don't trust yo' ass."

"Baby," Zuri pleaded. "It's okay. You're standing right here. I'll be okay."

Zuri stepped a few feet away to talk that bitch. Mehzani was lucky, because I would've punched that hoe out her shoes for talking that shit.

"Calm down, son. She okay," Zena added.

Moments later, I heard arguing and that was when I saw two more figures emerge from the car. The next thing I heard sent me running in her direction.

"Bitch, I told you you'll be seeing me soon. If I can't have you, this pussy-ass nigga can't either." Daman had his gun aimed directly at my baby.

"Zuurrii!" I screamed.

My feet couldn't get me there fast enough. It was like I was running in slow motion. Two gunshots rang out as I grabbed her by the waist. Both of us hit the ground hard. Shielding her body, I heard more shots being fired. The sound of screeching tires could be heard when the shots stopped.

Rolling over, I could see blood on my shirt and on Zuri's dress. Frantically, I screamed, "Call the ambulance."

Zuri had tears in her eyes.

"Baby, you gonna be okay. Help is on the way."

Zena and Coop ran to our aide. They both had a gun in their hand. "She hit, bruh?" Coop asked.

"Yeah."

Zena touched my shoulder. "So are you."

"I'm good, Ma."

"This bitch shot my baby." Zena stood up and cocked her pistol back.

When I looked around to see where she was going, I saw a body moving against the pavement. Zena shouted a few words that I couldn't understand and that was when I heard a single gunshot.

Boc!

While we waited on the paramedics, I rocked Zuri in my arms.

"Brick, I'm scared," she cried, "I don't want to die."

"You're not gonna die, baby. I promise. Just relax. Do you think God took us through all of that pain just to let it end like that? We were meant to be and you not going anywhere. You have to fight. Our babies need you and you know I can't raise Freddy Kruger, Michael Meyers and Jason by myself." I was doing my best to make her forget about the pain.

"They'll drive you crazy," she mumbled with a half-smile.

"Yes. I need you. What's a king without his queen?"

"A terrible ruler," she whispered.

The paramedics finally arrived and put Zuri up on the gurney. One of them saw the blood on my shirt. "Were you hit, sir?"

"Yeah."

"We need you to come over and get checked out."

"Help my wife. I don't need no fuckin' help."

Finally, they put her in the back of the truck and pulled off with me in the back. Up close and personal. During the ride to the hospital, I held her hand and prayed for a full recovery.

***

Two weeks later in Cuba

Zuri was making a full recovery after being shot in her chest. The bullet missed her heart by a few inches, so she was blessed to be alive. If it wasn't for me jumping in front of that second bullet, she would've been dead.

"How you feeling, love?"

"Like I'm ready to start our honeymoon."

"You know I been ready to slide up in that pussy. You supposed to be pregnant right now."

"Hey! Hey!" Zena walked in the room, interrupting my nasty talk. "You didn't hear that, did you?"

"I did. Five kids not enough?"

"Ten is the magic number."

Zuri's head swiveled in my direction. "For who?"

"Us."

"Listen." Zena leaned up against the dresser. "Bam, Braylin and Brayden are driving me crazy. I'm not watching anybody that's born after them."

"Where are they, anyway? You supposed to be watching them right now."

"They outside with their granddaddy. We too old to be running behind toddlers."

"I'm about to go out here and see what they doing."

"Did anybody find Mehzani and Gucci?" Zena asked with great concern in her voice.

"Nah. They didn't find them. I heard they left town."

As I stepped outside and inhaled the nice breeze, all I could do was smile. Watching my father play with his grandkids was worth more than all the money in the world. Life was truly good to me right now. My family was safe and Zuri was finally free from the grips of perverted-ass Daman. The night he shot her, he was shot in return by either Zena or Coop. Mehzani and Gucci pulled off, leaving him on the scene. Zena saw him and dumped a slug right between his eyes. That was her payback for all the foul shit he did to Zuri. Ma was definitely an OG. Now I understood how Zuri was able to adapt to my thuggish ways. It was in her bloodline, but I brought it out of her. My baby will forever be CORRUPTED BY A GANGSTA!!

Don't stop just yet, because it's not over for the Riccardo Gang just yet. Stay tuned, because Janae and Chance, aka Skeet, have a story to tell and it's filled with drama. Married to a Cartel Princess.

The End

Submission Guideline

Submit the first three chapters of your completed manuscript to ldpsubmissions@gmail.com, subject line: Your book's title. The manuscript must be in a .doc file and sent as an attachment. Document should be in Times New Roman, double spaced and in size 12 font. Also, provide your synopsis and full contact information. If sending multiple submissions, they must each be in a separate email.

Have a story but no way to send it electronically? You can still submit to LDP/Ca$h Presents. Send in the first three chapters, written or typed, of your completed manuscript to:

LDP: Submissions Dept
Po Box 870494
Mesquite, Tx 75187

DO NOT send original manuscript. Must be a duplicate.

Provide your synopsis and a cover letter containing your full contact information.

Thanks for considering LDP and Ca$h Presents.

Also, follow me on social media and be on the lookout for full length novels from the following short stories…

Beauty & the Beast

Thug Luvin'

For the Love of a Thug

COMING SOON!!

Gunz & Blaze: His Bonnie, Her Clyde

Foreign & Domestic: The Price You Pay for Love

She Can't Have You

Married to a Cartel Princess

Corrupted by a Gangsta 4

THE COST OF LOYALTY **III**
By **Kweli**
SHE FELL IN LOVE WITH A REAL ONE **II**
By **Tamara Butler**
RENEGADE BOYS **III**
By **Meesha**
A GANGSTER'S SYN II
By **J-Blunt**
KING OF NEW YORK V
RISE TO POWER III
COKE KINGS III
By **T.J. Edwards**
GORILLAZ IN THE BAY III
De'Kari
THE STREETS ARE CALLING II
Duquie Wilson
KINGPIN KILLAZ IV
STREET KINGS 2
PAID IN BLOOD 2
Hood Rich
SINS OF A HUSTLA II
ASAD
TRIGGADALE III
Elijah R. Freeman
MARRIED TO A BOSS III
By **Destiny Skai & Chris Green**
KINGZ OF THE GAME III
Playa Ray
SLAUGHTER GANG II
By **Willie Slaughter**
THE HEART OF A SAVAGE II
By **Jibril Williams**

FUK SHYT II
By Blakk Diamond
THE DOPEMAN'S BODYGAURD II
By Tranay Adams

Available Now
RESTRAINING ORDER **I & II**
By **CA$H & Coffee**
LOVE KNOWS NO BOUNDARIES **I II & III**
By **Coffee**
RAISED AS A GOON I, II, III & IV
BRED BY THE SLUMS I, II, III
BLAST FOR ME I & II
ROTTEN TO THE CORE I II III
A BRONX TALE I, II, III
DUFFEL BAG CARTEL I II III
By **Ghost**
LAY IT DOWN **I & II**
LAST OF A DYING BREED
BLOOD STAINS OF A SHOTTA I & II
By **Jamaica**
LOYAL TO THE GAME
LOYAL TO THE GAME II
LOYAL TO THE GAME III
LIFE OF SIN I, II
By **TJ & Jelissa**
BLOODY COMMAS I & II
SKI MASK CARTEL I II & III
KING OF NEW YORK I II,III IV
RISE TO POWER I II

COKE KINGS I II

By **T.J. Edwards**

IF LOVING HIM IS WRONG...I & II

LOVE ME EVEN WHEN IT HURTS I II

By **Jelissa**

WHEN THE STREETS CLAP BACK I & II III

By **Jibril Williams**

A DISTINGUISHED THUG STOLE MY HEART I II & III

LOVE SHOULDN'T HURT I II III IV

RENEGADE BOYS I & II

By **Meesha**

A GANGSTER'S CODE I &, II III

A GANGSTER'S SYN

By J-Blunt

PUSH IT TO THE LIMIT

By **Bre' Hayes**

BLOOD OF A BOSS **I, II, III, IV, V**

By **Askari**

THE STREETS BLEED MURDER **I, II & III**

THE HEART OF A GANGSTA I II& III

By **Jerry Jackson**

CUM FOR ME

CUM FOR ME 2

CUM FOR ME 3

CUM FOR ME 4

CUM FOR ME 5

An **LDP Erotica Collaboration**

BRIDE OF A HUSTLA **I II & II**

THE FETTI GIRLS **I, II& III**

CORRUPTED BY A GANGSTA I, II III, IV

By **Destiny Skai**

WHEN A GOOD GIRL GOES BAD

By **Adrienne**
THE COST OF LOYALTY
By **Kweli**
A GANGSTER'S REVENGE **I II III & IV**
THE BOSS MAN'S DAUGHTERS
THE BOSS MAN'S DAUGHTERS II
THE BOSSMAN'S DAUGHTERS III
THE BOSSMAN'S DAUGHTERS IV
THE BOSS MAN'S DAUGHTERS **V**
A SAVAGE LOVE **I & II**
BAE BELONGS TO ME I II
A HUSTLER'S DECEIT I, II, III
WHAT BAD BITCHES DO I, II, III
SOUL OF A MONSTER
By **Aryanna**
A KINGPIN'S AMBITON
A KINGPIN'S AMBITION **II**
I MURDER FOR THE DOUGH
By **Ambitious**
TRUE SAVAGE
TRUE SAVAGE II
TRUE SAVAGE **III**
TRUE SAVAGE **IV**
TRUE SAVAGE **V**
TRUE SAVAGE **VI**
By **Chris Green**
A DOPEBOY'S PRAYER
By **Eddie "Wolf" Lee**
THE KING CARTEL **I, II & III**
By **Frank Gresham**
THESE NIGGAS AIN'T LOYAL **I, II & III**
By **Nikki Tee**

Destiny Skai

GANGSTA SHYT **I II &III**

By **CATO**

THE ULTIMATE BETRAYAL

By **Phoenix**

BOSS'N UP **I , II & III**

By **Royal Nicole**

I LOVE YOU TO DEATH

By Destiny J

I RIDE FOR MY HITTA

I STILL RIDE FOR MY HITTA

By **Misty Holt**

LOVE & CHASIN' PAPER

By **Qay Crockett**

TO DIE IN VAIN

SINS OF A HUSTLA

By **ASAD**

BROOKLYN HUSTLAZ

By **Boogsy Morina**

BROOKLYN ON LOCK I & II

By **Sonovia**

GANGSTA CITY

By **Teddy Duke**

A DRUG KING AND HIS DIAMOND I & II III

A DOPEMAN'S RICHES

HER MAN, MINE'S TOO I, II

CASH MONEY HO'S

By Nicole Goosby

TRAPHOUSE KING **I II & III**

KINGPIN KILLAZ I II III

STREET KINGS

PAID IN BLOOD

By **Hood Rich**

LIPSTICK KILLAH **I, II, III**

CRIME OF PASSION I & II

By **Mimi**

STEADY MOBBN' **I, II, III**

By **Marcellus Allen**

WHO SHOT YA **I, II, III**

Renta

GORILLAZ IN THE BAY **I II**

DE'KARI

TRIGGADALE I II

Elijah R. Freeman

GOD BLESS THE TRAPPERS I, II, III

THESE SCANDALOUS STREETS I, II, III

FEAR MY GANGSTA I, II, III

THESE STREETS DON'T LOVE NOBODY I, II

BURY ME A G I, II, III, IV, V

A GANGSTA'S EMPIRE I, II, III, IV

THE DOPEMAN'S BODYGAURD

Tranay Adams

THE STREETS ARE CALLING

Duquie Wilson

MARRIED TO A BOSS… I II

By **Destiny Skai & Chris Green**

KINGZ OF THE GAME I II

Playa Ray

SLAUGHTER GANG II

By **Willie Slaughter**

THE HEART OF A SAVAGE

By **Jibril Williams**

FUK SHYT

By **Blakk Diamond**

Destiny Skai

BOOKS BY LDP'S CEO, CA$H

TRUST IN NO MAN
TRUST IN NO MAN 2
TRUST IN NO MAN 3
BONDED BY BLOOD
SHORTY GOT A THUG
THUGS CRY
THUGS CRY 2
THUGS CRY 3
TRUST NO BITCH
TRUST NO BITCH 2
TRUST NO BITCH 3
TIL MY CASKET DROPS
RESTRAINING ORDER
RESTRAINING ORDER 2
IN LOVE WITH A CONVICT

Coming Soon
BONDED BY BLOOD 2
BOW DOWN TO MY GANGSTA

www.ingramcontent.com/pod-product-compliance
Lightning Source LLC
Chambersburg PA
CBHW070446260626
47161CB00004B/1222

* 9 7 8 1 9 5 1 0 8 1 1 6 4 *